Willow replaced the receiver and ‗‗‗‗‗‗,
realizing with a sickening lurch of fear that ‗‗‗
not know where the fire escape might be. There
seemed to be no signs on the walls of the office that
were not already on fire. The choking, vile-smelling
smoke was getting worse. The sullenly smoldering
carpet was alight, and the flames had reached
more than halfway to her office. The noise was
appalling and to her horror she saw that chunks of
the ceiling were sagging down through the rolling,
threatening flames.

———————————— ★ ————————

NATASHA
COOPER
Rotten Apples

W★RLDWIDE®

TORONTO • NEW YORK • LONDON
AMSTERDAM • PARIS • SYDNEY • HAMBURG
STOCKHOLM • ATHENS • TOKYO • MILAN
MADRID • WARSAW • BUDAPEST • AUCKLAND

For the staff of my local tax office,
all of whom have treated me with great courtesy and
fairness during our long association.

ROTTEN APPLES

A Worldwide Mystery/July 1997

First published by St. Martin's Press, Incorporated.

ISBN 0-373-26244-2

AUTHOR'S NOTE

As far as I know, there is no Inland Revenue Tax District located in the Vauxhall Bridge Road. The office at the center of this novel, together with all the men and women who staff it, is wholly imaginary and has no counterpart in the real world. Indeed, every character in the novel shares that unreality. Any resemblance to an actual person, living or dead, is entirely coincidental.

ACKNOWLEDGMENTS

Many people helped me while I was writing this novel, and I should like to thank them all, in particular: Patricia Millbourn, Mary Carter, Owain Franks, Jennifer Kavanagh, Lucy Ferguson, Gerald Johnson, and the Press & Public Relations Department of the London Fire Brigade.

David Canter's *Criminal Shadows* (HarperCollins, 1994) was extremely helpful, as indeed was Tolley's *Guide to Inland Revenue Investigations*.

PROLOGUE

HE NEARLY WENT AWAY when he found the front door bolted against him and saw that her bedroom curtains were shut. It was the middle of the afternoon and there was only ever one reason why she wanted that sort of privacy. He hung about for a minute or two until the thought of the match got him going again. Someone had nicked his good racket and he had to get the old one.

He went round the back of the house, climbed over the garden wall and let himself in through the back door. Seeing hard little clumps of dry earth from the flowerbeds clinging to his trainers, he wiped them carefully on the hairy mat. She always nagged if he walked dust or mud into the house. He crept as quietly as possible up to the attic, where all her old junk was kept. A disgusting snorting sound came from inside her bedroom as he passed the door. He tried to block his ears.

Searching the box room, he did his best not to think about what might be happening downstairs or who the snorter might be. Eventually he saw the racket, wedged between the guitar that she hadn't played in years and a rickety wardrobe full of clothes that he'd told her were too gross to wear. He grabbed the racket, tucked it under his arm and went downstairs, keeping to the outside of the treads so that the boards did not creak too much.

As he got to the first-floor landing, he stopped and listened at the door of her room. Slowly he realised that the continuing, rhythmic sound could not be made by someone having a bonk after all. On the other hand it was not exactly like snoring, either. He found that he had to know what was going on and silently opened the door.

His tense muscles let go at once. She was alone, lying on her back under the dark-blue duvet. He'd only ever heard her snore once before, and that was after a boringly long lunch with a lot of wine one summer in Italy. She had stretched out on a long chair by the pool and slept her way through the afternoon, snuffling and groaning in a way that was really embarrassing. Luckily it also embarrassed the Italian who had brought the wine. He had gone long before she woke up. Which was great, even if it did get up her nose when she found out.

She looked as though she must have had another good lunch, but he did not mind that so much since she was alone. And he thought she looked quite pretty, even though her mouth was open and she was dribbling. He stored that bit of information to remind her next time she had a go at him for breathing through his mouth.

Her skin was much paler than usual and her wavy blonde hair was spread out over the blue pillow. She looked just like one of Botticelli's angels. It usually annoyed him when one of her men said that, but for once he saw what they meant. His face started to hurt again as he thought of them all.

He had never told anyone how much he wanted her to love him; he'd rather have died. And he'd never told anyone, least of all her, that there were times when she took him to hell and back. He whispered her name and then said it again, louder. She did not even move, let alone open her eyes and talk to him. He hated her.

His hands closed into fists and his eyes screwed up as he fought for self-control—and lost.

It seemed hardly more than a minute before he left her room, and he had no idea of the time until he reached the hall and happened to look at the clock. Then he knew he'd have to run all the way back if he weren't to get caught.

They made a great fuss about the ease with which he broke out of the school buildings, and they blamed him for going to her house whenever he needed anything. They seemed to want him to suffer for the way he kept on losing stuff, instead of just getting replacements from her. There were times when he thought that they were mad.

Something made him look back when he was half-way to the back door, and he saw an envelope addressed to him in her writing. He made a face and stuffed it in his pocket without opening it. Once he had got over the garden wall again, he ran like hell. No one saw him.

ONE

WILLOW ACQUIRED a third name just at the moment when her fragmented life seemed to become whole. Willow King to her civil service colleagues, and 'Cressida Woodruffe' on the jackets of her novels, she was Wilhelmina Worth on her marriage certificate.

Looking across the sunny breakfast table at her husband about fourteen months after the wedding, she decided that they had done pretty well by each other. Tom glanced up, as though he could feel her satisfaction, and grinned at her over the top of his newspaper.

She pushed up her smooth red fringe and held it in a bunch on the top of her head in a gesture that was becoming familiar to him. She looked so different from the woman he had first met that he almost laughed. In those days she had veered between utter dowdiness and exaggerated glamour. In the first guise she had worn spectacles, tight hair and no makeup; in the second she had hidden herself behind expensive designer clothes, clever cosmetics and a riot of cascading curls.

But for the past year or so she had worn her hair simply in a long gleaming bob. Her clothes were calmer, too—still well cut to show off her tall, slim figure, but less absurdly extravagant than they had once been. There were even days, when they were alone, when she was prepared to let him see her bony nose and pale eyelashes undisguised by makeup.

'What are you looking so pleased about?' he asked cheerfully.

'I was just thinking that we've probably beaten the odds already.'

'What, in still being married after such ages?'

'Not quite.' Laughing, she let her fringe flop down again. 'I think it's more that we've got this far without rows. I'm not sure that I ever believed that would be possible.'

Tom leaned forward to take another warm croissant from the napkin-lined basket between them. 'What about that time I forgot to tell you I had to go to Paris and you were consumed with wrath?'

'Oh, come off it, Tom. That was only irritation; not real wrath,' said Willow, doing her best to make light of an episode that had been difficult to forget.

Anger was something she had found easy to accommodate in the old days when she had lived alone. Since taking up with Tom she had come to feel wary of it in either of them.

'And it's long gone, as you very well know. I think we're safe enough now. Don't you?'

'Yes, I do,' he said, smiling at her with warming approval. 'And I know what you're talking about, too. But I find I'm a bit superstitious about saying that sort of thing and...'

'You, superstitious? You're the most rational man I know.' Willow blew him a kiss. 'It's one of the things I love about you.'

He bowed graciously, the effect only slightly marred by the fact that he had just put a large piece of well-buttered croissant in his mouth. She watched him with amusement and then suddenly sighed. He swallowed quickly and asked her what the matter was.

'Nothing important. I was just wishing that I'd never accepted this wretched job. What with you on the second shift and me having finished the book, we could have had some time to play.' She shook her head, making the hair fly across her face.

'You'd have hated it,' he said, picking up his cup to drink the last of the coffee in it. 'Having nothing to do while your agent reads the new novel? You'd be climbing the walls.'

Willow nodded. She knew that Tom did not need to be told what she was thinking. Then her green eyes began to sparkle once more. He looked wary, recognising mischief.

'This may sound like a line out of one of my early books,' she said, 'but there are times when I begin to think that you might really know me better than I know myself. And that's an appalling admission.'

'Shocking!'

There had been occasions during the past fourteen months when his own reactions and behaviour had surprised Tom into thinking that he knew his wife a great deal better than he knew *him*self. He decided not to bother her with that idea just for the moment and reverted to the previous—easier—subject.

'You've always been a sucker for secret worlds, Will. How could you of all people have resisted the chance to suss out the Inland Revenue?'

She smiled at him, enjoying the incongruous mixture of his sloppy dressing gown and the immaculate breakfast table. With his unshaven face, broad shoulders and broken nose, he looked intensely masculine—almost dangerous—in the midst of their highly civilised dining room.

The walls were painted a pale apricot colour that made it look bright even on grey days. When the sun was sparkling through the two long windows, as it was that morning, the effect was of sizzling light. There were still a couple of croissants in the basket on the pristine white damask table cloth. The breakfast service was of French flowered porcelain and the butter lay in a silver dish. A posy of mixed pinks was casually arranged in a low glass bowl, clashing with the burnt-orange colour of the home-made marmalade and Tom's plum-coloured dressing gown.

'I think you're probably right,' she said.

'About what?' He grinned, and added quickly: 'Not that I'm ever wrong, of course.'

Willow made a face. 'I only meant that you're right about the irresistibility of spying on the Revenue, but I probably shouldn't have admitted it. You've been right about too many things recently and I don't want you getting delusions of in-fallibility.'

'That could never happen in this house.'

'What do you mean?' said Willow, sounding less amused than she had been a moment before.

'Mrs Rusham makes it perfectly clear that she can only just tolerate my presence. That keeps me nice and humble,' he said drily.

Willow's relief that Tom had not been nursing a secret sorrow emerged as a burst of laughter, and she swiped at him with her napkin, forgetting that it was full of croissant crumbs. 'You're not unique in that. Disapproval comes naturally to her. I've been paying her wages for years and she still hasn't started to approve of me.'

'Maybe not,' said Tom as he put his hand up to feel his hair. He examined the crumbs sticking to his hand and wiped it on his napkin. 'But she's a lot cosier with you than she is with me. There are times when she looks at me as though she's about to sentence me to bread and water for a week.'

'Idiot,' said Willow, laughing again just as the door opened to reveal Mrs Rusham, looking as forbidding as usual in the white linen lab coat she wore instead of an apron.

'I thought you might like some more coffee,' she said as she laid two clear cups of foaming cappuccino on the table and removed the empty ones.

Willow was amused to see that Tom was flushing slightly as he started to pick the rest of the crumbs out of his hair. As soon as the housekeeper had left the room, Willow drank her coffee and then walked round the table to pat her husband's crunchy head.

'You needn't be afraid of bread and water while I'm alive,' she said, giving the announcement its maximum drama.

'Ah, Will,' said Tom, reaching up to hold her face next to his own, 'my champion!'

'Take care today, Tom,' she said as she pulled herself away from him.

'I always do,' he said, raising one hand to wave her off while he picked up the newspaper with the other.

Willow collected her handbag and the jacket of her bright-green linen suit, made up her face and put a pair of small but richly dark emerald earrings into her earlobes. She grimaced at herself in the mirror, enjoying the lavishness of her jewels and yet amused by her own pleasure. Once, things like the emeralds had provided her with a hedge against reality, but those days were gone. Now, she just enjoyed the way they looked.

Pleasurably satisfied with herself and her life, she went to the kitchen to say goodbye to Mrs Rusham, for whom she had considerable if unexpressed affection. They had always respected each other's privacy, and, never trying to become friends, had achieved a relationship that succeeded in spite of its apparent lack of warmth.

'It was a good breakfast. Thank you.'

'I'm glad you liked it,' said Mrs Rusham, smiling tightly. 'Will the chief inspector be in to dinner tonight?'

'Yes, I think so. Pretty late. If you could leave us both something in the fridge, that would be splendid.'

Willow knew that she was smiling in memory of Tom's bread-and-water fantasy, but she could not help it. Mrs Rusham's housekeeping had always been as lavish as her show of feelings had been meagre.

'I must go or I'll be late. See you tomorrow.'

The other woman nodded, and Willow left the house. As always, she turned at the corner of the street to look back.

She and Tom had sold their flats before the wedding and pooled their resources to buy the long, low house, which had been built across the front of a mews on the edges of Belgravia at the beginning of the last century. By the time they found it, the fabric had become dilapidated, the stucco had been falling off the three small Dutch gables in chunks, the paint had been peeling everywhere, and the glass in two of the circular windows in the gables had been badly cracked. But with money, care and an excellent builder, they had transformed it. Restuccoed and painted cream, with a new roof, new drains, wires and pipes, it had become a comfortable house with a kind of eccentric charm that suited them both.

Leaving it all behind her, Willow walked through the hot, white, tidy streets of Belgravia to the messier environs of Victoria Station, through the tatty edges of Pimlico and so to the broad, thunderous artery of the Vauxhall Bridge Road. It took her nearly twenty minutes, but after eating two of Mrs Rusham's croissants, even without the quantities of butter Tom liked to spread on his, she thought that the exercise was no bad thing. As she walked she considered the job she had been asked to do.

A week earlier, only a little more than a month after the General Election had ushered in a completely new government, she had been summoned to Whitehall to see George Profett, who had been made Minister for Rights and Charters. Never having encountered him before, either in the flesh or in any of the media, she had gone to his office full of curiosity.

He had surprised her. With his worn clothes, thin, lined face and very straight, untidy, blond hair, Profett looked quite unlike the archetypal politician, and Willow could not imagine what had attracted him to the life in the first place. But there was no doubt that he had been a clever choice for the job of being seen to protect citizens' rights.

Having been brought to believe that they had been manipulated by a bunch of arrogant muddlers and amoral chancers for the past few years, a large part of the electorate had given voice to a longing for government by figures of undeniable probity and firm principles. George Profett's very lack of suavity made him look as though he had plenty of those.

As Willow watched him, wondering whether he would be able to stand up to the rough and tumble of ministerial life, he recited a hesitant little speech about the new cabinet's concern that the rights of individuals might have been eroded during the long stint of the previous government.

It had been decided, he told her in conclusion, that he should collect a team of civil servants to look into certain specific cases of suspected abuse. From their reports decisions could be taken on what needed to be done to beef up the various citizen's charters.

'And you seemed just the type of person I have been looking for to investigate a case at the Inland Revenue,' he said, watching her through his thick spectacles.

'Really?'

'Yes. I gather that you've been part-time for some years now, are considering early retirement and have an income that does not depend on your civil service pay, all of which suggest that you will be wholly independent. Your experience as the

Assistant Secretary (Finance) at the Department of Pensions helped put you at the top of my shortlist, as indeed did your investigative experience.'

Willow asked herself uneasily how the minister had come to know of her detective skills. The few investigations she had tackled over the past few years had been made on a strictly amateur basis, and she had hoped that no one connected with her professional life had heard anything about them.

She saw that her silence was making Profett uncomfortable, but that did not worry her. Like most civil servants, she believed that a certain degree of mental discomfort was necessary for any minister. Without a reasonable amount of fear of their officials, elected politicians tended to make all sorts of precipitate decisions that could take their departments months to unravel.

'Are you at all interested?' he asked when the silence became unbearable.

'Could you give me a bit more information about the job before I decide?'

'The case is that of a woman called Fiona Fydgett—Doctor Fydgett in fact, the art historian. You've probably heard of her.'

'No, I don't think I have,' said Willow, adding, in an attempt to console him for her ignorance, 'but then I don't move in that world.'

'Ah. Well, she took an overdose a short while ago. The Inland Revenue had been investigating her financial affairs, and there's been a suggestion that it was their activities that drove her to suicide.'

He paused, obviously waiting for Willow to comment. She raised her darkened eyebrows. The minister took off his tortoiseshell spectacles and rubbed his eyes. He looked very tired. Willow thought that he was probably worn out with the effort of switching from opposition to government. It must have been a huge shock for all the members of the party to find themselves in charge after an election that no one had ever expected them to win.

'If the Revenue investigation was the cause of Doctor Fydgett's death,' Profett said, screwing up his myopic eyes so that he could still see her, 'it is crucial for us to establish whether or not it was carried out properly.'

'I can see that, but didn't the inquest establish the reason why she killed herself?' asked Willow.

'No,' he said with a determined smile that she thought was supposed to express complete frankness and which in itself made her suspicious. 'That surprised me, too. Never having had anything to do with either sudden death or the law, I hadn't realised that coroners are there only to decide the immediate cause of death, not to investigate motives or impute blame to anyone. If a crime has been committed, so I'm told, then it's up to the police to investigate and the courts to apportion guilt.'

'And no crime was suspected in this case?' said Willow, wanting to be absolutely clear about what she was supposed to be investigating.

'None. Which means that Fiona Fydgett's death is of no more official interest.'

'Except to you.'

'Except to my department. In the circumstances we can't just let it go. I have to be certain that no members of the Inland Revenue exceeded their brief or misused their powers.'

'I see,' said Willow. 'I don't want to raise unnecessary objections—it sounds like an intriguing assignment—but I thought taxpayers' complaints were ultimately the responsibility of the Treasury. Besides, haven't the Revenue themselves got some kind of investigative machinery? I'd have thought they'd be far more suitable than me, and they'd know at once what they were looking for, which no outsider could.'

'They have, of course. There's the Board Investigation Office. And there's the Revenue Adjudicator, who's been doing such a good job for aggrieved taxpayers, but this is a rather different enquiry. As it has to do with citizens' rights, I'm handling it rather than one of the Chancellor's team. And in some ways it's your very lack of experience that makes you what I want.'

'Oh?'

'Yes. I want to know all about the way they think and work and deal with people. I want an assessment of the feel of the office and what the staff think about what they're doing. The ideal would be for me to see it all for myself, and, since I can't do that, I think I'm more likely to get the kind of whole picture I want from an observer like you than from an insider. It's possible… Look here, are you going to take the job on?' He smiled suddenly, displaying an unexpected charm.

Willow, her interest tickled as much by the man himself as by the job he had described, nodded. 'Yes, I think I am.'

'In that case, to be absolutely frank, what I want is to be certain that this death isn't the result of some kind of canteen culture within the Inland Revenue. Will you find out for me?'

'I'll do my best,' she said, succumbing to the charm.

TWO

THE INLAND REVENUE building was a large, ugly, flat-fronted, red-brick edifice with grimy windows and a generally unwelcoming air. Giving her name to the man in the glass-fronted cubicle by the door, Willow was admitted. Apparently scowling, he told her to go to the third floor, waved her towards a door marked 'Private' and reached for the telephone on his desk.

Wondering whether the taxpayer's charter would ever manage to change such surliness, and whether that kind of thing should figure in her report, Willow took a creaky lift up to the third floor and stepped out into a semi-open-plan office furnished with grey-metal desks and an astonishing assortment of chairs. Looking from side to side as she tried to decide which way to go, she saw a short, dark-haired woman rushing towards her from an open door at the far end of the room.

'Willow King?'

'Yes. Are you Kate Moughette?'

'That's right. Come along and meet Len Scoffer. He handled the Fydgett case and can give you everything you need.' Kate's speech was so fast that Willow found it hard to sort the hurried syllables into comprehensible words. 'One of the other FT Inspectors, Jason Tillter, used to work on Fydgett's affairs a few years ago, before—'

'I'm sorry,' said Willow, breaking into the torrent of sounds, 'but could you just stop for a moment and explain FT?'

Kate turned her head briefly, looking astonished. 'It merely stands for "fully trained",' she said, no more slowly than before. 'If you need to talk to Jason, he'll be back in the office later this morning. I can't give you much time myself, I'm afraid. I'm very pushed at the moment. But then I had little to do with the Fydgett files and so that ought not to present any problems.'

Walking behind her, trying to adjust to Kate's speed of talking, Willow remembered the few things that the minister had said about her. 'She's shaping up to be a bit of a heroine in the Revenue, apparently. She's still not particularly senior— only the equivalent of a principal—but she's increased the tax take enormously in her local office, and in a year or two they'll promote her and give her a bigger district. If she manages that as well as the current one, they'll push her on towards the very top at Somerset House. They call her "Little Miss Muffett", but from what I've heard she'd see off a tarantula any day, let alone any British spider.'

Yes, thought Willow, following her down the long room and ignoring the curious stares of the junior tax staff, I bet she would. She looks quite powerful in spite of being so short.

Like many people who had been teased for their height in childhood, Willow had an instinctive contempt for those who did not share her inches. The habit was so ingrained that sometimes she did not even notice what she was thinking. On that occasion she did and set about making amends. For some time she had been conducting a private campaign to control her tendency to mockery and disdain.

She decided that Kate Moughette's suit was admirably designed for her height and well tailored, too. It was made of wool, but so light and fine that it must have been cool enough even for that hot June day. The colour was a particularly appealing shade of pale greyish lavender, which set off her glossy black hair to advantage.

Noticing the dust in the corners of the big room and the indelibly grimed paintwork, Willow thought that Kate must spend a fortune on dry cleaning and wondered how she could afford it on the salary most principals earned. There was a premium paid to those who served in the Inland Revenue rather than the ordinary civil service, but Willow did not think it could be much.

Kate stopped in the doorway of an office, effectively blocking Willow's view into it. 'Len, this is Willow King. I told you about her last week. She's here for the merk.'

'"Merk"?' said Willow instinctively. Kate turned, looking impatiently at the newcomer.

'MRC. It's what we call the Minister for Rights and Charters here.'

'Oh, I see. I thought it must be a contraction of "merkin", and I couldn't imagine what the context might be.'

Kate's lips tightened and her little eyes narrowed, which told Willow both that she was aware of some of the odder parts of the English language and that her sense of humour was slight. Anyone who did not automatically smile, or at least grimace, at the idea of a pubic wig would have to be treated with caution.

'This is Len Scoffer,' she said coldly. 'I'll leave him to tell you anything you need to know.'

Kate darted off without waiting for either of them to say anything. Willow smiled politely at the owner of the office and took stock of him.

He was in his early sixties, broad but at the same time stringy looking. He had a crumpled face and very short, stiff, grey hair that stuck up all over his head. The jacket of his greeny-brown suit was hanging over the back of his chair and he had things like steel springs clasped around his biceps, bunching up the overlong sleeves of his sharply ironed white poly-cotton shirt. His string vest was clearly visible through it. He made no move to smile or stand up to greet the newcomer.

Willow could not prevent a sinking feeling, having come across plenty of men like him before. They were intelligent, sometimes chippy, often pigheaded, nearly always completely honest and usually intolerant of anyone who did not share their own bleak outlook on life.

'Is she always as rushed as that or is there a crisis on?' Willow asked, smiling in an attempt to enlist his sympathy.

'She doesn't believe in wasting taxpayers' money. Nor do I.' Scoffer had a rasping voice that made it clear his sympathy was not on offer. 'Politicians do that much too easily. I can't think what they want you to look into the Fydgett case for. It was all perfectly simple.'

'Nevertheless, that's what I've been sent to do,' said Willow with another uncharacteristically ingratiating smile. 'And I'll need your help if I'm to do the job properly.'

'The woman's suicide had nothing to do with us. But if you must have the files, those for the last three years are on the press there.'

'On that what?' asked Willow, flummoxed.

Scoffer's thin lips twisted into a sneer. He pointed to a bat-tered dark-green filing cabinet opposite his desk on which were balanced a pile of cardboard folders.

'Thank you,' said Willow, feeling the full blast of his an-tagonism. She assumed that Scoffer, like most people she had ever dealt with, used aggression as his first means of defence. The prospect of being blamed for someone's death was enough to make anyone feel defensive.

'Do you think that there's somewhere I could sit and read the files?' she asked, politely enough. Watching his unyielding expression, she gave in to temptation: 'Or would that be a waste of taxpayers' money?'

'Cara!' yelled Scoffer. Willow took an involuntary step backwards. 'Cara! Come in here, will you?'

A moment later a scared-looking, brown-haired young woman dressed in a full blue skirt and well-washed black T-shirt looked around the door.

'Yes, Len? What have I done?'

'Nothing for once, unless it hasn't come to my attention yet. This is Willow King, sent by the Merk to investigate the Fydgett case. Those are the files. Take them and her to Mrs Patel's old office and tell her anything she needs to know.' He looked down again at the file on his desk, making it quite clear that in his opinion he had done all he needed to satisfy the minister.

'Would you like to come this way, Ms King?' said Cara politely.

Relieved to be treated as a human being, Willow smiled at her and followed her out into the big general office. There was amusement and mockery on the faces of several of the people sitting there, who must have heard everything that Len Scoffer had said. Once Willow would have felt humiliated by their amusement and therefore angry, but she had grown out of all that—or most of it.

Cara opened the door to an office about half the size of Scoffer's. It looked out over the busy main road.

'Will this be all right for you, Ms King?' she asked doubtfully.

'Yes, I think so,' said Willow, noticing that the metal desk itself was clean enough and that there was a telephone and a relatively stable-looking chair. It was covered in a surprising flowered nylon material that looked positively revolting above the orange carpet, but she thought that she could probably suppress her aesthetic faculties for a week or so. She opened the window to clear the air and recoiled from the noise and the smell of car exhaust from the road outside.

'And do please call me Willow,' she said when she had shut the window again. 'What's your name?'

'Caroline Saks, but I'm always called Cara.'

'And what are you?'

'A TO(HG), that is—'

'I know: a Tax Officer (Higher Grade),' said Willow, calculating that Cara's rank was the equivalent of an Executive Officer in the ordinary civil service. 'Did you have anything to do with Fiona Fydgett's case?'

'I do most of my work for Len, so yes, I did do some things. Would you like a cup of coffee?'

'Perhaps later when you're having one anyway. I'm perfectly certain that it's not your job to be making coffee for stray visitors.'

'Oh, no. We've got a machine out there. You know, a slot machine thing. Do call me if you need anything, and please don't take Len's...um, too seriously. His bark really is worse than his bite.'

'I see,' said Willow, thinking that Cara looked too frightened to reassure anyone about anything. 'Thank you.'

Cara backed out of the door and Willow sat down to read her way through the case of Fiona Fydgett, art historian, suicide, and possible tax dodger.

BY THE END OF the morning Willow thought that she had come
to understand a lot about Fiona Fydgett's career and income,
but nothing at all about her character. The files gave a confusing impression of that. From some of the letters she had
written in her flamboyant black script, she seemed to be both
casual and arrogant, but there were other letters, too, occasionally written in the same hand but more often typed, which
read as though they had been composed by a woman as fearful
as Cara Saks.

Fydgett's income had been made up of publishers' advances
and royalties, fees from an elitist travel agent, whose art tours
to Italian cities she sometimes escorted, fees for advising several art galleries on the attribution of paintings, a salary from
a famous institute of art history, and once or twice profits from
the sale of paintings she had picked up cheap and sold very
well.

It must have been a pleasant existence, Willow thought,
until Len Scoffer's increasingly aggressive letters had started
to spoil it. Fiona Fydgett had clearly spent her life in the company of like-minded people, moving between the scholarly and
commercial art worlds in London, Paris, Geneva and New
York, and being paid to travel to some of the most beautiful
places in Italy. To have earned the sums neatly typed at the
bottom of her annual accounts, she must have been successful;
she had obviously worked hard.

Her salary from the academic job was taxed under the
PAYE rules, and the profits from the sale of paintings were
treated as Capital Gains, but all the rest formed the profits of
self-employment and were taxed under Schedule D.

From the file, it appeared that Len Scoffer believed that she
owed just under five thousand pounds of extra tax. Willow
had not managed to work out how he had arrived at that figure,
but she could not help wondering why a woman like Fiona
Fydgett would have felt she had to kill herself over it. It did
not seem to be enough for anyone to die for, and Doctor Fydgett's net income for the preceding year had been well over
fifty thousand pounds. Surely if Scoffer's investigation had

been upsetting her, she could just have paid the tax and disputed the amount later.

Rereading the file in search of clues, Willow was interrupted by a knock at the door. It was immediately followed by a light, sarcastic, male voice, saying: 'You must be the important Willow King. How delightful to meet you! Jason Tillter.'

Willow looked up and saw a tall, thin, brown-haired man, who looked a little younger than Kate, standing by the door. Although he was smiling, there was a sneer in his expression; and, although he was holding out his hand with all the patronising graciousness of a visiting dignitary, he was standing too far away for Willow to take it without getting up and crossing the office. She had always disliked people who played the sort of games Jason seemed to be attempting and so she ignored his hand and merely said: 'How do you do?'

'Oh, aren't we superior?' he said, raising his eyebrows. 'Who rattled your cage this morning?'

Astonished by his quite unprovoked impudence, Willow looked at him with her jaw dropping until she realised that she must be looking gormless and shut her mouth with a snap.

'I'm sorry I wasn't here when you came,' said Jason with a return to his earlier regal manner.

'There's no reason why you should have been,' said Willow. 'I understand that you had an urgent meeting.'

Jason swung into the dingy office, rearranging the knotted silk cufflinks in his striped shirt, and sat down opposite her. He crossed his legs and leaned back. 'Now, what can I tell you?'

'I don't know that I need you to tell me anything just yet,' said Willow, examining him carefully. He and Len had been so gratuitously unpleasant that she was beginning to feel sorry not only for Fiona Fydgett but also for any other taxpayer who had had dealings with either of them. 'And I'm sure you have plenty of urgent work waiting for you.'

His self-satisfied expression tightened in irritation. A moment later he was smiling again. 'Whatever you say. I just thought you might need some help with the natives here. They're not like ordinary people, you know. I'd have thought

a stranger might need a little assistance, in translation if nothing else.'

'Well, I'm doing fine at the moment, thank you,' said Willow, thinking of Len's description of his filing cabinet as a
'press', but determined not to allow Jason to feel any sort of
control over her investigation. 'I expect that there will be
something you can help me with before I'm done, but just at
the moment I am acquainting myself with the Fydgett files.
There'll be plenty of time for questions later.'

'You'll discover pretty quickly that poor old Scoffer loathes
answering them. He's like Little Miss Muffet in that, if in
nothing else. I suspect that you're in for quite a rough time,
Ms King.'

'Is that so?' said Willow, resisting the strong temptation to
flatten Jason with some unanswerable piece of verbal brutality.
She compromised with a smile as patronising as his own. 'I
won't keep you from your work any longer. It was good of
you to make yourself known to me.'

When Jason eventually left her alone, she shook her head
and turned back to one of Doctor Fydgett's letters, which read:

Dear Sirs,
    With reference to our recent meeting, I wish to make
several things entirely clear:
    1. I have never concealed any income from your de-
partment and I will not be blackmailed into paying tax
on money I have never received.
    2. The only irregularity you have managed to estab-
lish since the commissioners decided four years ago that
my gains from the sale of paintings were Capital Gains
and not business profits was a genuine error on my part
of mistaking some dollar invoices for bills in pounds ster-
ling. I have apologised for that and frequently expressed
my readiness to pay the tax owing.
    3. The maximum tax I could possibly owe is less than
two hundred pounds. Your assessment for £4786.00 plus
interest is iniquitous.
    4. Your suggestion that I should pay that assessment

since it would be cheaper for me to do so than to continue
to fight you is outrageous. Your further suggestion that,
unless I settle with you now, you will investigate me
every year so that I shall never be free of you, is an
unconscionable threat.

Yours faithfully,
F. Fydgett

c.c. Malcolm Penholt, MP

There was a piece of paper pinned to the letter. On it someone,
perhaps Len Scoffer, had written:

Unwarrantably misleading impression of meeting. No
threats, no blackmail, merely an explanation of the risks
she faces in refusing to pay the assessment. Both sides
of any future action carefully presented, including likely
costs of going to court. LS also pointed out, after FF had
complained of having to pay accountants so much, that
if she had complied with first requirements for documents
her tax would have been paid by now and she would have
saved accountant's fees.

'I wonder,' said Willow aloud. She turned back to the beginning of the file to reread all the letters Scoffer had ever written
to Fiona Fydgett.

His first enquiry in the campaign that led to the demand for
£4786.00 had been couched in vague terms, and merely asked
whether Doctor Fydgett was sure that she had included all her
sources of income on her latest tax return.

Her accountant had answered that letter, confirming that all
her fees, commissions, royalties and salary had been included,
together with the income from her few shares, the tax-free
income from some National Savings Certificates, which he had
not included on the form, and interest from a building society
account and two separate accounts at her bank.

Scoffer's next letter, dated three months later, was more

accusatory in tone and reiterated the suggestion that Doctor Fydgett was concealing a further source of income from the Inland Revenue. It was again answered by her accountant.

Some time later she had written in her own hand, angrily refuting the suggestion that she was doing anything dishonest, and accusing Scoffer in turn of misusing his power, even using the emotive term 'abuse of process'.

He had obviously been infuriated by that for he had written back only a few weeks later with a cold, peremptory demand that she should submit copies of all her cash books, invoices, remittance advices, bank statements, and building society pass-books for the previous six years for him to check, together with details of all the travelling she had done and the cost of subsistence in the countries she had visited. He also asked for details of all the paintings she had bought and sold in the four years since the commissioners had ruled in her favour.

Doctor Fydgett had informed Scoffer that she was reluctant to provide so much information unless he gave her some reason for his mistrust of her accountant's figures. She wrote several times to tell him that she would be delighted to give him evidence of whichever figure it was that he disputed, but that he would have to tell her which it was before she could help him.

All he ever told her was that the Inland Revenue had received information that suggested she was concealing income and that it was her duty to provide whatever evidence he demanded.

Willow could not find anything in the file to show what the information was that Scoffer had received, or why he had believed that the tax Doctor Fydgett owed was £4786.00 rather than any other figure. Willow pushed the file away from her and got up to put her head round the door.

'Do you know where Jason Tillter is?' she asked the nearest person, a bored-looking young woman who was riffling through a pile of tax returns.

'Over there,' said the young woman, pointing with her chin across the room.

Willow nodded at her, unsmiling, and walked between the

rows of desks to the far wall, where Jason was arguing with another woman, who was trying to give him a file with a large yellow and white tag on it.

'But it requires immediate action,' she was saying plaintively. 'I'm only doing my job. It's not my fault someone gave it a tiger tag.'

'Don't be so ballsachingly boring, Moira. Give it to Len,' said Jason.

'I can't. It's your file. If you won't take it, I'll just put it on your desk with all the red tagged ones for this week. You can't get away from it.'

Catching sight of Willow, Jason shrugged and grabbed the file without a word.

'Yes?' he said to Willow, turning his back on the furious clerk. 'Can I give you some help after all?'

'I think you probably can if you still have time.' She smiled insincerely at him.

'Shoot,' he said, leading the way into his office. It was larger than the one she had been given and the desk had a square of grey 'leather-look' plastic glued to the top. Jason dropped the disputed file on it and sat down, putting his hands behind his head and stretching.

'I have one main question,' Willow said as she took the spare chair. 'Why are initial enquiries to taxpayers suspected of cheating made in such very vague terms?'

Jason's smile expanded to show his excellent teeth. He brought his hands down to the desk and leaned forward to say confidingly: 'Because it shakes the tree.'

'I beg your pardon?'

'It's common practice to ask general questions if we think we've discovered one anomaly because it tends to frighten a bent taxpayer into telling us about all sorts of other little fiddles we knew nothing about. It nearly always pays off.'

'I see. And do you, I mean you plural as in you officers of the Inland Revenue rather than you personally, ever get tax assessments wrong?'

'But of course we do,' he said, looking both astonished and superior, as though that were something self-evident that she

ought to have known. She did, of course, having had some
wrong assessments herself and having read of plenty of others
in the newspapers.

'Why?'

'Do you want the party line or one of the others?' Jason sat
up straight again.

Willow tried to suppress her growing amusement behind a
chill exterior. 'Try me with both sorts.'

'Okay. The official explanation is that if taxpayers all gave
us full and accurate information on time there would be no
mistakes.'

'And the others?'

'The politer explanation is that mistakes occur because of
inadequate training in the new provisions of the Finance Act
each year.' Jason looked at her across the desk, clearly enjoying himself. 'And of course the real one is that if you pay
peanuts you get monkeys and monkeys produce a lot of crap.'

'Yes, I see,' said Willow, struggling even harder to maintain
her mask of severity until she remembered Fiona Fydgett and
what had happened to her. At that all amusement vanished.
'Why are your errors considered to be different from those
made by taxpayers who receive no training at all in the provisions of the Finance Act or anything else?'

'Because we're honest even if some of us are stupid,' said
Jason easily. 'Taxpayers are all dishonest.'

Willow blinked. 'All of them?'

He laughed. 'You don't need to look so surprised. When
you've worked for the Revenue for as long as I have you get
pretty cynical about taxpayers' so-called honesty.'

'Do they ever pay more than they owe?' asked Willow,
mentally filing his chilling—and wrong—opinion for her report.

'Occasionally, but it's a rare one who actually does that.
Quite a lot don't claim back what they're entitled to, but that's
slightly different.'

'But what happens if you've overestimated an assessment
and they pay it?'

'When it becomes clear that's what happened we pay them a refund.'

'With interest?'

'If we've kept their money for more than twelve months.' Jason put up his dark eyebrows. 'Why do you ask?'

'And yet they have to pay interest from the instant any tax is overdue. Do you think that's fair?'

'My dear girl, it's hardly for me to answer a question like that,' he said. Willow, who thought that he must have been at least ten years her junior, did not give him the satisfaction of reacting to his calculated insult. 'If you don't like the law, write to your MP.'

'Doesn't it even surprise you?' she asked.

'Nope.'

'I see; thank you.' Getting up, Willow wanted to lay a hand on the top of her head to make sure it did not fly off, pushed up by the force of her rage on behalf of her fellow-taxpayers. Such unequal treatment seemed worse than merely unjust. At the door of Jason's office, she caught sight of Cara Saks.

'Did you hear any of that?' Willow asked as she left Jason's room.

Cara nodded, still looking scared.

'Well, what do you think?'

'I think it's outrageous actually,' she whispered, 'but it doesn't do to say so where Len can hear. He wants a word with you.'

'Fine,' said Willow, looking down at her watch. 'Tell him that I'm going out for lunch now and that I'll be back at my desk in an hour's time. I can see him whenever he wants to come after that. I'll be here probably for the rest of the day.'

'Actually,' said Cara, screwing up her face so that it was no longer at all pretty, 'I think he expects you to go to him.'

'Tough,' said Willow robustly.

For some time she had been waging war on any bullies she encountered in any area of her life, and she was beginning to think that Scoffer might be one of the worst. She retreated into her own office, beckoning. Cara followed, looking nervous. Willow shut the door and said quietly: 'You owe it to yourself to stand up to anyone who tries to tyrannise over you. Even if they are senior to you, you mustn't let them do it.'

'I'm sorry,' said Cara at once, hanging her head.

'No, you're not. You're just trying to stop me criticising you by agreeing with me, but I'm not criticising you: I'm only giving you a bit of friendly advice. If you give in to bullies or apologise in the hope that they'll stop tormenting you, they just get worse. Now, nip along and tell Mr Scoffer to come here after two. He can't kill you, and words may be horrible, but they don't actually do you any harm unless you let them. Okay?'

'All right,' said Cara, backing towards the door and looking even more scared.

As soon as Cara had gone, shutting the door behind her, Willow decided that she had had enough of tax inspectors for the moment. She wanted to find out something about the real Fiona Fydgett rather than the confusing paper version of the files and rang the number that the minister had given her for the dead woman's sister.

'Five Plough Court,' said a heavy male voice.

'Oh,' said Willow, feeling stumped. 'Um, I was trying to get in touch with Ms Serena Fydgett. Have I got the wrong number?'

'No. I'll put you through.'

A moment later Willow was speaking to Fiona's next of kin.

'And so,' she finished her explanation of who she was and what she was doing, 'I wondered if I could come and talk to you about it all.'

'Yes, all right,' said Ms Fydgett, sounding both less surprised and more co-operative than Willow had expected. 'I've got a string of conferences this afternoon, and I'm in court tomorrow, but I could see you here in chambers afterwards, say at five, if that's any good to you.'

'That's fine,' said Willow, at last realising what Five Plough Court must be.

She could not think why the minister had not told her that Serena Fydgett was a barrister. He seemed to have been remarkably economical with useful details about the people she was likely to encounter during her investigation. A charitable interpretation of that could be that he had not wanted to influence any of her judgments, but there were other, rather more sinister, possibilities. They made her uneasy.

'I'll see you then,' she said, betraying none of her thoughts. 'Five Plough Court. Is that in the Temple?'

'That's right. I'll expect you at five. Goodbye.'

Willow put down the telephone, collected her handbag and left the building. She was not at all hungry, but she was restless and thought that some fresh air would probably help.

It was not until she was striding up the Vauxhall Bridge Road towards Victoria that she realised what she really wanted was to go to Tom's office in Kingston and persuade him to have lunch with her. She had an extraordinarily strong impulse to talk to him.

Smiling at her own absurdity, she dismissed the idea. Both of them had always managed to give the other space and time in which to work undistracted, even in the days before they had decided to marry. She consoled herself with the thought of a late dinner together when she would tell him about her day and hear about his.

THREE

BACK IN THE OFFICE an hour later, her feet aching but her mood better, Willow returned to her files. Only a few minutes after she sat down, the office door opened with a bang. She took her time before looking up and then deliberately closed the file and moved it to one side.

'Yes, do come in and sit down, Len,' she said calmly. 'What was it you wanted to see me about?'

He shut the door and came to stand in front of her. His feet were well spread apart and his hands were clenched.

'I do not appreciate being sent impertinent messages by the junior staff,' he said at last.

Willow raised her eyebrows. 'I find it hard to believe that Cara Saks was impertinent. I have found her to be very polite, if a little over-retiring.'

Scoffer grunted.

'She told me that you wanted to see me,' said Willow.

'That's correct, and it would have been more courteous of you to—'

'Mr Scoffer,' said Willow quietly, 'don't let's get into an argument about manners. If you have something to tell or ask me, please do so. Otherwise, I still have plenty to read. And do sit down. You look absurd, looming over me like that.'

With surprise overtaking the aggression in his face, he said nothing. Willow waited, also in silence, wanting to pressure him into speaking first. Eventually he pulled up a chair and sat down.

'There are things you need to know about the Fydgett woman before you draw any conclusions from the files.'

'Oh?'

'Yes. She was unstable as well as dishonest.'

Willow watched him, wondering why he had not given her that piece of information during their first encounter.

'As far as I can see, you have no evidence of dishonesty at all,' she said. 'In fact I cannot see from the figures here why you should have asked her for any of the extra tax. Are there some more data that have not yet found their way to the file?'

'There's plenty there.'

'Where?'

'Pass me the file and I'll show you.'

Disliking his peremptory tone, Willow nevertheless did as he asked. He turned the pages, tearing one letter as it pulled against a pin. It seemed extraordinary to her that the Revenue used pins rather than paperclips. She had already pricked her fingers twice and left beads of blood on some of Fiona Fydgett's letters.

'Here,' said Scoffer, holding the file towards her but just out of reach.

Willow had to get up to take it and ripped a hole in the knee of her tights as the fine lycra caught on a sharp edge of metal under the desk. It did not improve her temper. Having read the letter, one of the typed ones, she looked up at the inspector again. 'All it says here is that she miscalculated some dollar expenses.'

'That's right. She claimed them in pounds until we forced her to admit that the invoices she eventually submitted were for dollars.'

'But even if that were not a genuine mistake, which I would have thought was worth considering, the difference, at the most advantageous possible exchange rate, can't have come to more than a couple of hundred pounds.'

'Yes,' said Scoffer after a pause. 'That's about it.'

'Then why have you been chasing her for over twenty times that in actual tax?'

'For various reasons.'

'Such as?'

'Now, don't you take that tone with me, young lady…' Scoffer was beginning as Willow stood up.

'Mr Scoffer, don't be so stupid. I don't wish to have to pull rank.'

He looked as though he might burst into speech. Willow

smiled provocatively, hoping that he would be angry enough to betray himself, if there was anything to betray. When he said nothing, she went on: 'Look at it from my point of view. I have to be sure that you did not take a personal dislike to Doctor Fydgett for some reason and persecute her until she killed herself.'

'That's ridiculous and offensive. I did no such thing,' said Scoffer, not moving from the chair. His whole posture suggested that what he wanted to say to Willow was: you forced me to sit down, I'm not going to get up now.

'Very well. Then explain to me how you see your dealings with her.' Willow thought that she had achieved a tone of polite enquiry but Scoffer looked even more obstructive, and so perhaps she had not.

'I sent her a standard letter requesting confirmation that she had no other sources of income,' he said through his teeth. 'If she had answered honestly and clearly and in time, we would have raised an assessment based on the true figures, she would have paid the tax, and that would have been the end of that.'

Willow sat down again and pulled forward the pad on which she had been scribbling questions she wanted to ask.

'What was the source of income you thought she had? I couldn't find any notes in the file.'

'Among other things, undeclared profits from the sale of paintings.'

'Based on what? She's declared capital gains on sales in two of the past three years. What makes you think that there were any more?'

Scoffer did not answer.

'All right, we'll take it from the beginning,' said Willow with a sigh. 'Why did you send her such a vague letter in the first place? If what you suspected was that she had been selling more paintings than she admitted, why didn't you ask her about that specifically?'

'Standard practice.'

Willow wrote herself a note, remembering Jason's explanation, saying as she wrote: 'What was the information that you told her you had received about her?'

'What information?'

'You wrote to Doctor Fydgett that you had received information that she was concealing sources of income. Here.' Willow found the relevant letter and showed it to him. 'Was that just because you guessed she was selling paintings? It doesn't sound like it.'

Scoffer said nothing.

'What did you mean?' Willow went on. 'I haven't found anything on the file to justify a tax demand for £4786.00. Was that the capital gains tax on these phantom picture sales or income tax of some kind?'

Scoffer was beginning to look uncomfortable. Willow was glad to see that he had a conscience, even though it appeared to be the equivalent of a primitive single-cell organism rather than a fully developed animal.

'Well?'

'Since her death, we've discovered that the information we received may in fact have been mistaken. There's no need to look like that. It was not our error.'

'Tell me more.'

'You'll have to talk to Kate Moughette about that. If you've finished with me, I'll get back to the work I'm paid to do.'

'Just before you go, would you tell me whether it is true that it is a deliberate policy to try to frighten taxpayers of whom you're suspicious?'

'Who told you that? It's ridiculous.'

Willow smiled. 'I have in the past heard it said that inspectors sometimes send hugely exaggerated assessments in order to frighten taxpayers into producing accounts or documents of some sort. I wondered whether that was what you had been doing in the Fydgett case.'

Scoffer looked witheringly at her. 'You clearly know nothing about the way we work. All assessments are calculated to the best of our judgment. Indeed we have to sign a certificate to that effect at the time the assessment is raised.'

'And if your judgment turns out to have been flawed, what happens then?'

'Unless there was reason to know that at the time of raising the assessment, it's just too bad.'

'I see,' said Willow, thinking about it. After a moment, she added: 'When you decide to send a taxpayer a large assessment based on something other than figures provided by that taxpayer, do you make any kind of enquiries first? I mean such as checking whether he or she, who may well be innocent in any case, is intelligent, healthy or strong enough to deal with the tactics that you use?'

'Certainly not. We're not social workers. We can't be expected to mess ourselves up in other people's feelings. If you do that you become like that fool Cara. She's actually been known to cry in meetings with taxpayers when she's supposed to be merely taking notes.'

'Really?'

'Yes, causing maximum embarrassment to everyone concerned. She's a real Belfast Post Room case. She appears unable to remember that it is the business of this office to assess the full tax owed and the collector's to make certain that it is all paid. Taxpayers' feelings are not our responsibility.'

Scoffer's contemptuous expression was so offensive that Willow let herself show a little of her own dislike. His face changed at once and he pointed one stubby finger at her and wagged it.

'Do you know how much the black economy loses the exchequer?'

'No, I've no idea.'

'It's been estimated to be the equivalent of something like five pence on the basic rate of tax, and no one can be sure it's not more. That fact alone justifies everything that we do.'

Willow raised her eyebrows. 'And what about the costs that are incurred by mistakes made in offices like this?' she asked, quite politely.

'I don't know what you mean.'

'I'm quite sure that you do.' Willow tried not to let his aggression stoke up her own. 'It must cost a great deal in time, paper and postage every time you send out incorrect assessments and have to put them right. Then there are the repayment cheques sent out just a week before you ask for precisely the same amount back again. And the assessments you raise for less than a pound. And what about the costs incurred by poor communication with the collector so that time is wasted badgering innocent taxpayers, and sending in bailiffs or even bankrupting people for money they don't actually owe?'

'If all taxpayers provided full and honest information on time, there would be no need for any of that, and communications with the collector would be much easier to keep up to date.'

'Do you really believe that?' asked Willow.

'It's obvious. Tax cheats cost this country a fortune it cannot afford.'

'I'm not talking about them,' said Willow, holding down her own anger with difficulty. 'I'm on your side as far as loathing tax-dodgers goes. But I am here to look into the way you dealt with a woman who doesn't appear to have been cheating at all. And I am becoming concerned that she may have been a victim of a deliberate policy. If that is so, something needs to be done to ensure that other people who may be equally unable to cope with it do not suffer as she did.'

'If they are honest, they have nothing to fear,' said Scoffer doggedly. 'Unfortunately you have to face the fact that nearly everyone in any kind of cash-based business is on the fiddle. We have to remember that until they show themselves to be honest.'

'Whatever happened,' asked Willow more coldly than she had yet spoken to anyone in the tax office, 'to the basic principle of English law, that you're innocent until proven guilty?'

Scoffer got up, smiling. 'Didn't you know that the Revenue is different?' he asked. 'As far as tax assessments are concerned, the onus is on the taxpayer to prove that an assessment is incorrect. How strange that you're ignorant of something so fundamental!'

Without waiting for a comment, he turned and stumped out of her office. Willow looked after him, wondering how innocent taxpayers could ever prove they had not received any cash payments if the Revenue were convinced that they had. She was deeply relieved that her own tax affairs were dealt with by a very different kind of inspector. Although she had had no direct contact with him, the letters and assessments he sent her had always been reasonable, even when they were wrong, and his responses to her accountant's corrections had always been impeccable and quick.

By a quarter to six the building was almost completely empty. Willow, who had agreed to see the minister in the House of Commons at half-past six to report informally on her first day's investigation, put her files away and walked out into the main office. The metal desks with their loads of files, loose papers, typewriters, computer screens and sad little heaps of mess looked infinitely depressing. The ferocious power that unhappy taxpayers like Fiona Fydgett seemed to feel issuing from such rooms seemed hard to take seriously.

Perhaps it was not surprising that Scoffer had no idea of the terror he might be visiting on his innocent suspects. And perhaps it was no wonder that anxious taxpayers appeared shifty to him as they tried to contain their fear and deal with demands that they did not always understand, even if they considered them justified.

Reaching the door of Kate's office, Willow pushed it open and looked in.

'Ah, yes, come in.' Kate was frowning as though she had a headache or an intractable problem. She did not look at all pleased to see Willow.

'Thank you. I thought it just as well to wait until the staff had gone before we had a chat,' said Willow, taking a chair without being invited to sit down.

'I can't imagine what you might need me for.'

'No? Well, very little really so far. Len Scoffer referred me to you when I asked him about the information this office received about Fiona Fydgett's income.'

'Did he? As you must know, all financial information we receive is confidential.' Kate's rapid voice had slowed, but her coldness had not thawed at all.

Willow looked at the rising star of the tax gatherers, widened her lips in an attempt at a smile, and said: 'But I've been sent here by the minister expressly to look into everything that was said and done during the investigation into Fiona Fydgett's affairs.'

'That makes no difference to the confidentiality of information received by this office.'

Willow thought that Kate sounded as though she were reciting a training manual. Two can play at that game, she decided, filling her mind with civil service formality.

'The minister needs to be fully briefed if he is to be able to defend you and your staff when questions are asked about your treatment of taxpayers. And they will be asked, you know, if not by Doctor Fydgett's Member of Parliament in the House, then by the media. She had a lot of influential friends and relations. You won't be able to cover up for much longer.'

'We have not been covering anything up,' said Kate Moughette, even more icily. 'Make your point, and don't try to threaten me. We're fire-proof here.'

'There was no threat, and I have made my only point: that I am here to report to the minister on everything that you or your staff said or wrote to and about Fiona Fydgett. Everything. Surely that's clear enough?'

'Perhaps. But I would need specific authority to give you any more information.'

'In other words, the files I have been given to read so far are fakes.'

'Certainly not.' Kate Moughette sounded genuinely outraged, which Willow felt was quite an achievement in the circumstances. 'They have merely been edited in line with our duty of confidentiality.'

'I see,' said Willow, not certain of the interaction between the Data Protection Act and the Official Secrets Act, or how far her own powers of search extended. Had she realised how much obstruction she was likely to meet, she would have made the minister give her much clearer instructions in the first place.

'Well, I'm due to see the minister this evening. I shall ask him for clearance.'

'You can do whatever you like. It won't change anything.'

Willow raised her eyebrows. Long accustomed to the odd ways of some eccentric civil service colleagues, she was still surprised by the strength of the resistance Kate and her staff were showing. 'Fine. Well, I'd better go or I shall be late for him. I'll see you in the morning. I should like to see the rest of the information by then.'

'We'll see. Good night.' The dark head bent once again over the papers and calculator on the desk.

'One more thing,' said Willow, remembering Len's demand for all his suspect's records, whether or not they were relevant to his specific enquiry, and recognising the potential usefulness of such a tactic.

'Yes?' said Kate without looking up.

'I shall also be explaining to the minister that I need to see the files—unfilleted—of all the other investigations you are carrying out at the moment.'

'That's impossible.'

'We'll see,' Willow echoed with childish satisfaction as she left.

FOUR

WILLOW REACHED the House of Commons half an hour later, having walked slowly along the Embankment, enjoying the warm evening light over the Thames, stopping outside the Tate for a moment to check the posters for any new exhibitions she or Tom might want to see.

One of the bluebottles at the door of the Palace of Westminster took her name, matched it with some secret list and then directed her to the terrace. Willow, who had visited ministers at the House often before, was surprised. In the past she had always been received in their offices.

She knew her way and, having nodded her thanks to the policeman, walked off in the direction of the terrace. She could never be sure whether she was more amused or irritated by the building's church-like gothickery. Considering the sleazy deals, the bullying of reluctant back-benchers, and the sometimes mind-numbing hypocrisy that were generally accepted there, the pretentions of its architecture seemed absurd.

Reaching the terrace, she breathed in the scent of the river, which came through the wafts of cigar smoke, aftershave, alcohol, sweat, and petrol from a passing motor launch, and thought how much had changed during her years in London. When she had first arrived in the capital nearly twenty years earlier, the Thames had been a disgusting mixture of animal, vegetable and mineral waste, and it had smelled of all of them.

Recently, she had heard, salmon had been seen not far from London, and otters were beginning to return to the upper reaches of the river. But the colour of the water was still the same shade of dull, thick *café au lait* it had been when she had stood beside it as a raw, aggressively self-sufficient mathematician from Newcastle.

There's a moral in that somewhere, she told herself piously, and then added with more familiar self-mockery, but I can't imagine what it might be.

'Ah, Minister,' she called, seeing George Profett waving to her from the edge of the terrace. She made her way to his side, adding, 'How pleasant it is out here.'

'Not at all. It's good of you to make the time. By the way, do you know Malcolm Penholt?' The minister turned to smile at the man beside him, adding, 'Malcolm, this is Willow King. She's a civil servant, loosely attached to my department at the moment.'

'Ah, yes,' said the other man, who was much more like the politicians to whom Willow was accustomed. Despite his smoothness and his carefully chosen clothes, Penholt looked as though he might be very good company. He had round dark eyes that seemed full of light in his broad, tanned face, and his wry smile was attractive. His well-controlled dark curly hair was only just beginning to recede and grow grey at the temples. He looked as though he must have been in his later forties.

'You did excellent work a year or two ago on education in prisons for the Home Office,' he said. When Willow did not react, he frowned, adding with a delightful hint of amused anxiety, 'I'm not making a fool of myself, am I? That report was one of yours, wasn't it?'

'Actually it was John Misterton's,' said Willow, smiling at his technique as well as his knowledge of her past, 'but in a way you're right; I was Secretary to the Commission. How do you do?'

She assumed that the minister had introduced them because Penholt had been Fiona Fydgett's MP, and waited for one of them to say something about her. No one said anything at all until the minister handed Willow a drink.

'Thank you,' she said, adding, in an attempt to get the conversation going, 'It's awful of me, but my memory's much worse than yours, Mr Penholt. I'm not sure which constituency you represent.'

Both men laughed.

'Fulham and Chelsea,' said Penholt casually. 'One of the few that remained staunchly Tory at last year's débâcle.'

'Oh, of course,' said Willow, remembering a little just in time. 'You were the only Conservative MP to increase his majority. How could I have forgotten?'

'Merely the civil servant's obligatory blindness to politics, I suspect,' Profett said wryly. 'Well, it was good to talk, Malcolm. We'll speak in due course. I'll keep you posted.'

'Good, George,' said the Conservative obediently. 'Good to see you. Thanks for the drink. Pleasure to meet you, Miss King.'

'All mine, Mr Penholt.'

He raised a hand in an elegantly casual wave and disappeared into the throng.

'So he was Doctor Fydgett's MP?' said Willow.

'Yes, he was. Naturally he's concerned about what happened to her, but he's a good bloke taken all in all, and he's given me a chance to find out what was going on before he starts to make capital out of it.'

'That seems remarkably charitable in the circumstances,' said Willow, wondering why the minister was refusing to look at her. She could not decide whether he or Penholt was behaving more oddly in the circumstances. As far as she could see there was nothing to stop an opposition MP making a huge and public fuss about the possible injustice done to his constituent. 'Did he know her well?'

'Just what are you implying?' he asked, withdrawing his gaze from the far end of the terrace.

'Nothing at all.' Willow let herself seem puzzled. 'It was an idle question: making conversation and all that.'

'Oh, I see. I don't think he knew her particularly well, although they had some friends in common. Now, how are you getting on with them all in the Vauxhall Bridge Road?'

'I'm not yet,' said Willow carefully. 'I'm afraid that they're all being pretty obstructive so far.'

'I suppose that was only to be expected.'

'No doubt, but if I'm to do a proper job, I shall need more information. The files they've given me have been censored, and I've been denied access to any others. Can you compel them to hand over any information I need?'

'That may be tricky. Aspects of their work constitute official secrets, or so I understand from my more experienced colleagues.'

'Well, there's no problem there. I signed the Official Secrets Act years ago, when I joined the civil service. I belong to the same club, even though they can't bring themselves to believe it.' Resentment was oozing into her voice, and she corrected it at once. 'Will you talk to your relevant colleague and get an instruction through to Little Miss Muffet?'

'I'll do my best.' The minister smiled at her reference to Kate's nickname. 'But I'm sure you know what civil servants can be like: need-to-know basis and all that.'

'Yes, indeed,' said Willow with a smile of her own. 'But the people who decide who needs to know what are sometimes kept in the dark by the very people who need to know, because they don't want irrelevant people knowing what it is they're doing—and therefore needing to know. Don't you agree?'

'It sounds a little complicated,' he said with the first glimmer of real humour Willow had seen in him, 'but I think I get your drift. I'll do what I can. So you've nothing for me so far?'

'Nothing specially about Fydgett, but I must say that your anxieties about a canteen culture may have been well founded.'

'Aha. What leads you to that conclusion?'

'Various conversations I've had that point up the hostility some of them seem to feel towards their "customers", a conviction that taxpayers are dishonest, and an apparent certainty that any errors made by taxpayers are deliberate, whereas any made by Revenue staff are wholly innocent and always excusable. But I'll put it all into the report.'

'What's your opinion of Kate Moughette?'

'I'm not sure yet. She seems efficient, but that may be merely because she speaks so fast. She dresses surprisingly lavishly, but I'm sure that's not the sort of thing that would interest you. I haven't seen or heard enough to form any fair judgment of her competence yet.'

'Pity.'

Willow stared at him for a moment and saw a faint flush staining his angular face. He had not given her any indication that he had been expecting an assessment of Ms Moughette.

'Minister, will you tell me something?'

'If I can.'

'What is it that you really expect me to find out from this investigation?'

'I can't imagine what you mean,' he said, gazing at the far end of the terrace again as though he were determined not to catch her eye. She wanted to say that she could not imagine what he might be trying to hide. 'I've told you that I want to find out whether Doctor Fydgett's death was caused, in any way or to any degree, by the activities of anyone in that tax office. Didn't I make that clear?'

'Yes you did, but I feel as though I'm being kept in the dark about something that you know or suspect, which could be relevant to the assignment you have given me.'

The minister glanced down at his watch, an expensive-looking, very thin Piaget. It seemed an uncharacteristically luxurious item for such a high-minded, almost ascetic, man.

Don't let your suspicions run away with you, Willow apostrophised herself. It was probably a present from someone or bought in the days before he even entered Parliament. She told herself that she was becoming paranoid and wondered whether she could have been infected by something in the air of the tax office.

'I'm afraid I really am going to have to leave you now, Willow. There are things I must do before tonight's main debate. Do stay, if you'd like. I'm sure there must be people you know here.'

'One or two,' said Willow, looking around. She caught sight of Elsie Trouville, who had been Home Secretary during the last government and whom she had always liked. They waved to each other. 'But I'm due home for dinner. I ought to get back.'

'Keep me informed, won't you, and I'll let you know about your powers of search and so on. At your home number?'

'Yes, please. My housekeeper will answer the telephone if I'm not there, and if she's out too there's an answering machine.'

'Splendid. I can't thank you enough for the work you're doing,' he said, with what Willow thought was probably his constituent-charming smile. His washed-out blue eyes looked distant again. He ran one hand through his thick, straw-blond hair. 'Well, good night to you.'

Willow followed him back into the building and made her way through the vaulted stone corridors to the street. Various people nodded to her as she passed, and one civil servant, with whom she had worked years earlier, stopped to chat for a moment.

He seemed surprised to see her but asked no questions. Instead he launched at once into telling her how high he had risen at the Treasury. Bored, but aware that if she continued to postpone her retirement she might find herself working with him again some day, Willow smiled and nodded in all the right places.

'Nothing's ever wasted that happens to a writer,' her literary agent, Eve Greville, had once said when Willow had confessed to a lowness of spirits that was affecting every aspect of her life. 'All the worst things come in useful in the end.'

And so do the boring and the trivial, she told herself as she eventually extricated herself from her erstwhile colleague. Reaching the fresher air of Old Palace Yard a few minutes later, she cast a glance up at the statue of Henry V. It looked even more magnificent than usual with the reflections of the evening sun glowing orange on the polished bronze.

She crossed Parliament Square and walked along Birdcage Walk to avoid the noise and bustle of Victoria Street. Cutting up through St. James's Park, enjoying the light on the water of the lake and the mixture of greens in the leaves and grass, she made her way on into Green Park, walking diagonally past the palace.

As she went she rehearsed the events of her day so that she

could make up an amusing account of it to entertain Tom when he got home. Strung up from his work dealing with serious crime and wanting distraction, he often needed her to tell him stories before he could relax.

Laughing at some of her own jokes, Willow told them this way and that until she was satisfied, interrupted only by a large man who looked as though he had just come off a building site, who grinned at her and said: 'You can talk to me, love, if you like.'

Aware that she was blushing, irritated with herself and yet a little amused as well, Willow walked on much more quickly. Quite soon she reached the boundary of the park and stood at the edge of the road, watching the roaring, angry traffic that forced its way round Hyde Park Corner. Contemplating the few crossing points above ground, she decided to save time and use the subway.

The smelly dankness made her wish that she had not given in to impatience, but she hurried on, looking neither right nor left and pretending not to see the beggar who tried to stop her.

Lurching up from his bed of matted blankets, papers and bits of cardboard, he put out both hands and shouted at her that he was starving. The smells of urine, dirt and alcohol that rose from his clothes and bed nauseated her, but they might not have been enough to stop her giving him money if he had not frightened her as well. Ashamed, but excusing herself with the knowledge that she subscribed to several charities for the homeless, she held her breath as she passed him, shaking her head, and did not breathe easily again until she reached the far side of the huge roundabout and was climbing the steps up into the open.

She was soon back in the broader, quieter, more peaceful streets of her familiar neighbourhood, where no beggars ever lay in cardboard boxes, unfed, unwashed, unhappy and frightening.

Willow knew that Mrs Rusham would have left the house twenty minutes earlier and that Tom would be unlikely to return for a while, but that suited her. Despite her complete happiness with him, she cherished the hour or so that she usually had to herself at the end of each working day. It gave her time to take stock, and, if she had been writing, to return from whatever fantasy world had been engaging her.

Planning to have a bath and perhaps a glass of wine from the latest mixed tasting case she had ordered from the Wine Society, she rounded the last corner before the mews and saw with surprise that several of the windows in the house were wide open.

Either Mrs Rusham had had a mad fit of absent-mindedness before she left the house, Willow thought, or there was something wrong. Hurrying along the street, fishing in her large, squashy suede shoulder bag for her keys, she thought of burglars and wondered if she ought to get some help before she let herself in.

There was no one around, and she thought that she would look an idiot if she summoned a busy policeman on such slim evidence of danger. Nervously unlocking the front door, Willow called out: 'Hello?'

There was the sound of hurrying footsteps and the kitchen door opening. Mrs Rusham came out into the hall, looking quite unlike herself without her white overall. It was a moment before Willow realised that her imperturbable housekeeper had been crying.

'Mrs Rusham,' she said at once, moving forward. 'Whatever's happened? Are you ill? What is it?'

Mrs Rusham shook her head, gasped out an apology, and then said: 'It's Mr Tom.'

'Mr Who?' asked Willow, wondering whether one of Mrs Rusham's relations was in trouble. Then it hit her. In a quite different voice, she said: 'My Tom?'

'Yes. He's been shot.'

Willow felt as though her insides were being sucked out of her. There was pain, dizziness, a terrifying coldness and the awful, eviscerated emptiness in the centre of her body.

'Not dead,' she said, not making a question of it.

'No.' Mrs Rusham gulped again and made a visible effort to pull herself together and give all the necessary information as quickly as possible. 'He's in Dowting's Hospital with wounds to his chest, and he has a fractured skull. They think he must have hit his head awkwardly as he collapsed. He's on a ventilator and drips. They say that he's holding his own. I thought I'd better wait for you. I couldn't just leave a note about something like that.'

'Thank you,' said Willow mechanically, her mind refusing to absorb the full impact of the news, even though her body was reacting to it all. She held on to the wall with her left hand and rubbed her damp forehead on the shoulder of her suit jacket. Her eyebrows clenched together as she tried to force her brain into some kind of rationality.

'Where did it happen?' she asked eventually.

'Somewhere in Kingston. It was his office who rang. They wouldn't give me any details. We've all been trying to find you ever since. They got the news at about half-past six.'

'I was at the House of Commons. I'd better…' Willow took her hand down from the wall and looked at the fingers. They felt as though they ought to be swollen, but they showed no signs of change. It seemed extraordinary that any part of her could be the same as it had been ten minutes earlier.

'I'll get over to Dowting's now.' Willow frowned. She couldn't see properly or think and her voice sounded peculiar. 'And you'd better get off home, I expect. At least, hadn't you?'

Mrs Rusham nodded, blew her nose hard, and blundered back into the kitchen to fetch her shopping bag and jacket. Willow stayed in the hall, unaware that the front door was still open behind her. It was not until the pressure of the keys began to hurt her palm that she realised she was still gripping them in her right hand. She moved jerkily to drop them on the pewter plate on the hall table where she and Tom always kept their keys when they were in the house.

'Holding his own,' she repeated aloud. It sounded dreadful.

The telephone started to ring. Willow did not want to talk to anyone; she moved towards the stairs so that she could change into some clothes that would be comfortable enough for a night spent in a chair by a hospital bed.

Hearing Mrs Rusham coming out of the kitchen again, Wil-

low stopped half-way up the stairs. Something moved slug-
gishly in her brain and she realised it was gratitude. She managed to unclench her lips and smile.

'It was good of you to wait so long.'

'It was all I could do,' said Mrs Rusham, sounding more
like her usual efficient, unemotional self. 'I'll set the alarms
and lock up when you've gone. Oh, I do hope… Well, that
won't do any good. I'll see you tomorrow.'

Willow nodded and went on upstairs, tripping over her feet,
which felt twice as large as usual, and trying to ignore the
buzzing in her ears and the clenching pain in the pit of her
stomach. It was not until she had buttoned up her loose trousers that she realised it was her own muscles that were gripping tight around the emptiness. She made herself relax them.
The pain seemed less intense at once, but she still felt sick
and very cold.

'Tom,' she said experimentally. 'Oh, God! Tom. Pull yourself together and get a sweater. You need to be warm. It won't
help him if you have hysterics. Get going. Tom. Take some
money and don't forget the keys. Keys. Car keys. They're on
the bunch by the door. Check the fuel before you set off. Tyres
are all right. You know that. Take the keys. Oh, Tom, please
hang on. Holding his own. Help him, for God's sake.'

Muttering to herself, she dressed and went downstairs again.
Mrs Rusham was standing in the kitchen doorway, but she
said nothing, for which Willow was dimly grateful. They nodded to each other, lips tight and eyes anxious.

Willow went out into the street to unlock her car.

FIVE

THE DRIVE across the river to the big hospital could take no more than eight minutes in the early morning or at night, but then, at the tail end of the rush hour, it took Willow forty-five minutes, creeping along the Embankment and sitting for ten minutes on the bridge itself, breathing in the exhaust from the car in front of her. She could not work out what the burning smell was for ages and even then did not think to shut the ventilators.

Her brain still would not work properly and yet she could not make it ignore what might be happening to Tom. She tried to stop herself thinking by reciting childhood jingles, multiplication tables, and rules for this and that, even running through the proof of Pythagoras's theorem as it had been laid out in her O level maths book.

Eventually she reached the far side of the bridge, skirted the roundabout and found a parking space close to the accident and emergency entrance of the big hospital. She backed her car with difficulty and eventually left it slanting selfishly into the next space.

The smell of the old hospital greeted her in a waft of familiar comfort. It was made up of floor polish, food and drink from the visitors' canteen, disinfectant, recycled air and something else she had never been able to identify. Nowhere else in the world smelled like Dowting's Hospital.

Willow knew lots of people who hated it and everything it represented, but to her it offered instant reassurance. She had never been admitted to the place except to have part of herself mended, and she had never visited friends there who had not been cured of whatever ailed them. Some of the tension eased in her neck and shoulders, and as she walked across to the reception desk she moved less clumsily.

'Where will I find Detective Chief Inspector Worth?' she asked.

A blankly official expression deadened the smile on the receptionist's face.

'I'm his wife, Wilhelmina Worth,' she said, reaching down into the depths of her bag for some identification. She found her driving licence and offered that.

'Thank you, Mrs Worth,' said the man, his expression changing to one of intense sympathy. 'May I say how sorry I am?'

'Thank you, but I'd rather you told me where to find him.'

'Of course. He's in a private room at the end of Sidney Ward in the ITU, that's the Intensive Care Unit. Tenth floor.'

'Yes, I know the way. Thank you.'

Willow made herself wait for a lift, knowing perfectly well that, however long it was before an empty one appeared, it would take less time than climbing ten flights of stairs. Eventually the green bulb above the third lift in the row lit up and a moment later the doors sighed open. There was already an inhabited bed and a green-robed porter inside, but Willow pushed herself in beside the bed and pressed the button marked ten. She turned to smile apologetically at the patient, and, seeing that he was unconscious, raised her eyes to meet the gaze of the porter.

'You going to ITU?' he said. 'Visiting's over.'

'I know. It's my husband. He's in a single room. They'll let me go in, won't they?'

'He the policeman?'

'Yes.'

The porter leaned across his sleeping charge, holding out his large, black hand. Willow took it and felt the first tears prickling at her eyes. She was at once touched and appalled by the man's wordless sympathy. That Tom's plight should already be known throughout the hospital made it seem as though he were in even worse danger than she had suspected.

The lift stopped. She looked up to check where they were and when the doors opened stepped out in the quiet dimness of the intensive care wards. A young nurse walked towards her, carrying a stainless-steel kidney bowl that seemed to be full of rubber tubing.

'Can I help you?' she asked kindly. Willow, who had half expected to be told she should not be there, could not speak for a moment. The nurse turned away to put down her bowl and came back to put a hand on Willow's arm, waiting patiently.

'My husband,' she said at last. 'Tom Worth.'

'Come along. He's down here. I'll take you. He's very fit. He's got a good chance.'

Willow could not answer. She walked through the door that the nurse was holding open and stood at the foot of Tom's bed, just looking.

His eyes were closed and his long, black lashes lay fanned out over the huge, grey-brown arcs under his eyes. His skin was the colour of old, dried-out putty. A great wodge of bandages covered the right of his head and another lay over his naked chest. There seemed to be tubes plugged in all over him.

'It's just the ventilator, a saline drip, a discharge outlet from the chest wound, and a catheter. Don't let them frighten you.'

Willow hardly heard the nurse's voice or noticed when she left the room, quietly closing the door behind her.

Quiet-footed men and women came in and out of the room at intervals during the evening. Someone brought Willow a chair and made her sit down. Later someone else talked to her, trying to persuade her to go to the canteen and eat or drink. She just shook her head and knew that they were whispering about her just outside the door. That did not seem to matter. Nothing mattered any longer except what might be happening to Tom.

As she sat watching him, she had to bite the insides of her cheeks to stop herself yelling. All she could think was that he might die, and all she could feel was a kind of nauseating panic.

It occurred to her later that grief was a lovely word, full of overtones of large-mindedness and dignity, quite unlike the mean, selfish terror that obsessed her as she sat by Tom's still body. She wanted to think only of him, but she could not do it. Every idea in her mind was connected with herself, with her fears and her guilt. Every snappish word she had ever spoken to him returned to accuse her, along with all the moments of insensitivity when she had hurt him or been thick about something he needed. She thought with loathing of the months she had spent dithering as she refused to let herself believe she loved him, or he her.

'What a waste!' she said, oblivious of the nurses just outside the door. 'Oh, Tom, I'm so sorry.'

Stop thinking, she commanded herself, knowing that she could not alter his fate however much she tormented herself with her own failings. And it was just possible that her mood might affect him. Rationally she knew that it was unlikely that he could sense anything about her presence in the room, let alone what might be going on in her brain, but for almost the first time in her life she thought that rationality might not be all important. Her mind, perhaps searching for something to distract itself, threw up a memory of his confession of superstition only that morning.

Willow did not wipe away the unaccustomed tears because she did not even notice that they were sliding down her cheeks and dripping on to the thick sweater. Tom's words echoed and re-echoed in her brain: 'I'm superstitious about that...'

'Stop thinking,' she commanded herself.

Her vigil was interrupted soon after ten by someone more ruthless than any of the nurses or the doctor who had spoken to her earlier in an effort to persuade her to leave. She did not hear him open the door, but she felt his hand pulling at her shoulder. Shocked at the contact, she turned her head fast and saw a tall, dark, angry-looking man in a crumpled grey suit. Although they had met only three times before, she recognised him at once as Superintendent John Blackled, Tom's immediate superior.

'Hello, Jack,' she said hoarsely, before she coughed to clear her clogged throat. She became aware of her damp cheeks and wiped them with the palms of both hands, pushing outwards and downwards from the sides of her nose and then shaking her hands to get rid of the dampness. 'What happened to him?'

'I'll tell you all about it, but not in here.'

'He hasn't recovered consciousness yet. He can't hear us.'

'You never know with head injuries. It's just possible that he can hear. Get weaving.'

Willow breathed deeply and then followed the superintendent out of the dim room, looking over her shoulder at the bed. Despite her protests, Blackled took her downstairs to the visitors' canteen and bought her a bowl of salty, orange-coloured soup and a roll.

'I know that the unmatchable Mrs Rusham will have left you something much better at home, but you ought to eat. You don't have to finish the bread, but you must have the soup.'

'I don't think I can swallow,' said Willow carefully, having picked up the spoon and put it tentatively into the soup. Blind obedience to authority had never appealed to her, but she recognised his good intentions.

'Don't be so self-indulgent.'

Stung, Willow looked up at him, blinking.

'Come on,' he said, more gently. 'Don't make a great drama out of it. It's bad enough as it is.'

A small but real smile pulled at her lips, as she remembered Tom's telling her that his boss was always known as 'Black Jack', as much for his impatient toughness as his actual name. The pinprick of amusement spread a little warmth into her as it usually did. She swallowed half a spoonful of soup.

'So tell me what happened,' she said when she had got it down.

'We still don't know.' Blackled was relieved to see that a little colour had come back into her grey face. 'He was on his way back from a meeting at the local nick. They've been having trouble with some violent kids down there and he'd gone to advise. Not really part of his job, but he's a mate of the DCI there, who thought he might be able to help. Tom wasn't due to meet any of the little scrotes themselves and there was no obvious risk. The desk sergeant says he left them at ten to six. At one minute to, they got a call from someone who said he'd found a man shot and bleeding in an alley just a few streets away. They called the ambulance, told the man to wait and went out in strength to see what had happened. Then they called us. We tried to get hold of you, both at home and the office.'

'I know. I was in the House of Commons with the minister. Who was the man who found him?'

'Young, black, good Samaritan apparently. They checked him out, of course, but he's got no form and his place of work still has time clocks, if you can believe it. He'd left only five minutes before he called us. No marks on his hands. No weapons. He really seems to be clean.'

'He'd hardly have waited for your lot to appear if he wasn't, would he?' said Willow with some of the old tartness. Black Jack nodded. 'Did he see anyone?'

'He says not.'

'Do you believe that?'

'No reason not to. He must have known that he'd be a suspect and it would have been easy to make up a story about seeing someone run off. But he didn't. Like I say, he's clean.'

'Thank God he was there,' said Willow, closing her eyes and feeling all the panic again, mixed with fury at whoever had fired the gun, and a less fair rage at the man opposite her.

'Right,' he agreed, apparently unaware of her anger. 'The bleeding was pretty severe as it was. Drink your soup.'

She took a little more and then gave up, announcing that she was going back to Tom.

John Blackled got to his feet. 'You can't do anything for him, and you look like hell. You ought to go to bed. Come back in the morning. They've got your number. They'll ring you if there's any change.'

As Willow stood up, he put his arms around her and held her head against his broad shoulder.

'Don't worry, Will. We'll see you right. You're family now.'

Outraged, she pulled herself away. No one but Tom called her Will. She recognised Blackled's good intentions, but she could not respond to them. Shaking her head, she told him again that she was going back up to the ward.

'Okay, Will,' he said, making her grit her teeth. 'I understand. You go on back to him if you must. And don't worry. We'll get them. We always get the bloody little toerags in cases like these.'

What good will that do, Tom? she asked silently. She knew that Blackled was talking about cases where cops are killed and that he was overstating his case. Backing away from him for a few yards, she saw that his expression of sympathy was turning puzzled and then irritated. She thought that he would have found it easier if she had leaned on his shoulder and wept and begged for help. That had never been her style. Turning away abruptly, she walked fast towards the lifts.

Much later the nurses managed to persuade her to go home by promising to telephone if there were any changes in Tom's condition. Willow stumbled out of the Intensive Care Unit and down to the big foyer of the hospital, quiet by then and empty but for one old woman sitting at the end of one of the rows of seats in her dressing gown, smoking. Willow nodded to her and went out to find the car, which got her home in nine and a half minutes.

The house seemed very empty when she let herself in, and the thought that she had once wanted an hour's solitude there at the end of every day before Tom got home seemed absurd. Mentally groping for the anger that had helped her keep uncomfortable thoughts under control in the past, she tried to hate the criminals who had fired the shots, the police officers who had not protected Tom, and the doctors who had not brought him round. But it was herself she hated most.

Having double-locked the front door and tried to think what she usually did at that time of day, she remembered that Mrs Rusham would have left dinner for two in the kitchen. Some of it probably needed putting away or at least covering. Willow opened the door of the huge fridge and nearly wept again as she saw two of Tom's favourite dishes, laid out under transparent perspex covers.

There were two small, dome-shaped, cucumber mousses,

looking very pale within their circles of dark-green watercress, and two plates of fish salad, with scallops, prawns and baton-shaped pieces of salmon and halibut, carefully arranged between strips of radish, tomato, and radicchio. A small jug of some kind of pale-green sauce stood beside the plates.

Hardly aware of what she was doing, but desperate for some kind of contact with Tom, Willow reached into the cold depths of the fridge and took out one of the mousses before taking a spoon from the nearest drawer. The smoothness of the mousse made it easy to swallow, even though she was not at all hungry, and the slight astringency of the cucumber was paradoxically comforting.

Having finished the first mousse, she picked up the other one and started to eat that, too. Half-way through the third spoonful, the possibility of Tom's dying closed her throat and she sank down on to the floor, leaned her head on the edge of one of the fridge shelves and suddenly burst into deep, howling tears.

The sobs seemed to be pulled up through her chest by an irresistible force as she gulped and choked. Tears poured out of her rapidly swelling eyes, making them burn, and her nose filled with disgusting fluid. Thoughts of Tom and herself, of life, pain, terror, and bitter coldness, flashed through her mind, chasing each other, never lasting long enough to be rationalised. Hardly able to breathe, nauseated and blubbering, Willow felt out of control and physically revolting.

Her spasms did not even begin to subside for nearly five minutes. Then, fighting for mastery, she hauled herself up from the floor, shut the fridge door at last and went to wash at the sink. As she was splashing cold water over face, rubbing at her eyes with her sticky fingers, reaching for kitchen paper to blow her nose and dry her face so that she could start washing it all over again, a phrase came into her mind.

It's your fault.

'Don't be ridiculous!' she said loudly, but it did not help.

Part of her mind was convinced that if she had not been so afraid of what loving Tom might do to her he would never have been shot. Another part taunted her with the idea that it must have been her relaxation that had brought disaster on them both. If she had kept herself braced, as she had always done in the old days, Tom would have been safe and she would have been all right, too.

Furious with herself for letting such unhelpful ideas addle her brains, she picked up the sodden balls of kitchen paper, flung them into the immaculate bin and went upstairs.

The sight of their bedroom almost overset her again. They had argued amicably for days about how to have it decorated and had settled eventually on ivy-green walls with white paintwork and furniture. The curtains were of thickly lined white cotton damask edged with a four-inch linen fringe dyed to a slightly lighter green. An old, much faded Savonnerie carpet woven in cream and pink and green was laid on the polished parquet floor, and a sunny painting of an eighteenth-century *fête champêtre* with a woman on a swing, hung between the windows opposite the bed.

Willow, who had bought it before she had even met Tom, had liked it for its frivolity and never cared that it had been described in the auction catalogue as 'After Fragonard', that it had no provenance and might even have been a copy of something once seen by a Victorian maiden aunt. But, for once, its exuberant jollity seemed out of place and garish, and she looked away.

There was a round table at either side of the big bed, which was covered with a simple white woven cotton throw from Gozo. On Willow's side the table looked almost cluttered, carrying as it did the telephone, a pile of books, a glass vase of pink and white roses, a silver Thermos of Mrs Rusham's iced lemonade, a bottle of pills and a box of handkerchieves, as well as the creamware lamp that was matched by one at Tom's side.

His table was quite different. There were no flowers, for he refused to have any near him while he slept in case they stole his oxygen, and apart from the lamp there were only two books. One would be whichever new novel or biography he was in the middle of reading. The other, Willow knew, would be by John Buchan.

It had once amused her to discover how much Tom liked the simple tales he must have first read when he was about eight, but she had come to understand that they represented a kind of safety for him. Whenever he was involved in a particularly difficult or troubling case, he retreated to Buchan's world, where villains were wholeheartedly evil and heroes triumphed, where honest women looked like boys and sang like nightingales, and where there were no horrible moral dilemmas. Good was good and bad was bad and never the twain did meet.

Determined not to resort to the sleeping pills that had always worried Tom, Willow undressed and got into bed and tried to read his copy of *Mr Standfast*. She could not get absorbed in it and after half an hour gave up and turned out the light, only to lie uncomfortably awake for hours. The cool linen sheets turned into hot, ridged, uncomfortable traps beneath her exhausted body, and the extra-fine goosedown pillows seemed lumpy and stifling.

At one moment she turned on the light to stare at the little brown bottle of Temazepam, which she kept as a kind of talisman beside her bed. The theory was that knowing the pills were there would stop her being too afraid of insomnia to let herself sleep. That night they were a talisman of another kind, in spite of Tom's remembered disapproval of suicide.

'I think it must be one of the cruellest things anyone can do to their family—and friends,' he had once said at the end of a particularly heartbreaking case.

Willow had been surprised, knowing that Tom's years in the police had given him ample evidence of all sorts of more obvious cruelties. Thinking about them did not help her sleep, and nor did the glass of milk or the brandy or any of the three soothingly familiar novels she tried to read. Eventually, soon after three in the morning, she succumbed to her old terror of sleeplessness and took two pills.

SIX

WAKING LATER THAN USUAL the next morning, Willow reached for the telephone to ring the hospital even before she got out of bed. The nurse who answered the telephone in the ITU said that there had been no change in Tom's condition during the second half of the night, but that that was not necessarily a bad thing.

'I need to speak to the consultant,' said Willow.

'There's nothing more he can tell you, Mrs Worth.'

'I know, but I need to speak to him.'

'He won't be here again until ten. I'll tell him then, if you like, and ask him to ring you. Where will you be?'

Willow dictated the number of the tax office, thanked the nurse and put down the receiver. Hearing the sound of Mrs Rusham's activities in the kitchen, Willow went downstairs to tell her the news.

Mrs Rusham listened calmly, nodded, and then said in a tightly controlled voice: 'Would you like your breakfast before or after your bath?'

Willow saw that all the other woman's defences were up again and followed her lead by announcing calmly that she would bathe and dress before breakfast.

As she was washing her feet a few minutes later, she thought about the words she would use to tell Tom how wrong he had been about Mrs Rusham's feelings for him. Her warm smile faded a moment later as reality returned and she knew that he might never be able to hear anything she told him again. But she kept her terrors under control. Mrs Rusham was not the only person whose defences were back in place.

By the time Willow left the house, having breakfasted on coffee, fruit, and a fishcake made from some of the uneaten fish from the previous night's dinner, she was superficially in command of herself. Her green suit had makeup all over the left shoulder, where she had wiped her forehead the previous evening, and so she had left it at the end of the bed for Mrs Rusham to take to the cleaners and chosen another suit from her large wardrobe. It was made of linen in a chestnut colour that made her hair look particularly vibrant, and she wore it with a thin shirt of buff silk. A string of pearls was fastened round her neck and a pair of matching earrings glowed softly in her earlobes.

She felt much too gaudy, but she was determined to look as normal as possible. The thought of having to answer sympathetic questions about Tom from any of Kate Moughette's staff was horrible. With luck, Willow thought, they would not even know that she was married to him.

No one said anything at all to her when she arrived and she walked into Mrs Patel's old office, determined to concentrate on her work for the minister.

Tom's consultant could not tell her anything when he eventually rang her, and he sounded irritable when she asked her unanswerable questions.

'Is he going to live?' she said at one moment, needing to put her worst fears into words.

'We hope so. We are doing all we can to ensure it, but I cannot give you any guarantees at the moment. When there is something to tell you, you will be told. Until then, there really is nothing more I can say. We are doing all we can.' The impatience in his voice was barely controlled by his undoubted sympathy.

'I know. Thank you. I'd like…I would like to know more details of the actual damage his brain and chest have suffered.'

'As soon as there is any news, you will have it.'

'If I were to come in at lunchtime would you be available to talk?'

'No, I'm afraid not. I'll be operating. I could see you briefly…' There was a short pause. 'Yes, the day after tomorrow at nine-thirty if that's any good to you, although there's no guarantee that we'll know any more by then.'

'I understand that. Thank you. I'll be there at nine-thirty. Goodbye.'

Breathing deeply, Willow pulled forward the notes she had written the previous day and tried to make sense of them. Her brain seemed to be quite useless and it was not until much later that she even remembered her meeting with the minister or that she had asked him to arrange for her to see the remaining confidential information about Fiona Fydgett.

By that time Kate had gone out to lunch. Willow decided that she, too, might as well go out, even though once again she did not particularly want to eat anything.

Returning to the office from a steamy café, where she had lunched on a cheese-and-salad sandwich and a can of Diet Coke, she discovered that Kate was still not back in her office. Len Scoffer was at his desk, sitting with a Tupperware box in front of him, eating his way through a solid looking pork pie. There was a tomato awaiting his attention beside a small bar of chocolate and a glossy green Granny Smith apple. He put the half-eaten pie down in the box when he saw her and wiped his mouth and his hands on a paper napkin before saying, 'Yes, Miss King?'

'I believe that an instruction has come through that I am to have access to those parts of Fiona Fydgett's file that were weeded yesterday, and also to files concerning the other investigations you're carrying out at the moment.'

'I have had no instructions about the Fydgett files, but Kate asked me to give you those.' One short bony finger was pointing towards a new pile of folders on top of his green filing cabinet. Willow picked them up. 'You'll find that they're all investigations that Kate set up when she first came here. A few have already been resolved, rather oddly in some instances; others not yet. She's about to have a go at transport— mini-cabs, taxis and private bus firms—but until now she's been targeting the building trade.'

'Really?' said Willow, noticing that Len was being more forthcoming than usual. She wondered why. 'Why should she do that?'

'Come on, you're not that naive. Hasn't a plumber ever quoted you two prices: one in cash and a higher one for a cheque, which he'd have to record in his accounts and on which he would have to pay tax?'

The patronage in his voice irritated Willow out of her apathy and she said, 'No. My housekeeper deals with all that sort of thing. Thank you for these. I'll be back for the Fydgett papers later.'

She did not wait for any reaction and returned to her own room to read through the first batch of new files, acquainting herself with the realities of financial life as a self-employed plumber, electrician, roofer and carpenter. Their letters were both less and more informative than Fiona Fydgett's. None had her way with words and yet through many of their papers came personalities that were much more distinct than hers.

The electrician, whose name was Daniel Hallten, was apparently facing bankruptcy, but he had eventually entered into an Independent Voluntary Agreement, under which he had agreed to pay his creditors a monthly sum over a period of three years. If he failed to make any of the payments he could be made bankrupt, but provided he kept them up he would be allowed to continue to trade, and in the end he would have paid his creditors only thirty pence in each pound he owed.

Willow thought that behind the aggression of some of his letters he was a worrier and intended to do right by the tax inspectors once he understood the system. He simply found it hard to grasp the way they worked and they seemed unable to find words that would explain it to him.

Joe Wraggeley, the plumber, had no such troubles. He seemed a far more insouciant character and his business appeared to be fairly successful, not least after the ferociously cold winter before his last set of accounts. Len Scoffer had disputed his figures for that year. It was clear that Wraggeley had been under surveillance of some sort, for Scoffer had challenged him to produce details of various specific jobs that had not figured in his accounts at all.

Could it ever be worth while, Willow asked herself, to have such a man watched for the sort of debts that were claimed by Scoffer? Wouldn't it cost more to trap the plumber than his unpaid taxes were worth?

Recognising a most unsuitable reaction for a civil servant, she reminded herself of her long-held and unchangeable belief that people who live in a country ought to pay its legitimate taxes and ignored the final pathetic letter in which the plumber undertook to pay the whole of the last assessment together with the accrued interest and penalties, but begged to be allowed to pay in instalments over several years.

There was no time to look at any of the other cases before her meeting with Serena Fydgett, and so Willow quickly locked away the files in the deep bottom drawer of Mrs Patel's desk.

Willow waved at Cara Saks as she left and was glad to see her smile more confidently than usual. Turning away, Willow found herself face to face with Jason Tillter.

'So how's it going?' he asked her with his usual wide but unconvincing smile.

'Interestingly,' she said. 'I'm glad to have run into you because I've got another question which I suspect you will answer more frankly than most others here.'

'Yes?'

'Is there any acknowledgment among inspectors of the basic unfairness of a taxpayer's treatment depending so much on the personality of the inspector dealing with his or her case?' Seeing that Jason was looking at her blankly, Willow added: 'Clearly some inspectors are a great deal harder to deal with than others. Doesn't it seem unfair that some taxpayers therefore have to suffer much more than others before their cases are settled?'

'No. It seems funny.' Jason produced one of his most dazzling smiles.

'I beg your pardon?' Willow could not see anything at all funny in the idea.

'Since all taxpayers are dishonest, it's a matter of the greatest amusement to us when one of them comes up against a real screwball like…well, no names no pack drill. You know who I mean.'

Willow looked at him. After a moment she said quite coldly: 'Are any of your cases under investigation at the moment?'

'Naturally. We're targeted to investigate a certain percent-age of cases and we get paid bonuses for cases settled, though not, of course, for extra tax collected. Why do you ask?'

'I'll need to see the files of those cases. I'm going through a batch of Kate's just now, but I'll be through with them in a day or two. Will you have yours ready please?'

'I'll have to—'

'Kate is fully aware of what I'm doing,' said Willow before he could complete his objection or explain why he was sud-denly looking so angry. 'Good evening, Jason.'

SHE REACHED the Temple half an hour later and walked into its leafy calm with a sense of relief. The peaceful and civilised air of the place was illusory, she knew, for the barristers who worked there could be quite as ruthless in their own way as any tax inspector. But the quiet of the narrow roads between the beautiful old buildings was a great deal pleasanter than the great barrack-like building on the Vauxhall Bridge Road with the traffic thundering up and down outside and pumping acrid fumes into the air.

It took her a while to identify Plough Court, which was not a building she knew, but she found it in the end. Inside it proved to look very much like other sets of chambers she had visited, with cream-painted walls and stone stairs edged with plain, black-painted iron banisters.

Serena, too, proved to look very much as Willow had ex-pected. She had removed her wig and gown, but Willow thought she would have known her anywhere as a barrister. She was a big woman, tall as well as broad shouldered, and there was a flamboyance about her ostensibly severe clothes and a firm confidence in her well-rounded voice that seemed quintessentially of the Bar. Plenty of barristers were not at all like their stereotypes, Willow had found, but enough of them were to provide amusement in easier times.

'Do sit down,' Serena said, gesturing towards a comfort-able-looking leather chair opposite her desk.

As Willow obeyed, the light from the window behind the desk fell on her face and Serena gasped. In a much less fruity voice, she said, 'You look ill. Are you up to this? Would you rather we put it off?'

Willow shook her head. 'I'm better working, I think, while I...' Remembering Tom's perceptive assessment of her inability to wait, workless, for news of her agent's reactions to her new novel, Willow was afraid that she might burst into tears. Determined not to give way to a habit she had always despised, particularly in front of a stranger, she concentrated hard, once more biting the scraped insides of her cheeks. When she could speak again, she said: 'You know that I'm looking into the Revenue's conduct of your sister's case.' To her regret her voice came out cool and almost uninterested. 'I gather that you had serious reservations about the tax inspector's behaviour. Can you tell me why?'

Willow watched the barrister frown and remembered that it was only a matter of weeks since her sister had killed herself. She said more warmly: 'I'm sorry if it troubles you to talk about it. I do realise that it's all very recent and that you must feel raw still. But—'

'Of course it troubles me,' said Serena impatiently, 'but the sooner it's sorted out the better. I believe that Scoffer was unnecessarily aggressive in his dealings with my sister, that he allowed his personal feelings to affect the way he treated her, and possibly that he threatened her with an annual investigation that would eventually cost her far more in accountancy fees than the tax he was claiming.'

'Why is that no more than a possibility?'

'Because the only evidence I have is a copy of a letter that she wrote, protesting about an oral threat he made during a meeting. There's no corroboration. That wouldn't be anything like enough to stand up in court.'

Serena covered her eyes for a moment. Willow, feeling almost as embarrassed as though she herself had burst into tears, said quietly: 'Shall I go?'

'No, don't.' Serena looked up again. There were no signs of distress on her face, only anger. 'In some ways, I think, it actually helps to talk. I...'

When it was clear that Serena was not going to finish her

sentence, Willow tried to prompt her. 'Tell me. I'm here to help investigate what happened to your sister and why, so that the minister can ensure that nothing like it ever happens again.'

'Yes, I know. And, believe me, I am grateful, particularly since you don't look to be in any state to be investigating anything.'

'I'm all right. What were you going to say just then?'

There was an uncomfortable silence. After a while Willow said: 'If it helps at all, I think I can understand something of what you must be feeling. My husband is badly injured in hospital at the moment, and—'

'Well, unless you caused his injuries, you won't understand,' said Serena harshly. Seeing that Willow was looking blank, Serena added as though to a rather stupid child: 'I feel guilty about what happened to my sister.'

'Guilty,' repeated Willow, whose naturally suspicious mind had been seething with memories of faked suicides. Hoping that she sounded merely interested, she said: 'Why?'

'Because I ought to have known how they were treating her and done something to help. But I've been snowed under with work. I...' Serena visibly took control of herself, and added in her court voice, 'You can't live other people's lives for them, but I could have done more to help.'

Nor die their deaths, thought Willow in a sudden panic, completely distracted from her extravagant suspicions. I must concentrate on the Fydgetts and stop thinking about Tom for the moment. I can't. I must.

'I still don't understand,' she said, trying to keep her mind on her job.

Serena sighed and fiddled with a Mont Blanc pen that had leaked ink all over a document in front of her.

'If Fiona had only told me what was happening, I could have protected her from the worst effects of what Scoffer was doing. I don't take tax cases myself, but I know plenty of people who do. We could have sorted it all out easily enough without any of the anguish that she seems to have suffered.'

'In that case, why didn't she tell you what was happening?'

Serena shook her head and then looked back at Willow. 'That's what's tormenting me,' she said, sounding puzzled by her own lack of reticence. 'If only I hadn't been so angry with her about something else, I'd probably have heard all about it. As it is, all I can do now is make certain that her estate doesn't pay a penny more tax than is due and take care of Robert for her.'

'Robert?' said Willow, once more diverted from all the things she ought to have been asking.

'Her son.' Serena looked surprised, as though she had expected Willow to know everything about the Fydgett family. 'He's fifteen. His father deserted them both before he was born. Fiona's had many... Fiona often fell in love, but she never married again. We're a cousinless family and both my parents are dead. Apart from me, Rob has no one.'

Willow closed her eyes, trying not to think of what would happen to her if Tom died.

'What is it?' asked Serena with such concern in her voice that Willow trembled. 'Is it your husband? I'm sorry if I sounded unsympathetic just now. It's difficult just at the moment to remember that our tragedy isn't the only one in the world.'

Unable to hold out any longer, Willow blew her nose hard, and explained about the shooting. Serena put a few skilful questions and Willow did not stop talking again until she heard herself explaining about the permafrost in which her emotions had been encased for her first thirty-eight years, and the way that Tom had thawed them out. Horrified to be opening her private life to a stranger, whom she had no reason to trust— or to bore—she finally put a mental gag on herself and managed to stop talking.

Serena, who had been listening in silence, said, 'I heard about the shooting on the news last night, of course, but I hadn't made the connection between him and you. I am so sorry. It must be appalling for you not knowing whether he's going to survive.'

Taken aback by the other woman's bluntness, and yet at the

same time relieved that she had not commented on any of the emotional outpourings, Willow just nodded.

'Where is he?'

'Dowting's. I've every respect for them there. If anyone can help him, they can.' Willow shook her head. 'But that's not what we're here to discuss.' She tried to think of something relevant to ask and, failing, added: 'Tell me more about the boy, your nephew.'

'He's at St Peter's in Chelsea; a boarder,' said Serena readily, not pointing out that Robert was not germane to the enquiry either. She seemed as relieved as Willow to be able to talk about something else.

'A London boarding school? Isn't that a bit odd given that your sister lived so close?'

'Not really. Fiona was—often preoccupied, and she had to travel so much that it seemed best for him to board, even though her house is only about ten minutes' walk from the school. From what I picked up from them both, it always sounded as though he'd been reasonably happy there.'

'Been?'

'Yes. As you can imagine he's quite different now.'

'Deeply unhappy, I'd have thought.'

'I'd have thought so, too, but he's gone cold on me. I don't know that I expected him to cry in my arms exactly, but he won't let any feelings out at all... He actually quite frightens me at the moment.' She frowned.

'Why frightens?' asked Willow.

'There must be so much going on under the surface,' said Serena quickly, 'and not knowing what he's thinking at all worries me. He seems hostile, and yet he doesn't appear to think it's my fault that she's dead, and so I don't understand it. I suppose the hostility might just be a mask, but for what? He's a big lad, too, for his age,' she added with apparent irrelevance.

Willow was about to ask a question when Serena shook her head so violently that she loosened one of the hairpins that skewered her dark hair into a bun at the nape of her neck.

'I've had him out of school each weekend since it happened,

so that he knows he's still got a home and...well, some kind of support. But so far it seems as though I'm doing no more than driving him even further into himself.' Serena coughed. 'I can't think why I'm telling you all this.'

Willow smiled at that, feeling for the first time that day as though she did not have to pretend about anything. 'Perhaps because I let go and told you far too much about myself. It's a weird feeling, isn't it?'

Serena only nodded.

'It's going to be difficult for you, though, isn't it: altering your life to fit a schoolboy into it, particularly a hostile one?' Willow went on, only too glad to be distracted from her own troubles and forgetting all the questions she ought to have been asking. 'Is he likely to do well academically? That might help.'

Serena's face brightened with a tolerant smile that made Willow think young Robert might eventually be lucky in his guardian.

'I think so, probably. He's certainly got brains, although his results aren't particularly good so far. I'm not sure what he'll do in the end. As a small boy he used to say he'd like to be a burglar because he liked seeing the inside of other people's homes.'

'Presumably he's got over that now,' said Willow with a laugh. She sobered up as she thought about the loneliness that might make a child yearn to be inside other people's houses.

'Definitely. The last I heard was that he's decided to go in for architecture or possibly town planning. Apparently he's been working on a project about utilities and ways of improving their provision and maintenance in large cities.'

'He'll be blessed by all Londoners if he can think of ways to do that which don't entail digging up newly surfaced roads and pavements every five minutes,' Willow said with real fervour. 'But back to your sister for a moment. I must just get one thing clear at least. Do you believe that Scoffer was responsible for her death or not?'

Serena sighed again and looked down at the piles of paper on her desk. 'Partly, but perhaps not entirely. That's why I

want to know what you find out. It would help to discover…'
She shook her head as though she could not bear to say any
more.

'Why not entirely?'

There was a long pause, before Serena said abruptly: 'She
had tried to kill herself before.'

Willow frowned. Once again she could not understand why
the minister had kept such important information from her.
Previous suicide attempts, at least, must have come up at the
inquest.

'You're very frank,' she said at last.

'It's no secret. She…well, she was often ill. Scoffer probably didn't realise that and wouldn't have known how to deal
with it even if he had; I don't believe that excuses the way he
treated her.'

'No,' said Willow slowly as she absorbed the significance
of what she had just heard, 'no, I don't suppose you do. Did
she leave a letter?'

'Not this time,' said Serena, looking up. At the sight of her
face Willow forgot enough of her own misery to feel sympathetic. 'But on the two previous occasions when she was
found unconscious with an overdose inside her there were letters.'

Willow started as her suspicions returned.

'Oh, you don't need to look like that,' said Serena at once.
'There was not the remotest doubt that she'd done it herself
or even that she'd meant to do it. She'd seen her doctor that
morning and got a new prescription for anti-depressants. She
picked up the pills from the chemist and went straight home
to swallow the lot with a large whisky. The front door was
bolted on the inside and the back door locked. There were no
signs of a break-in. No one else had been there.'

'But no one really knows why she did it this time.' Willow
looked across the desk at the self-controlled, intelligent woman
on the other side, and told herself to stop being silly. Serena
would hardly be talking so frankly if she had had a hand in
her sister's death. It frightened Willow to think how seriously
her judgment had been affected by what had happened to Tom.

'No, but several people knew that the tax investigation had been upsetting her, and her papers underline that.'

'"Several people"? Who?'

'Oh, old friends of ours, like her MP, and even one or two people she'd bought pictures from. I didn't know at the time, but some of them have been in touch with me since she died. Apparently Scoffer was convinced she'd been understating the gains she'd made on her paintings and he'd approached some of her buyers and sellers to check up on the information she'd given him.'

'What?' Willow was outraged that there were no copies of such letters on the file she had read. She assumed that Scoffer had removed them until it struck her that Serena might be lying in an attempt to arouse extra sympathy for her dead sister, or even to press the blame for her death more firmly on to Scoffer than the evidence warranted. Willow reminded herself that hearsay, such as Serena had offered, was not proof of anything at all.

'I know,' said Serena, unaware of Willow's wavering sympathy. 'It's no wonder Fiona was getting in such a state. Her reputation could have taken quite a beating from gossip generated by his activities. After all, it's not as though all the picture buyers and sellers were friends of hers, who'd have known she'd never lie. Some were perfect strangers, who might have believed anything of her—even that she'd cheated them. It must have been utterly ghastly for her.'

There was a long silence as Willow tried to absorb the implications of what she had learned.

'Have you any photographs of her?' she said eventually.

'Yes,' said Serena, looking as though she had been jolted by the change of subject. 'Why?'

'It's irrational,' Willow said, 'but I feel that if I knew what she looked like I might be able to understand a bit more about what went on between her and Scoffer, which would help me come to the sort of conclusions I've been asked to make.'

'Okay. They're all at home. I'll bung one in the post for you.'

Willow thanked her, talked for a few minutes more, and left for the hospital.

There was no change in Tom's condition. She sat with him in complete silence for four hours, sometimes certain that he would regain consciousness, at others coldly convinced that he would die. Eventually she gave in to common sense and took a taxi back to the mews, trying to deaden her own raw feelings without rebuilding the self-defensive walls that she had been working to dismantle ever since she and Tom had decided to marry.

Finding that the insides of her cheeks were clamped between her teeth again as she unlocked her front door, she deliberately relaxed her jaw muscles and tried to turn her mind to more productive things. She wished that she had prepared better for her meeting with Serena and not been so easily and completely distracted. If only she had drawn up a proper list of questions as she would have done in the old days before the shooting, the interview would have been of much more use.

Later, lying in a cool bath, with the skin of her fingers and toes slowly puckering in the scented water, she thought about Fiona Fydgett's alleged suicide attempts and knew that the investigation was going to be much more complicated than she had ever thought it would be.

SEVEN

THE FOLLOWING MORNING Willow went straight into Kate Moughette's office to ask for a copy of Serena Fydgett's letter of protest to the Chairman of the Inland Revenue. Kate's neatly painted lips tightened in irritation, but she found a photocopy of the letter without difficulty. Willow smiled insincerely and took the piece of paper back to her temporary office.

Dear Sir Roland,

My sister, Doctor Fiona Fydgett of 1 Castlereagh Street, Chelsea, whose tax affairs have been under investigation by some of your officers, killed herself last week. While I do not suggest that their treatment of her was the sole cause of her suicide, I must protest about the way they have handled her case; and I would ask you, as a matter of urgency, to review the Inland Revenue's policy on disputed tax assessments and to consider instituting some different form of training.

Taxpayers are now called 'customers', and I would suggest that if the customer cannot always be considered to be right, there should at least be an acknowledgment that the people with whom the customers are dealing may sometimes be wrong as well. It is also essential that proof of wrongdoing is established before customers are treated as guilty. I know that the onus is on taxpayers to prove their innocence, but while your officers are waiting for that I suggest it would be more productive if they refrained from treating taxpayers as criminals.

There is, I understand from my sister's solicitor, a serious allegation in her papers to the effect that the inspector in charge of her case actually threatened that if

she did not agree to pay the disputed assessment he would
see that she was investigated every year until she died.
He pointed out that she had already protested that she
could not afford to pay her accountant to deal with the
first investigation and therefore would not be in a position
to challenge any future assessments. It seems more than
possible that, unable to face the prospect of such investigations, draining both her fragile emotional energy and
her purse, she killed herself.

In any case, such a threat seems to me not only to
constitute abuse of process, but also to be tantamount to
blackmail.

Yours sincerely,
Serena Fydgett

Willow read the letter through several times, wishing that she
had the minister in front of her so that she could cross-examine
him. She would also have liked to talk to Malcolm Penholt to
find out precisely what Serena had meant by describing him
as 'an old friend of ours', and how much of her story about
her sister he would be prepared to corroborate.

Fiona Fydgett's history was sad, but, as far as Willow could
see, it was no real threat to the new government. However
appalling the investigation might have seemed to Fiona herself, any questions or criticisms that were raised about it could
be countered by the fact that she had never tried to use the
well-publicised system for complaints against the Revenue,
and indeed that she had tried to kill herself at least twice before. The minister must have known both of those facts, even
if he had not mentioned them to Willow. Could he really have
been motivated only by a desire to collect enough ammunition
to persuade his colleagues to beef up the Taxpayer's Charter?

Willow pushed aside the list of criticisms she had made for
her report on Scoffer's conduct and, as she did so, her concentration broke and the thoughts she had been holding at bay
all morning flooded into her conscious mind.

Tom will die, she said to herself. If he does, I'd rather be dead. It would have been better never to have loved him at all than to face this. All my life I've protected myself against this particular pain, and now I've lost my last defences against it; not even lost them, actually chosen to dismantle them. I must have been mad.

With an audible growl, pushed out through gritted teeth, she ordered herself to get back to work and picked up the telephone to tell Len Scoffer that she needed to talk to him again. His line was engaged and so she started to plough through all the other files she had been given, doggedly refusing to let herself think of Tom.

As the day wore on she felt as though she were getting to know many of the taxpayers who were, or recently had been, in dispute with Kate and Scoffer. Most of them seemed to her to be fundamentally honest, if sometimes rather silly, but every so often she would come across one like Joe Wraggeley, whose letters and tax returns would have aroused plenty of suspicions in her mind if she had been an inspector.

It was not until late afternoon that she found any cases that had ended at all strangely, and then she came across one concerning an architect called Simon Creke. He had got into a mess over an unprecedentedly successful year, during which he had won a lucrative architectural prize, as well as earning far more in fees than ever before or since.

When Kate had written to ask him whether he had had any sources of income other than those listed in his accounts, he had told her at once about the prize, claiming that his accountant (who was not chartered) had advised him that money from prizes was not taxable. Kate had disputed that, writing to explain that prizes from the competitions entered in the course of carrying out a trade or profession were indeed taxable. After an increasingly acrimonious exchange of letters, during which she had told the accountant that she would be imposing large penalties, she had effectively ordered both him and his client to come to her office for a meeting.

Kate's notes of that meeting made it clear that the accountant was sticking by his guns. Then there was an apparent gap in the files, after which there was a letter from a different accountant with plenty of initials after his name, dated seven weeks after the meeting, suggesting a protracted repayment schedule for the original tax demand, but making no mention of the penalties that Kate had written about in one of her earliest letters. The file made it clear that Simon Creke was faithfully repaying the tax but it gave no clues as to why Kate should have let him off the penalty.

Willow was still working when Kate walked past the open door of Mrs Patel's office on her way out of the building at seven-thirty.

'You're very dedicated,' Kate said, stopping in the doorway.

Taking the comment at face value, Willow smiled noncommittally, still determined not to tell anyone in the tax office about Tom or explain why she did not want to go back to her empty house. 'I haven't very long in which to prepare this report for the Merk, and I want to make it as comprehensive as possible,' she said, using Kate's nickname for the minister partly out of amusement and partly to try to build some kind of bond between them. 'I imagine the last thing you want is for me or anyone else to have to come back to ask more questions.'

'You're right there.' Kate also seemed to be making an unusual effort to be pleasant. She produced a smile but it looked more like a grimace than an expression of pleasure or affection. 'It's considerate of you. But you ought to stop now. I have a settled policy here that the staff work no longer than their contractual hours except in seriously dire emergencies. It's too easy for any group of people to sink into bad habits, egging each other on to stay later and later each day. All that happens is that they do less and less in each hour they spend, and ruin their private lives and mental health. I know you're not staff, but all the same...'

'I know what you mean, but I want to get this finished. Are you in a great hurry, or have you a moment to spare? There are one or two things I still don't understand, and I'd rather not make a fool of myself in my report.'

Kate looked at her watch, tightened her lips and then shrugged and came into the room, pulling her carefully looped scarf from around her neck. 'Okay, I can spare about ten minutes.'

'Well, it's this plumber really,' Willow said.

Kate smiled with a synthetic kindliness that raised most of Willow's hackles. 'We have quite a lot of those,' she said. 'Which is the case?'

Willow passed it across the shabby desk.

Kate opened it and quickly read through the first few letters and memos. 'All right. Wraggeley. Yes, I remember. What's the problem?'

'I just wondered why you went to the expense of having him under surveillance.'

Kate frowned. 'There's nothing here about surveillance.'

'No. But it's perfectly clear that it happened. The list of jobs you sent him and the sums of money you quote for his cash receipts show that you've either suborned someone on his staff or been having him watched.'

'No comment.'

'If the latter,' said Willow carefully, 'it must have cost a great deal more than the extra tax you finally got him to pay. I wondered how much of that sort of thing goes on?'

'That's hardly within your brief.' All attempts to be friendly had stopped. Kate looked as coldly obstructive as she had been on the first morning of Willow's assignment.

'I'm just interested,' said Willow, adding in an attempt to retrieve Kate's co-operation, 'I ought perhaps to say unequivocally that I entirely agree with you that people who owe tax ought to pay it. I'm merely exercised about the budgeting and costing of an operation like this. I wonder if it can ever be cost-effective.'

'So far, it looks as though it will be,' said Kate, sounding a little less annoyed. 'There's been an element of *pour encourager les autres* about it. Almost as soon as he realised that we had collected hard information about the black-economy parts of his business, we had a trickle and then a flood of revised accounts from other people in his and related trades.'

Willow could not help smiling at Kate's apposite choice of

words for the group of repentant plumbers. 'I see. That makes
sense. I was mildly concerned that you'd been going after him
out of expensive rage. Now, turning to the architect...'

Kate visibly twitched and covered the movement by reaching across for the file Willow was holding out to her. 'Well?'

'I don't quite understand why you should have let him off
the penalties you wrote about in this letter.'

'Surely you're looking for instances of Revenue brutality
rather than solicitude,' said Kate, her neat eyebrows meeting
across the top of her small nose.

'To be frank, I'm not absolutely certain exactly what I am
looking for, except that it must lie in oddities.' Willow paused
in order to smile. 'This definitely seems to me to be one of
those.'

Kate leaned back in her chair and crossed her legs, the picture of ease and confidence. Willow thought the picture might
be as untruthful as her own smile.

'It's perfectly simple, although several people in this office
have been whispering about it. No doubt you've heard some
of the tittle-tattle.' Kate's little nostrils flared in disdain. 'The
man was badly advised by his accountant—exceptionally
badly advised—and since he himself was more than willing to
provide every bit of information I asked for and pay everything he owed, it seemed inappropriate for me to impose penalties. He is paying the interest on the original sum without
demur.'

'Are you really allowed that much discretion over penalties?' asked Willow almost involuntarily.

'Certainly,' said Kate coolly as she looked at her watch
again. 'Now, if there's nothing else, I must be off.'

'Nothing,' said Willow.

Kate redraped the fine silk scarf around her neck, tucked
the ends into the collarless neck of her pale sage-coloured suit,
picked up her briefcase and left, shutting the office door behind her.

Wondering how many more of the expensive-looking pastel
summer suits Kate must have hanging in her wardrobes, Willow went back to her files. She had already called the hospital

and heard that there was still no change in Tom's condition, and the last thing she wanted was to spend an evening alone in the rooms she had furnished with him, trying to keep her thoughts under control. Work was more likely to do that than any book, piece of music or television programme. She did not even consider trying to see a friend; it would be impossible not to talk about Tom and anything that was said could only make her terror worse.

By ten o'clock her back was aching, her eyes were smarting, her nose was blocked, and smells of burning exhaust from the road outside seemed to have invaded every inch of her office. Blinking, she pulled a handkerchief out of her bag and blew her nose vigorously. It helped a bit, but there seemed still to be something wrong. After a second she decided that the burning smell was worse than just exhaust fumes and got up to investigate.

Opening her door, she saw to her horror that the whole of the wall at the far end of the long general office was on fire. Flames were licking around the doorjambs of Kate's office and Len Scoffer's, crawling up the wall and eating away at the ceiling. The grubby greenish carpet of the main office was smouldering in long patches that seemed to stretch out towards Willow like the fingers of some malevolent creature.

Transfixed in shock, for a moment she simply stared, choking in the acrid smoke with its foul smells of burning varnish, rubber, dirt, wood and plastic. Then she looked the other way towards the stairs and cried out.

Already her exit was blocked by a thick barrier of blackish grey smoke through which bright orange flames were shooting. She was caught between two advancing fires. Her eyes were streaming and the choking in her throat was threatening to make her sick as well. Desperately looking round the big room, trying to think what to do first, she noticed that the heavily sprung fire doors were hooked open in the passage between her and the stairs fire. Seizing her jacket from the back of her chair, she held it around her nose and mouth and ran forwards to unhook the doors. The brass was already hot and she swore, pulling back from it.

Taking the jacket from her face, and trying not to breathe in, she wrapped it round her hand. Choking in the smoke, despite holding her breath, and flinching from the heat that seemed strong enough to peel the skin from her face, she managed to force one stiff hook out of its brass eye. The door swung heavily towards her, almost knocking her off balance. She struggled across the wide corridor to the other door and repeated the operation. Just as the door was released from its anchorage, a rolling wave of fire uncurled itself along the ceiling towards her. Intense heat pushed her behind the swinging door and frightened her back into her wits.

She ran for the nearest telephone and punched in 999, knowing that she should have done that first. As she pressed the buttons, she saw that something had happened to the skin on the fingers of her right hand. It looked like crumpled cloth that had been pushed up in ugly wrinkles and somehow glued into place.

'Emergency. Which service are you calling?' said an efficient male voice, forcing her attention away from the horrible sight of her own hand.

'Fire,' gasped Willow.

'What's your telephone number?' asked the voice coolly.

Willow looked down at the telephone only to see that the card with the number was so old and scuffed that she could not read the figures. She craned towards the next telephone but could not see it.

'I'm not sure,' she sobbed. 'Hold on. I'll find out.'

'Too late,' said the voice irritably. 'You're through.'

'Fire brigade,' said an even more efficient voice.

'Thank God!' said Willow, wasting crucial time. She gave the address of the building, explained what had happened and what she had done so far. Her voice was almost calm for most of the time but every so often it wobbled or was overtaken by a cough.

'We're on our way,' said the fire brigade officer and gave her instructions to get to the fire escape without waiting to collect any belongings.

Willow replaced the receiver and prepared to run, realising

with a sickening lurch of fear that she did not know where the fire escape might be. There seemed to be no signs on the walls of the office that were not already on fire. The choking, vile-smelling smoke was getting worse. The sullenly smouldering carpet was alight, and the flames had reached more than half the way to her office. She could not see the wall that divided the inspectors' rooms from their staff. The noise was appalling and to her horror she saw that chunks of the ceiling were sagging down through the rolling, threatening flames.

Sobbing, Willow turned into her own small office and banged the door shut as though its varnished, veneered chipboard could keep out flames. Aware that she was disobeying the Fire Brigade's instructions, she seized her suede shoulderbag, stuffing into it the black notebook in which she had been writing, hung the bag crosswise over her back, and leaned out through the open window. The air smelled fantastically sweet, as though the dust and fumes pumped out by the incessant traffic had been miraculously cleaned. A streetlamp cast a wonderfully serene, unflickering light over the whole scene.

Suddenly hopeful, Willow got one knee on the sharp metal edge of the casement window and looked down to try to work out how she could climb to safety. The forty-foot drop seemed so much less frightening than the fire that she hauled herself up so that she was balanced on the narrow metal frame. She hardly noticed that it bit into her knees. 'Fires go up,' she said grimly. 'I'll have to get down.'

Hanging on to the sides of the window frame, she put one leg out over the sill and realised at once that she would have to go down the other way. Turning awkwardly half in and half out of the window, she saw that flames were already licking around the edges of the door, and the sight forced her to move.

With her back to the street, she re-clamped her hands on to the narrow metal window frame and gingerly launched herself down the wall. It was clear that her shoes were going to be a dreadful encumbrance and so she kicked them off. It seemed a long time before she heard them hit the pavement.

Keeping her mind deadened to the length of the drop, she felt around with her Lycra-covered feet for some kind of toehold. There seemed to be nothing. Her tights ripped against the brickwork and the skin of her big toes was scraped raw. Her hand, already painful from the burns on the palms and fingers, began to hurt seriously, and she knew that she would not be able to hold on for much longer.

Risking another look downwards in search of where to go next, she thought she saw the shadow of a gap in the brickwork about nine inches below her right foot, but she also saw the street and several upturned faces. Dizziness flooded her mind and she pushed her face into the brickwork in an effort to keep the sick faintness at bay. The roughness of the bricks rasping the singed skin of her face helped to control the vertigo and she arched and stretched her right foot until it found the crack in the bricks.

Carefully testing her weight, she took one hand off the window frame and instantly gripped the edge of the wider concrete sill. She breathed deeply and forced herself to move the other hand. The toehold was not deep enough to take her whole weight and she knew that she must move on quickly.

Her muscles began to quiver and she could not force herself to move either hands or feet. Terrified that she would fall, she hung spreadeagled against the wall, feeling the skin on her burned hands break agonisingly.

'Hang on, love,' said a voice from below her. 'You're doing okay. We've called the Fire Brigade. They won't be long. Hang on. The fire's above you. It can't come down and get you. If you fall we'll catch you. It's not far.'

Another male voice, more authoritative, said: 'You're not going to fall. Move your left hand down, about four inches. There's a gap in the mortar that'll be a great handhold. You're fine. The shaking will stop as soon as you move. Take your left hand off. Come on. You can do it.'

Feeling as though she were pulling against some tremendous suction, Willow did as she was told, scrabbling clumsily for the promised handhold.

'Aah!'

'That's right. Turn your fingers so that they fill the whole gap. Good. Now move your right foot. Just about eighteen inches below the level of your foothold is the top of another window. It's narrow, but it'll serve you so long as you don't let go of your handhold. Come on. You can do it. It's much safer than staying where you are. Come on.'

In the distance Willow could hear the consoling, exciting, threatening sound of sirens. There were several, not quite synchronised with each other.

I'm going to make it after all, she thought, relaxing just enough to move her right foot as she had been instructed. I'm not going to die.

It was not until a tough-feeling young fireman in a scratchy blue uniform pulled her into the safety of the cradle at the top of a crane that she remembered wanting to be dead. He put his arm around her shoulders, chuntering to her as his mates wound them down to the ground.

'You'll be fine, love. You did great. Don't worry now. We've called an ambulance. You'll be fine. All's well. See? They've got the pumps going.'

There was a slight bump and he guided her out on to the pavement. There was the sound of clapping and a hoarse cheer. Willow turned, every muscle in her body shaking even more than when she was pinned in terror against the excoriating brick wall. Her head felt as though it were floating a few inches above her neck and her throat was sore. She could hardly see.

'Thank you,' she muttered, frowning at the bunch of spectators, who were being urged away from her and from the building by an older fireman. A row of four gleaming, panting, quivering, scarlet and silver engines was ranged along the pavement and there seemed to be dozens of running, helmeted men, pulling out hoses, fetching ladders. One yelled out: 'We've got a real burner here.'

Then the water started, hooshing out of the hoses, filling their flatness out into great, fat worms. Willow moved as water drops ricocheted off the building into her hair and she tripped over a loose paving stone.

The young fireman steadied her and urged her towards the first-aid kit in his particular engine.

'Wait a minute,' she said, searching the faces of the growing crowd.

'There's a man there who was talking me down. A climber, I think. I must—'

'Anyone else in the building, love?' called an urgent voice.

'I don't know,' said Willow. 'Not on my floor. But I don't know about the others.'

'We can't find any, Matt,' shouted a voice from inside the building.

Willow's officer led her away to put a temporary dressing on her hands. Then the ambulance came. She tried to explain that she had to find the man who had guided her down the building, but the paramedics overrode her protests and whisked her away. With tears of pain and frustration leaking out of her sore eyes, Willow asked the green-overalled woman where she was being taken.

'Dowting's. Just across the river. You'll be there in no time and they'll give you something for the pain. It won't be long now, love. I promise. Hang on.'

Willow closed her eyes.

FIVE HOURS LATER she was lying, washed, bandaged and dressed, in a torn but clean hospital nightgown in a ward full of interested middle-aged women. Her burns were not severe, she had been told. She was very lucky. Yellow ointment had been smeared over her hands, and then they had been swathed in light, unconstricting gauze bandages. Her hair had been singed in front, as had her eyebrows, presumably by the burst of flames that had surged towards her as she forced the second door to close. But there was no serious damage. The sensation of peeling and burning on her face had been merely heat. The skin was intact, except for a couple of places where the brick-work had scraped it. The damage was not much worse than a bad day's sunbathing on the beach would have caused.

Looking down at her bandaged hands, Willow doubted the doctor's reassurances. The memory of the stretched and distorted skin on the first three fingers of her right hand was terrifying, worse even than the actual pain, but eventually the pills she had been given began to deaden her feelings.

The sharp pain in her hands and the rasping ache in her throat, nose and eyes were still there, but they seemed less immediate and her mind was soothed, too. Her thoughts slowed into easy lethargy. Someone else was responsible. She could let go for the moment.

SHE WOKE THE NEXT MORNING, feeling much less easy, choking and coughing, and feeling sick. Trying to find a tissue to spit into before she was properly awake, she banged her hand on the edge of the wheeled table at her side and cried out sharply. Holding the hand against her chest, still choking, she waited for the throbbing pain to stop.

She could not see properly and her eyes hurt too. Terrified that they might have been permanently damaged by the fire, it took Willow a while to remember that she had not taken out her contact lenses when she reached the hospital. There was nothing on her bedside table to put the lenses in and so she screwed up her eyes to try to ease the burning sensation, and decided to put up with it until she could think of something sensible to do with the lenses.

'Here, love, take this,' said a small, grey-haired woman at her side, offering her a bundle of paper handkerchieves. Willow nodded and accepted them, spitting gouts of blackened phlegm into them.

'Sorry,' she muttered when the spasm was over. 'Disgusting!'

'Don't you fret. You've had a bad time. You really have. You were having a terrible nightmare just now.'

Willow tried to haul herself up the bed, leaning on her wrists and wincing.

'Hold on,' said her rescuer. 'Bet, come over here and help.'

'Coming, Lil,' said a taller, plump woman from a bed near the door. She pulled an orange quilted dressing gown over her blue nightdress and hurried over. Her blue eyes were alight with interest and concern. She helped her friend push Willow up against the banked pillows behind her back.

'Aren't there any nurses?' she asked painfully, when, panting, they stood back.

'Oh, yes, but they're doing the changeover at the moment. You know, night staff to day. They have to talk about us, so they don't have time to do anything for a bit. But they'll be round soon. They're good girls, you know,' said the woman called Bet.

Willow smiled at them both. 'What are you in for?' she asked, but before they could answer she was coughing again.

Bet bustled off in her quilted dressing gown and fluffy slippers and poured Willow a glass of water, saying, 'Go on, Lil. Get her some more hankies. Can't you see she needs them?'

Willow, astonished by their kindness, coughed and spluttered, drank the water, and began to breathe normally again. Bet assured her that the trolley with early tea would be round soon and asked if she could get anything in the meantime. Willow, tired out by the effort of coughing up the smoke and dust, shook her head.

'D'you know which floor we're on?' she asked suddenly. The two women turned, beaming.

'Ninth,' they said in unison, obviously glad to be able to help.

Thinking of Tom, lying just one floor above her, made Willow swing her legs out from under the white cellular blanket.

'Oh, I don't think you ought to get up,' said Bet, 'not for a bit. Wait till the nurse's seen you.'

'Don't be silly, Bet,' said Lil. 'She'll need the toilet. All that coughing! Think what it does to your bladder; and she probably hasn't been at all since they brought her in.'

'We'd better help her, then. She shouldn't go on her own. She might pass out.'

'It's all right,' said Willow, smiling at them both and trying not to wince as the scorched skin of her face stretched. 'It's my hands and my lungs that are the trouble, not my legs. I'll be fine.'

She walked gingerly out of the ward, and knowing that they were watching, held herself as straight as possible in spite of the shakiness of her legs. Having used the lavatory, as they expected, she turned out of the ward through the swing doors and called the lift.

It was not until she was walking into the Intensive Care Unit that she noticed the cold on her back and realised that the nightgown she had been put into the previous evening was gaping all down the back, secured by only one pair of tapes.

'What are you doing?' called a nurse, hurrying round the desk half-way down the corridor. 'Who are you?'

'Tom Worth's wife,' she said, noticing how hoarse she sounded. She could not recognise the nurse but thought that was probably because she still could not see clearly. 'I need to see him.'

'So you are,' said the nurse, peering at her. 'I'd not have recognised you like that. But you're hurt; burned, isn't it? You shouldn't be up here. Where've you come from? I'll take you back at once.'

'Floor below. Don't know the ward. Please let me see him.'

'Come along. I'll take you back.'

'I must see Tom first.'

With a small, strong hand under Willow's right elbow, the nurse led her to Tom's room and let her stand at the foot of his bed for a moment. His face was still the odd pale-beige colour that had worried her so much when she first saw him after the shooting, and he appeared not to have moved at all since then. At that moment Willow could not believe that he would ever look any different.

'There's been no change,' said the nurse, stating the obvious, but she added with brisk kindness, 'That's not bad news. He's holding his own. Come along now. We must get you back to bed.'

EIGHT

THE FOLLOWING DAY Willow was told that her bed was needed for an emergency admission and that she would be allowed to leave after lunch. She went bearing a prescription for painkillers and a pink card to remind her of the date of her first outpatient appointment. The nurse who saw her off told her not to touch the dressing on her hands until she came to the hospital's burns clinic again after the weekend.

'But if you are worried or have any bad pain, let us know at once. All right?'

'All right,' said Willow, longing to get out of her filthy, stinking clothes and find her old spectacles, which would at least help her to see the world's sharp edges again. She took a taxi back to the house and let herself in.

It struck her belatedly that she ought to have telephoned from the hospital as soon as she came round the previous morning to let Mrs Rusham know what had happened and when she might be home. She was just rehearsing an explanatory apology when Mrs Rusham emerged from the kitchen, wiping her hands on a teatowel. At the sight of her employer she smiled, apparently bearing no malice at all.

'Mrs Rusham,' said Willow at once, determined to make amends, 'I should have rung you yesterday. It was inconsiderate of me to disappear without a word like that. I am sorry.'

'Please don't apologise. You could hardly help being taken to hospital with burns. I was very concerned for you when I read the newspapers yesterday morning, but once I had rung the hospital to enquire how you were, everything was fine.'

'I'm glad,' said Willow, wondering for the first time what might lie behind Mrs Rusham's refusal to expect anything from anyone and to keep all her own feelings and needs so tightly controlled. Both characteristics had been so useful in the days when Willow led her secret double life that she had never even considered their oddity. Now, after they had shared a much more human anxiety over Tom, Willow did find her housekeeper's restraint curious, and she was even beginning to feel guilty for all the years of treating Mrs Rusham as though she were an unfailingly efficient robot.

'I must get out of these revolting clothes and then make some telephone calls,' she said, putting her keys on to the pewter plate in the hall.

'Do you need any help getting undressed?' asked Mrs Rusham. 'Your hands look quite badly damaged.'

'It's really just the bandages,' said Willow. 'I'm sure I'll be able to manage.' She swayed suddenly and put out a hand to steady herself against the wall, adding, 'But I think I might spend the rest of the day in bed. Could you bring my post and stuff up there in a minute or two?'

'Certainly. A great many people have phoned and sent flowers. I'll bring them up so you can see them as they are and then I'll put them in vases. Would you like some in your bedroom?'

'Just a few, thank you, Mrs Rusham,' said Willow as she straightened up.

It was harder than she expected to undress, and her hands felt as though they were being burned all over again by the time she had finished, but she had managed to unzip and un-hook everything she had been wearing. Having pulled a clean, soft, white-cotton nightdress over her head, she searched for her old spectacles and fumblingly took out her lenses, sighing in relief and blinking. It would probably take a while for her eyes to adjust to seeing through spectacles again, but at least they were not as painful as the lenses had become. One of them slipped from her bandaged hands and disappeared in the pile of the carpet. For a moment its loss seemed important until Willow remembered that she had a spare. She decided to let it disappear into Mrs Rusham's Hoover in due course.

Getting into bed a moment later and lying back against the extra-soft goose-down pillows, Willow wished that she had been able to bathe and wash her hair, but the hospital had warned her not to get her hands wet. Mrs Rusham would probably have helped her, but they were not on the sort of terms that would let either of them go through such intimacy without embarrassment. Bathing would just have to come later, Willow thought. At least the nurses had washed her.

As she slid down the bed, she became aware of more damage to various bits of her body that she had not noticed at the time. There was a powerful ache across her shoulders and down the top of each arm, and her neck felt as though she had been racked.

'Superintendent Blackled is very anxious to talk to you as soon as you feel up to it,' said Mrs Rusham, returning with her arms full of flowers. 'These are from him. And here's the number where you can find him this morning. He said he wouldn't be in his own office again until late this afternoon.'

She held out a huge fan-shaped arrangement of orange, red and yellow roses, pinks and freesias. Willow shook her head, thinking that anyone who could send a fire victim a bouquet of flame-coloured flowers must be more insensitive than Blackled had ever seemed during their few encounters.

'Who are the others from?' she asked, admiring the chaste mixture of white, cream, and the palest of lemon-yellows.

Mrs Rusham opened the small, thick envelope, drew out a card and brought it to the bed.

'Serena Fydgett,' Willow read with difficulty. It seemed remarkably kind of Serena to have taken such trouble for a virtual stranger.

There was a ring at the street door downstairs. Mrs Rusham laid the flowers on the end of the bed, crackling their transparent bags, and handed Willow a sheaf of telephone messages.

Willow squinted at the various notes, trying to decipher their messages before dropping the small squares of paper on the floor by her bed as she finished them. She did not dare let herself think about her hands and whether the doctors had been over-optimistic in their reassurances.

'More flowers,' said Mrs Rusham, returning with a blue-and-white mixture wrapped in cellophane and tied with shiny blue ribbons. She detached the note.

'You read it,' said Willow, deciding that she did not want to use her hands or her eyes at all if it was not necessary.

'It's from the minister,' said Mrs Rusham, displaying more instinctive deference than Willow would have expected. 'I'll put all these in water. Would you like anything to eat or drink?'

'Something cold and fruity to drink would be nice.' Willow looked down at her swathed and padded hands, adding, 'Have we got any straws? I'm not sure I could hold a glass comfortably.'

When the housekeeper had gone, Willow wished that she had asked her to put the telephone on the bed before she left. Swearing at the pain in her hands, she managed to pull the telephone off the table at her side and tumble it into her lap. When she had wedged the receiver between her ear and her shoulder, she pressed the numbers from the piece of paper Mrs Rusham had given her and asked to speak to John Blackled.

'Will? That you? Good to hear your voice. It's a bit hoarse, isn't it? But I gather you're okay. I called the hospital and they said you'd been discharged. How are you feeling?'

'Sore and sick. Altogether vile really, but okay. What can I do for you?'

'Not a lot. I just wanted to find out how you were feeling. Oh, and I was wondering if maybe I could pop in later with one of my colleagues.'

'Oh yes?' Willow knew that her rasping voice had grown cool. Blackled's casualness seemed horribly artificial.

'Yes. I don't want to worry you or anything, but we need to eliminate the possibility that you and Tom could have been targets of the same person.'

'What?' Willow, who felt as though the smoke had affected her brain as well as her throat and lungs, could not imagine what Blackled was talking about. A moment later it hit her. 'You're not telling me it was *arson,* are you?' she said.

'Probably. Almost certainly. We're not handling that investigation here, but we're in touch with the lads who are, and they want to talk to you. I thought it'd be easier for you if I came over with one of them so that you're not exposed to complete strangers in your bedroom. I take it you are in bed? You ought to be.'

'Yes, I am,' said Willow, trying to come to terms with the idea that someone might have started the fire deliberately. 'I'm compos, if dazed and a bit silly. When d'you want to come?'

'Any time. Now, perhaps. We could be with you in about half an hour. Suit you, Will?'

'All right,' she said, wishing that she could add a demand that he call her anything but that.

He arrived thirty-five minutes later with another man, whom he introduced as Chief Inspector Harness. Willow thought that he must be in his late thirties, perhaps a dozen years younger than Black Jack, and considerably more attractive, with well-cut fairish hair, neat features and big grey eyes. He was also much more tidily dressed than the older man.

Harness's finely striped cotton shirt was beautifully ironed and his dark suit looked as though it had been brushed and pressed within the last twenty-four hours, unlike his senior officer's, which as usual might have been slept in for every night of the previous month. Side by side the two made her think of Charlotte Brontë's description of Mr Rochester and St John Rivers as Vulcan and Apollo. The memory made her smile in spite of her increasingly uncomfortable thoughts.

She nodded to both men and was surprised when Harness came to the side of her bed to shake hands. When he saw the bandages over hers he flushed and smiled with unexpected sweetness.

'Silly of me,' he said in a light, rather charming voice. 'How are you, Mrs Worth?'

'I've been better, but I'll live.'

'It's good of you to see us at such a moment.'

Willow smiled at him, liking both his politeness and his gentle manner. She told Mrs Rusham to bring them both chairs and asked them if they wanted anything to drink. Both declined and Mrs Rusham left the room as soon as she had arranged two small white cane chairs to the left of the bed.

'What makes your ''lads'' think I might have been a target of the arson, if that's really what it was?' Willow asked, wanting to get the upsetting theory into perspective as soon as possible. She clung to her natural scepticism and added hopefully: 'It seems most unlikely.'

Black Jack wagged his big head from side to side, grimacing. 'It was an idea that passed through the minds of Harness here and some of his colleagues when they read in the paper that you're poor Tom's wife. He got on to me and, unlikely though it is that there's someone with a violent grudge against you both, I thought he'd better look into it straight away, if only to eliminate the idea altogether and get everyone on to more useful work.'

Willow turned to the other man, who appeared to be too sensible to waste time on such improbable fantasies. 'How were the fires started?'

'We've no details yet, Mrs Worth,' said Harness, taking a notebook out of the inside pocket of his suit. 'But we're pretty sure it was electrical, possibly attached to some kind of timing device, possibly—'

'Well, in that case,' Willow said without waiting for him to finish, 'it's highly unlikely that I was the target. Thank God for that!'

'Why unlikely?'

'No one could have known that I'd be in the building that late, even if they had any idea that I was working there at all. The timer must have been set to start the fire at, what? Half-past nine or ten at the very latest? That's well outside working hours. Whoever it was must have been after the building, not anyone in it.'

There was a particular stillness about both men that made Willow wary. 'What is it?' she demanded.

'What's what?' said Black Jack, smiling at her, his sharp teeth looking almost sinister in his artificially hearty grin.

'There's something you haven't told me, something important.' She looked from one man to the other and then back again. 'You've both got it written all over you. Out with it.'

'She's quick, isn't she?' said Jack to his colleague, clearly deferring to him even though Harness was his junior in rank. Willow's suspicion of them both grew, and with it dislike.

'Come on, tell me,' she said, almost shouting at them in frustration. She coughed and then swallowed in a useless attempt to ease her throat. 'I don't care which of you does it, but I want to know now. Or else you can go. I'm too worn out and sore to play games.'

The men glanced at each other again.

'You know her better than I,' said Harness. 'Up to you.'

Black Jack shrugged and turned back to Willow. 'All right, Will. It's just that we didn't want to worry you if you were a bit delicate, but you're clearly your old self again. They found a body when they'd put the fire out.'

Willow felt as though she had been plunged right back to the nightmare of heat and smells and terror. She shut her eyes, unable even to ask whose body it was.

'It's been identified as that of a Mr Leonard Scoffer, the tax inspector, we understand,' said Harness, watching her carefully. 'The body was found in his office. The identification is provisional until we get his dental records, but it's probably him.'

Willow was so surprised that she opened her eyes again, frowning as she tried to absorb the shock.

'That makes it not only arson but possibly murder as well,' said Blackled. 'It's certainly manslaughter. We have to get it sorted quick.'

Willow stared into the space between her two visitors as she remembered the sight of Scoffer's office before the flames had completely hidden it. She thought that his door had been shut, but she could probably have got through the flames and opened it if she had known anyone was there. The thought of what he must have suffered while she was escaping filled her with horror.

'Are you absolutely sure you didn't know anyone was around?' said Harness.

Willow nodded, wincing as a strand of hair caught on the edge of the pillow and pulled. She realised that her scalp must have been singed as well as the skin of her face. She also realised belatedly that Harness's tone had suggested that he suspected her of deliberately leaving Scoffer to die.

'I thought they'd all gone,' she said slowly. 'Kate Mough-ette was the last. And she didn't say anything about his still being there when she came to my office. Surely she'd have known. Their rooms were next door to each other.'

Something about Kate's appearance in her office seemed important, but Willow could not remember what it was. Frustrated, she shook her head against the pillow and then wished she had not as pain shot across her scalp.

'Odd was it, that he'd be hanging about so late?' said Blackled casually.

'Extraordinary,' said Willow, blinking and wishing that she knew exactly what the two men were thinking. 'Are they certain that he was killed by the fire?'

'Why do you ask that?' Harness's voice was hard with suspicion.

'He always left in time to catch the five forty-five back to East Croydon. I overheard someone say that on my first day. Can't remember how. The only reason I can think of that he might have been still there is if he'd been unconscious. No, that doesn't fit. Someone would have noticed. Although he did always keep his door shut when he could. He hated interruptions. Oh, God! It's...'

Willow realised that she was rambling and tried to stop thinking about Scoffer as a man and concentrate on the intellectual problem of how he had died and why.

'Have you talked to his wife? I imagine she'd know if he had any other plans for that evening.'

'I haven't,' said Harness, 'but some of my people are dealing with it now.'

'Are they sure what killed him yet? Has the pathologist done the post-mortem?'

'The body's pretty badly burned. They're doing the PM now. Last I heard there weren't any signs of violence, and they think he died of asphyxiation.' Harness was still examining Willow's face. He added deliberately: 'When a corpse is found slumped in the middle of a burned room, you can usually assume the person was killed by smoke and fumes. If he's by the door, it's more likely the flames got him.'

Willow felt sick. She could not speak, even to object to Harness's interrogation technique.

Black Jack smiled less wolfishly than usual. 'They do think that the main fire may have started in or around his office, but that could have been chance,' he said, 'which is why it occurred to one bright spark—sorry, unfortunate choice of words—that you might have been the target.'

'Don't flannel,' said Willow, finding it easier to be angry than to let herself feel anything real. 'They can tell precisely where a fire started and what started it these days. Either it was his office or it wasn't. He was a smoker. Pipe. Perhaps it wasn't arson. It could have been smouldering tobacco in the wastepaper basket, or perhaps a lit match dropped on to the visitor's chair. It was probably stuffed with the old sort of quick-burning foam.' She shook her head, remembering that the stairs had been on fire, too. 'But what was he doing there so late? I wish I could think properly.'

'Actually, Will,' Jack said, 'we hoped that you might be able to tell us what he was doing. After all, there were just the two of you in the building. Alone. You know the score. What was it all about?'

Willow closed her eyes and lifted a hand to push the hair away from her forehead, forgetting her bandages for the moment. The gauze felt very rough on her reddened skin.

'What on earth are you suggesting? That I was having a romantic assignation with Len Scoffer? Or that I wanted him dead because he was rude and unpleasant?'

'Don't be ridiculous,' said Jack, making the other man blink at him.

'Careful, sir. She's a sick woman.'

'She's not that sick.'

For the first time Willow wondered what Tom's colleagues thought about his late marriage and what they said about her in the canteen. She waited to hear what the two in front of her wanted to know.

'All right,' said Harness after a sticky silence, which neither of the others seemed prepared to break. 'First of all, satisfy my curiosity and tell me what you were doing in that tax office in the first place.'

'That's easy.' Willow relaxed against her pillows. 'I'm surprised you don't know. I was sent there by the Minister for Rights and Charters to look into an investigation they've been carrying out into the affairs of a woman who killed herself a fortnight ago. Her name was Doctor Fiona Fydgett. Clear?'

'As crystal.'

It struck Willow then that if she genuinely had been the arsonist's target, his motive would have been much more likely to be the need to stop her investigation into the Fydgett case than to get back at her or Tom for anything they had done in the past. She felt her neck muscles relax against the pillow. Tom might be safe after all in his hospital bed, and as soon as her burns had healed she would be able to look after herself.

'This Scoffer: was he the investigating officer on the Fydgett case?' asked Harness.

'They don't call it that,' said Willow, 'but yes, he was.'

The bedroom door opened before either man could ask anything else, and Mrs Rusham looked in.

'Is everything all right?' she asked. 'You know the doctors did say that you were not to overtax yourself.'

Willow was amused by the evidence of Mrs Rusham's imagination and caught a gleam of laughter in her black eyes.

'I'm fine. But could I have some more of that juice? My throat's wearing out.'

'Yes, I'll fetch some. And it's time for your next pills. Here they are.' Mrs Rusham bustled over to the side of the bed and rearranged the pillows, playing the part of a nurse for once, instead of her usual withdrawn housekeeper role.

Neither police officer looked at all embarrassed by her activities, which was probably what she had hoped to achieve. They merely waited until she had gone, when John Blackled said casually: 'To go back to the question I first started with: can you think of anyone who might have wanted both you and Tom harmed? It seems a bit much of a coincidence that the pair of you should have been involved in murderous attacks within forty-eight hours.'

Willow felt impatient as well as tired and her voice was sharp as she said, 'I've already explained why I couldn't have been the target of a fire set to go off at that time of night.'

'There might not actually have been a clock,' said Harness, drawling in an unconvincing attempt to sound casual. 'It's possible, but by no means certain yet. They'll probably know for sure later, but at the moment they're saying that it could also have been a radio signal or a flashing light.'

'What? Like a remote-control bomb?'

'That sort of thing. And if so, it could have been set off at any moment they chose. I don't want to worry you unnecessarily, but we need to investigate every possibility.' He watched Willow close her eyes again and added gently: 'You know the way we work. We have to find out whether they could have been watching you and followed you to the tax office. It is possible that it was you they wanted and Scoffer who just got caught in the cross-fire, rather than vice versa.'

Willow suddenly remembered the predatory tramp who had accosted her under Hyde Park Corner, and her old sensation of being protected from chaos by only a thin membrane of safety returned.

'What makes you think I've been watched?' No longer so certain that she could look after herself, she tried to hide her fears, but she did not think that she had succeeded.

'We don't think it's very likely,' said Harness soothingly, 'but we have to make sure. If you notice anything unusual, let me know at once. We'll keep you informed, of course.' He folded up his notebook.

'Oh hell!' Willow said loudly and then put a bandaged hand to her neck, as though that could soothe the pain inside her throat.

'What have you remembered?' asked Harness sharply.

'I can't think why I've been such a fool,' said Willow, afraid that her brain would never work properly again. 'Jack, you said it could have been someone who had a grudge against me and Tom.'

'Yes?'

'There are in fact four people who might think that we had injured them. As far as I know they're all still in prison, but…'

She tried to organize her thoughts so that she could explain succinctly that over the past few years she had been involved in the unmasking of four murderers.

'You needn't look like that,' she said in exasperation as Blackled cast up his eyes. 'I didn't set out to be a private investigator or anything. It just happened. But Tom was always around as well.'

Harness took out his notebook again and clicked the point of his Biro down on to the paper. Willow gave him the names of the people she had helped to put away.

'Thank you, Mrs Worth,' said Harness. 'That's very helpful indeed.'

She thought that he looked almost grim in spite of his delicate features.

'You will tell me if any of them are out, won't you?' Willow considered the various stories she had read of prisoners escaping while in transit from one gaol to another. 'Or even in an open prison.'

'Don't you worry. If they were convicted of murder they will have got life, and none of them will be out yet. But I'll get someone to check it right away. Well, I think that about wraps it up then, don't you, sir? We'll leave Mrs Worth to her ministering angel for the moment.'

Mrs Rusham, who had just returned with a jug of fruit juice, a clean glass and another bendy straw, looked at him as though he were a cockroach. She put the glass down on the table at Willow's side, poured in the juice and stuck in the straw, bending it into a right angle so that Willow could suck up the juice without having to move or lift the glass.

'Good of you to see us. I hope your hands heal soon, Mrs Worth.'

'Thank you,' said Willow mechanically.

If she had not been so physically weak, she thought she would have been able to control her terrors better. Making sure that her voice did not wobble, she said: 'Jack, before you go?'

'Yes?' He looked down at his watch, demonstrating the urgency of the many demands on his time.

'Have you got someone at the hospital to make sure Tom's not attacked again?'

'Naturally,' he said, smiling down at her with approval. 'Didn't you see the officer there when you last visited? He saw you.'

'No, I didn't,' she said abruptly and turned her face to the wall. She heard the two men whisper to each other and then leave the room.

Once she was certain they had gone, she rolled her head back on the pillow, took the straw between her lips and sucked some of the fresh, sweet fruit juice into her mouth. As she swallowed, she felt a momentary easing of her throat and tried to think sensibly.

The possibility that someone had been stalking both Tom and herself, and, having twice failed to kill, might try again, appalled her. She got out of bed and closed all the windows.

In the resulting stuffiness, she went back to bed and picked up the first of the newspapers Mrs Rusham had provided, turning the pages until she came to the report of the fire. She found that if she held the paper really close to her eyes she could see the print without her spectacles.

There was a picture of her apparently stuck to the wall and two columns of text about the fire, but, having read every word, she was no better informed. There was no report of any body, and Scoffer was not even mentioned, although Kate Moughette was named as the District Inspector in charge of the office.

Willow searched the other papers, turning the pages with difficulty, learning from one that she was a 'flame-haired tax heroine', and from the *Daily Mercury* that she was 'romance-writer wife of shot top cop'.

Mrs Rusham reappeared with a heap of envelopes, saying, 'Here's the post. Would you like me to open them?'

'Oh, would you?' Willow let the paper fall into her lap. 'That would really help.'

Mrs Rusham slit each envelope neatly with a blunt knife she had brought with her in the pocket of her white lab coat and handed the letters still folded to Willow, who reached for her glasses. She glanced at each letter and, with much of her usual efficiency, divided them into piles to be dealt with later. Bills went into one, letters about her books into another, and personal notes in a third. The usual crop of junk mail she handed straight back to Mrs Rusham for immediate disposal.

The last envelope was brown, about five inches by eight and stiffened. Mrs Rusham opened it with more difficulty than usual, having to pick a wide strip of Sellotape from the flap.

'It seems to be a photograph,' she said, handing it over. 'Ah, here's the enclosure.'

'Thanks,' said Willow, taking the short note, which must have been written before the fire and before Serena had sent the flowers.

Willow,
This is probably the clearest photograph I've got of Fiona, even though it doesn't give much idea of her character. Hope it'll be of some help.

S. Fydgett

PS I'm sorry I upset you by cross-examining you about your husband. My friends tell me that I treat everyone like an obstructive witness these days. It was good of you to be so patient with me. I hope that you get some better news of him soon.

Touched by the post-script, Willow picked up the photograph and stared at it. There was an enormous difference between the two sisters. Fiona had been remarkably pretty, unless the studio portrait had been heavily retouched. Where Serena's face looked solid, her sister's was delicate, with a pointed chin and wide blue eyes. Her blonde hair was short, fringing her face in feathery curls. She looked fascinating and mischievous, and very much the younger of the two.

The hints Serena had given that Fiona had had many lovers seemed credible. Reconstructing some of the other hints she had not even noticed at the time, Willow began to wonder how the two women had got on and whether Serena had grudged her sister those seductive looks and the lovers they had brought her. Willow had always despised people who thought that plain women were automatically jealous of prettier ones—or that it was looks alone that aroused love—but there had definitely been something ambivalent in the way Serena had talked about her sister.

Never having had sisters of her own, Willow had nothing to go on but instinct and the novels she had read. Some of them certainly suggested that tremendous jealousy could co-exist with genuine affection, but Willow could not think of anyone, either in life or fiction, who had gone so far as to kill her sister out of jealousy.

The telephone rang before Willow could remember precisely what it was Serena had said that seemed ambivalent or even try to retrieve the reasons she had given for her certainty that Fiona had committed suicide. Mrs Rusham got up to answer it.

'It's Jane Cleverholme, from the *Daily Mercury*,' she said a moment later, having covered the mouthpiece of the receiver with great care. 'Shall I say you're not available?'

'No, it's all right,' said Willow, holding out her bandaged right hand and trying to ignore her disappointment that it was not one of the nurses with good news of Tom. 'I'll talk to her. Thanks, Mrs Rusham.'

'Willow? Is that really you? Are you all right? You sound amazing, considering.'

'Jane, how nice of you to ring!' Willow made an effort to sound glad. 'How are you?'

'Oh, I'm fine. Much more to the point: how are you? It must have been frightful.'

'Yes, it was. Just that. Are you after more gory details for your paper?'

'Not exactly. I'm features editor now, and I was just thinking that maybe you might like to do a piece for us when you're better. You know, not precisely news; more on the lines of real-life adventures of an adventurous novelist.'

Willow waited, saying nothing.

Jane wheedled on: 'And then there's the romantic angle as well, isn't there?'

'What?' Willow felt as though she had been saying little else than that one bald word for days. For an angry moment she wondered whether the police had been offering the *Mercury* hints about a relationship between herself and Len Scoffer. It was not completely unknown for police officers to hand tabloid newspapers juicy little bits of information from a crime scene.

'You sound a bit hostile, Willow.'

'A bit is understating it. I'm feeling pretty tried just at the moment, and…and battered. I'll admit I owe you one, or several, for information in the past, but I'm hurt and worn out and bloody anxious, so come out with exactly what you're proposing or bugger off and let me sleep.'

Jane laughed. There was little amusement in the sound and it was tainted with self-consciousness. Willow longed for someone to talk to her straight for once.

'I do admire you, you know,' said Jane. 'After what you've been through. No, it's just that that spectacularly handsome climber—you know, Jonathan Fergusson-Miller—was the bloke who was guiding you down the wall last night. I thought it could make a great feature: romance, life-and-death danger, brief encounter sort of thing. We'd pay for a slap-up dinner, you know, for you to talk to him—with photographs.'

'How on earth do you know it was him?' asked Willow, momentarily distracted.

'Coincidence, really. One of my colleagues was there. She'd been to meet someone not far away and was on her way to Pimlico tube. She saw and heard what happened, and then she got his name on the off-chance it might be interesting. When we discovered that the heroine was you, it seemed that we'd struck gold. He's quite happy to contribute. He's planning a new expedition for next year and is in the process of raising funds now.'

'Cynic. I'll think about it and let you know.'

'But you won't go to anyone else with it?' Jane sounded worried.

'No, I won't do that,' said Willow, glad to feel even the tiniest bit of power.

'Thanks, Willow. You're a brick. Oh, er…I've been wanting to ask, but wasn't quite sure how to put it. How's Tom?'

'Holding his own. Goodbye, Jane.'

Willow cut the connection, not wanting to hear Jane apologising for insensitivity or asking any more questions. Willow would have to accept or refuse the idea of the article within a few days; but even that might be enough to help her regain some of her defences. The thought of making an ass of herself dining with the mountaineer for the benefit of the *Mercury*'s photographers filled her with disgust, but, on the other hand, her publishers were always wanting her to accept every scrap of offered publicity.

Willow was surprised at the way her mind divided itself into layers. At the base of them all was her anxiety for Tom; that was there all the time and it could rear up above everything else without any warning. But there were other layers, too: the fears that Harness and Black Jack had raised in her; anger at her own physical pain; curiosity about the fire; sympathy for Scoffer's family; concern about exactly what the minister had expected her to discover; anxiety about Eve Greville's reactions to the book she had just finished writing; gratitude to Mrs Rusham; and even mild amusement at Jane Cleverholme's opportunism.

As Willow thought about it all, the different layers seemed to melt into each other and suddenly give way to nothing, only to reappear an instant later and swoop away before she could grasp them. The painkillers she had taken pushed her into sleep before she understood what was happening.

NINE

AFTER AN UNCOMFORTABLE and anxiety-infested weekend, Willow woke at seven on Monday morning restless and agitated. She got up at once, knowing that she would sink into real depression if she had to lie in bed for any more days with nothing to do but worry about Tom, wonder who might have tried to kill her, and imagine what it would have felt like if she had not managed to climb out of the burning building.

Anything would be better than that. Best of all would be to get back to work and establish exactly what had happened to Fiona Fydgett, whether someone else had been involved in her death, who had set fire to the tax office, and why. Once she knew all that, and whether there had been any connection between Fydgett's death and the fire, she might be able to lay some of her worst nightmares to rest.

Peering under the bandages, she saw that the stretched and wrinkled skin of her hands had blown up into large, fluid-filled blisters, which frightened her less, even though they looked more revolting. Her fingers still did not bend easily, and her palms were sore, but she had begun to believe that the hands might one day work properly again and she was becoming less reluctant to use them.

She had learned to bathe without wetting them at all by dint of pouring a lot of detergent-based bathfoam in the water so that she did not need to use soap. That morning, for her first full day out of bed, she picked clothes with the simplest of fastenings, which her hands could manage. Her eyes were getting used to spectacles again and for most of the time she could see clearly enough.

When she got out of the bath and looked at herself in the mirror, she grimaced at her puffy, reddened face. There was nothing she could do about that, since she could not bear the idea of smearing cosmetics on her skin, but she was determined to have something done to improve her lank and ragged hair.

Her usual hairdressers opened for business at half-past eight, and she persuaded them to fit her in then without an appointment. She spent an hour answering tactful questions about Tom and about her own experiences in the fire as an apprentice washed her hair with as much gentleness as he could manage, and then the owner of the salon cut and styled it. Willow tried not to look in the mirrors until they had finished. She had to admit then that she did look a little better, and she felt as though she might be able to face Kate Moughette and her team.

They had been temporarily relocated in an empty government building south of the river, but Willow wanted to take a detour to the old offices so that she could have a look at the damage the fire had done. She could not imagine what clues she might be able to pick up from merely looking at the building, but she had to try.

A taxi was passing the door of the salon as she emerged and she asked the driver to take her to the Vauxhall Bridge Road. It was not until she had strapped herself into the seat belt with great difficulty that she noticed the driver watching her in his mirror.

Part of his big face was hidden, but she could see from the reflection of his left eye that he was looking at her. When she moved sideways to get out of his line of sight, his head moved, too. He looked at the traffic every so often, but his gaze always came back to her.

It was impossible not to remember Harness's idea that someone might have been watching her. And it was equally impossible not to realise just how easy it would be to follow someone through the streets of London in a black taxi.

Willow stared out of the window at the passing buildings, only occasionally glancing at the driver. Each time, she saw that he was still looking at her. She noticed with relief that there were handles on the inside of both doors so that at least she would be able to escape, and then tried to laugh at her fears.

Before her over-vivid imagination could drive her right out of her wits, the cab turned into the Vauxhall Bridge Road and drew up outside the tax office.

'Here you are, love,' said the cabbie, as Willow leaned against the seat, waiting until she had got her breath back.

'It was you, wasn't it?' the driver said as she handed over her fare. 'In that fire?'

'Yes, it was.' Willow sighed as she realised that the cabbie was a celebrity spotter rather than a murderer's sidekick. Feeling a complete idiot, she tipped him and turned away.

A surprising amount of the building had survived. There was no glass in the windows of the top three storeys, and ugly black marks defaced the brickwork above them all, but otherwise, from the road, the walls looked solid enough. She could not see the roof, which must have been below the ornamental parapet, but she assumed that much of it had collapsed.

From where she was standing, none of the hand- or footholds that she had relied on as she climbed down the huge wall looked large enough to have supported her. It seemed astonishing that she had not fallen and smashed her skull open on the pavement. Sanity-saving fury surged through her. If the fire really had been caused deliberately, she wanted the arsonist behind bars for a long time, whoever he—or she—might be.

What had been simply a calm investigation of the goings-on of a group of possibly over-zealous tax inspectors had been transformed into something urgent and personal. Willow knew nothing whatever about arson, but she had tracked down murderers before; and she could do it again.

'Please keep back, miss,' said a young policeman in uniform as she reached the steps. 'You can't come in here.'

She unclenched her teeth, held out her hands in their gauze bandages and smiled. 'It was me who climbed out. You must have seen it in the papers.'

'That's as maybe, but I can't let you in. If you left any property and it's survived the fire it will be returned to you in due course when the experts have finished,' said the constable, looking over her head as though he was afraid the anger in her face might infect him.

'It's not that,' she said humbly. 'I had no property except notes and I suspect they all went up in flames. I just wanted to know how badly the building's been damaged.'

'Couldn't say, miss.'

'But there are people in there, aren't there? I can hear them. Couldn't I talk to some of them?'

'My instructions are that no one's to go in. It's not safe.' The constable was still making certain that he could not catch her eye. 'I must ask you to move on.'

'Very well,' she said, resigned.

It was not his fault after all that he had been put on the steps to keep out all comers, but it was a pity that he had not let her talk to whoever was assessing the evidence inside. Somehow she would just have to persuade Blackled to pass on anything he learned.

Having hailed another taxi, she gave the address of the temporary tax office. The route took the cab almost past the door of Dowting's and for a moment even her determination to track down the arsonist was overtaken by anxiety for Tom.

He had still been unconscious when she had been to see him the previous afternoon, but she thought she had detected a slight improvement in the colour of his skin. Her eyes closed and she whispered his name over and over again until the taxi stopped outside the half-renovated office block.

'I could never stand that yoga stuff,' said the cabbie as she handed over three pound coins.

'Sorry?'

'You know, all that "om, om" chanting you were doing. The wife did it for an evening course once and tried to make me have a go. Thought I'd look a right charlie standing on me head, chanting "om, om, om". Does you good though, does it?'

'Sometimes. Thanks,' she said, taking her change and giving him a fifty-pence tip, which was really far too much for the two-pound-twenty fare. But the moment of amusement he had given her was worth at least that.

She remembered seeing a note on the desk of one of the tax officers that taxi drivers should be assessed as earning twelve-and-a-half per cent of their fares in tips, and thought of all the times she had handed over a bare ten per cent. The affronted expressions of the drivers had often annoyed her, but knowing that they might have been taxed on some much greater notional sum, she felt she ought to make some kind of reparation.

'Thanks, love. And don't mind me: you keep on with the "om, om". Did the wife good, or so she says. And I must say, it did make her quite supple, know what I mean?' He leered at her theatrically.

'Thanks,' said Willow again, still more amused.

Kate Moughette was sitting at her desk, staring at a piece of paper in front of her, when Willow looked into her office a few minutes later. She looked desperately worried. When Willow greeted her, Kate seemed to gather herself together and managed to produce a smile of a sort, even though her eyes did not change at all.

'Thank goodness you're all right,' she said with unusual slowness. 'Is it agony? Your hands, I mean.'

'They're not exactly pleasant, but not torture either. May I come in?'

'Yes, of course. D'you want some coffee?'

'That would be nice, if you've got time,' said Willow, not wanting to waste Kate's unusually co-operative mood. 'Although, come to think of it, if it's another of those machines, I'd rather have tea.'

'It's not,' said Kate, still talking slowly. Willow thought that she looked awful, ill and tired, almost as though she had not slept since the fire.

'There hasn't been time to get one. We've rigged up one of those dripping machines—you know, a filter thing.' She got up and left the office, to return a moment later with two cups of coffee.

Willow noticed that there was a long smear of greasy dust along the back of her jacket. It looked as though, unaccustomed to the dust pockets of her new office, she had leaned against one and spoiled the pearl-pink linen in a way she would never have done in the familiar surroundings of the old building.

'There,' she said, handing a cup to Willow. 'You do have milk, don't you?'

'Sometimes. Kate, are you all right?'

'Perfectly,' she said more crisply and then shrugged, adding, 'At least as much as anyone could be, knowing that Len's dead—and that most of the work we've all been doing for the past year and a bit has gone, though that's less important, of course.'

'Didn't they rescue any of the files?' asked Willow, frowning. 'They must have done. The building didn't look as though it had been that badly burned.'

'They salvaged some—quite a lot of the stuff in the presses actually. And a team of paper conservators are working on some of the rest now.' She looked at Willow, who, still not quite accustomed to the way her glasses made her see, thought that there was both anger and despair in Kate's small dark eyes. 'But a hell of a lot's gone. The investigation files that had been got out for you have been almost completely destroyed.'

'What do you mean, destroyed? The data must all be on computer somewhere. Don't you have some kind of off-site back-up?'

'We're not fully computerised yet.' Kate sounded exhausted. 'Didn't you know that? A lot of our stuff's still only on paper. The staff are reconstructing what they can, and we've been... The Collector's office is sending all the information they've got, but there are still going to be some hideous gaps. We're going to have to write to all our taxpayers to get copies of this year's tax returns all over again, and—'

'But we're only in July, months from the October deadline. Surely no one's sent a return back yet?'

'You'd be surprised,' said Kate, frowning, 'how many people actually read the instructions on the form to return it within thirty days. We'd had lots in, but now we've no record of how many. We'll just have to write to everyone and we're working on the letter now. It's a nightmare. And all the investigative work...' Her voice died.

'I suppose you'll just have to dump some cases,' said Willow, thinking about her report.

Kate shrugged. 'We can't do that. Not possibly. But reconstructing the information we'd already got is going to be difficult, and in some cases, you see, we'd made them hand over all their papers to us, so they won't be able to help even if they wanted to.' She frowned again and shook her head as though to free her mind of everything in it.

'But you don't need to listen to all this. There's not really much more for you to do here, is there? You'd read the Fydgett files before they were burned, and you've talked to everyone who dealt with her. I assume you'll just write up your report and go.' Kate's voice suggested that Willow's departure would be the only encouraging event in a disastrous week.

'That sort of thing,' said Willow, determined to preserve her entrée into the tax office and wishing she had insisted on seeing the missing Fydgett papers before the fire. 'But there are still plenty of investigation files I hadn't had time to read, which are presumably still in the presses and must be all right. I've seen none of Jason's, for instance.'

'Well, they're hardly relevant. He'd done no work on Fydgett's affairs for years. My predecessor made him hand the file over to Len as soon as she disputed the assessment of profits on her picture dealing. She claimed that they were Capital Gains while Jason's view was that they were part of her business and should be taxed as income. But that aspect of her affairs was sorted out long ago. Nothing he may have done then can possibly matter now.'

That's what you think, matey, said Willow to herself, feeling tougher. She was about to ask for more details of why Len had asked Fiona Fydgett for details of all her recent picture sales when there was a knock on the door and Cara Saks looked round it.

'Yes, what is it?' asked Kate, sounding brisk again.

Cara flinched. 'You asked me to find out what's happening about Len and the funeral and everything...' She paused.

Willow wondered how often Cara was asked to take on tasks that ought to have been carried out by a secretary, and why she agreed to do it.

'Well?' Kate's voice was sharp once more.

'Apparently the police can't release, you know, it—the body—until they've solved all sorts of problems, and Mrs Scoffer doesn't want to wait, and so she's having a sort of service at their local church on Thursday afternoon. She's invited us all to tea at her house afterwards. Are we going?'

'Yes: to the service at least. Anyone who worked closely with Len, and anyone else who wants to go. Tell them all, will you, Cara?'

'Which church, and what time?' asked Willow. 'I'd like to go.'

'You?' said Kate, astonished. 'You loathed him.'

'I hardly knew him, but I feel responsible for his death.'

Both the others gaped at her.

'If I'd thought…I mean, I ought to have found out if there was anyone else in the building before just getting out like that. If I'd been more aware of what was happening, I'd have realised he…'

'I don't think you should blame yourself.' Kate shook her head again and pushed her fingers through her usually glossy dark hair, tangling it. 'I had no idea he was there either, or I'd have chased him out long before. I can't think what on earth he was doing in the office so late. It's one of the things that's been bothering me so much. Why?'

'I can't imagine,' said Willow, reminded of her own interests. 'Look, I oughtn't to be holding you up like this. I'll get out of your way. Where's my office?'

'I'm afraid we haven't got any room for you at all,' said Kate quickly. 'We're horribly pushed for space here. Must you be in the same building as us to write up your report? Surely not.'

'Perhaps not.' Willow, realising that she was not going to get anywhere by antagonising Kate, pulled forward a piece of rough paper from the pile on the desk and scribbled a row of numbers on it. 'I'll do what I can at home and then arrange to come back at a time that suits you. Here's my number in case you need me. I've put the fax number as well. I'll ring you when I need to talk. Okay? Goodbye.'

Kate merely nodded and Cara said nothing. As Willow left them, she caught sight of Jason, leaning back in a chair and gazing up at the ceiling with an extraordinarily satisfied expression on his face. She stopped beside his desk, wondering whether it was only her antipathy that made her think it might have been he who had torched the building. Regretfully she decided that it was. No one who had just caused so much damage, let alone killed a colleague, would be fool enough to look so obviously pleased with himself. On the other hand, he was quite clever enough to know that, and undoubtedly subtle enough to try a double-bluff if he thought he could get away with it.

'Morning, Willow,' he said, looking her up and down. 'That was an impressive piece of PR, wasn't it? On the front pages of most of the broadsheets and all of the tabloids. Who'd have thought a bestselling novelist could possibly be concealed behind the serious "Miss King" we'd all learned to know and... What a tasty story!' He laughed and waited for a comment, but Willow was still enough in control of herself to avoid giving him any satisfaction. She waited to see what he would do next, although she was not sanguine enough to believe he would betray himself.

'It's lucky for you that Len died, isn't it?' said Jason, trying a bit too hard to get a rise out of her. 'The story wouldn't have run on beyond the first day if it hadn't been for his barbecued corpse.'

'It must take a peculiar set of values to find humour in a death like his,' said Willow, hoping to see him squirm. She was disappointed. He looked at her as blankly as though they were playing poker. 'I gather that you used to handle Fiona Fydgett's case until the picture-dealing conflict came up. I'd like to talk to you about it and her.'

He looked surprised, but before he could say anything there was a shout from the far end of the building.

'Jason! I need you.'

Both he and Willow looked round to see Kate beckoning. 'Hurry up.'

He looked at Willow, smiled provocatively, and said: 'When the boss lady calls, all must obey. I'm going to be all tied up for the rest of today and tomorrow; then there's Len's service, but I could see you the day after that, if you like.'

'We'll see,' said Willow, unable to believe he could be that busy, but determined not to join in his games by arguing with him. She had plenty of other people to see and things to do. He could wait. And the more background information she had before she questioned him seriously, the more effective she was likely to be.

Leaving the building, she decided to visit Tom while she was on the right side of the river. When she got to his room, she saw a nurse by his bed, changing the bag attached to his catheter. The nurse looked up and smiled before hooking the bag on to its frame at the side of his bed.

'I'll leave you to it. He's doing all right, you know.'

'Thank you,' said Willow.

When she was alone with Tom, she leaned forward until her forehead was lying on his arm. At the touch of his skin on hers all the old mess of feelings swirled around in her: all the love, longing, anxiety, anger and resentment.

The resentment made her so ashamed that she tried to persuade herself that it did not exist.

After a while she sat up, remembering something Tom had said to her one wet afternoon soon after their marriage.

'If I've learned one thing, Will,' he had announced after an unhappy misunderstanding that had taken them days to sort out, 'it's that pretending not to feel doesn't work. If you push all your uncomfortable emotions down below the surface they'll only start to rot everything else. I think you need to recognise them for what they are, get them into perspective and *then* forget about them.'

She thought about it for a long time, almost hearing his voice again.

'All right,' she said at last, watching his still face, 'I will admit to all the vile feelings if you really want, and I'll stop trying to push them down, but I'm going to need help.'

He did not answer, of course, just lay there with the machines breathing for him and dripping some fluids into him and pulling others out.

She could not help thinking of their last breakfast together, when it had seemed as though there was almost perfect communication between them. At that moment she had felt remarkably safe: with him, with herself and with all the feelings that she had resisted for so long. Looking at him now, it struck her that Tom might not have shared that safety. He had said he was superstitious and she had taken that to mean that he did not want to tempt fate with too much complacency about their emotional life. But what if there had been something else worrying him? For the first time it struck her that he might have been afraid of violence or even death.

Could he, she asked herself, have known something about the work he was planning to do that day that had frightened him? Had he had some kind of premonition of what would happen?

Theoretically she had always known that he, like every other police officer in London, was at risk. But she had never thought much about it. In her experience, it was officers on the beat or responding to incidents who were in serious danger. Senior detectives like Tom were much less likely to come face to face with violent thugs carrying guns.

Her insensitivity to his possible fear seemed monstrous and she longed for him to wake so that she could put things right. Suddenly that seemed much more important than any of her own needs.

TEN

'SERENA FYDGETT RANG,' said Mrs Rusham as soon as Willow looked into the kitchen on her return. There was a delectable, sharp smell of herbs and shallots being cooked in a reduction of wine vinegar.

'She sounded upset,' Mrs Rusham went on. 'I told her that you were at the office, but she said she'd rung there and they didn't know where you were.'

'I went to the hospital.' Willow's mind was too full of Tom to think about anything else just then. 'He's still hanging on, Mrs Rusham. There is still hope. Really there is.'

Mrs Rusham said nothing, but the sympathy in her dark eyes was enough to reactivate all Willow's private fears. She turned away, leaving Mrs Rusham to her pots and pans.

Later, when she was calmer, Willow remembered the message from Serena Fydgett and telephoned her.

'What the hell have you been saying?' said Serena Fydgett as soon as Willow had announced who she was. 'Your job was to look into how the tax people dealt with my sister's affairs, not to start slandering the rest of us.'

'I don't understand,' said Willow, who had been about to thank Serena for the flowers she had sent after the fire. Adjusting as quickly as she could to the aggression in the other woman's voice—and her own suspicions, which suddenly seemed less extravagantly wild—Willow added: 'Who do you think I've been talking to?'

'The police.'

'Don't be absurd.' Willow grabbed her fringe with one bandaged hand and held it above her head. 'I mean I answered everything they asked me last week, but the only thing that was remotely relevant to you was my explanation of the work I was doing for the minister.'

'But you must have told them that I blamed Scoffer for Fiona's death. No one else can have done it.'

'Except the minister, or perhaps her MP. Your name wasn't even mentioned. Are you telling me they've...' Letting her hair fly loose again, Willow stopped. It would be pretty insulting to ask whether Harness had charged Serena with arson and murder.

'Not only did they bang on my door at six-thirty this morning to question me about whether I had tried to kill Leonard Scoffer,' Serena went on furiously, 'but I've just found out that they've been harassing my nephew, too.'

'What?' said Willow, and then quickly followed it with a better response. 'That's absurd. They can't possibly suspect a schoolboy.'

'It seems—unfortunately—that they do. One or perhaps both of us. Even more unfortunate is the fact that Rob's headmaster believed he had the right to advise co-operation with the police. They had been grilling him over three hours before I got him out, with no more protection than that idiot headmaster. He hadn't even the wit to get a solicitor there. Though come to think of some of the ones who—'

'I'm appalled,' said Willow, interrupting without stopping to think. Her voice seemed to carry real conviction, for when Serena spoke again she sounded a little less angry.

'That's a relief.'

'And I can assure you that none of that can have been the result of anything I said,' Willow went on. 'Neither your name nor your nephew's was mentioned at any time during my session with the police, and I haven't even seen them since the day after the fire.'

'I'm sorry,' said Serena, sounding as though she were beginning to relax. 'It's only that I couldn't think why they'd have come up with anything so ludicrous unless you'd put them up to it.'

'I can promise you it wasn't me.' Willow thought of all the things she wanted to ask Serena about Fiona's death, the earlier suicide attempts (which only she had mentioned) and exactly what Fiona had done to make Serena angry with her.

'But they must have had some information from somewhere
to make them take such a dramatic step. I mean... Look,
wouldn't you rather talk face to face about all this? You could
come and have some lunch.'

'Why?'

'Oh because of lots of reasons, really.' Willow tried to produce a convincing excuse. 'One is wholly selfish,' she said. 'I
am so angry with the criminal fool who put me through hell
in that fire that I want him prosecuted as fast as possible. It
sounds as though the police are barking up completely the
wrong tree. If you and I pool our information, we'll get there
much quicker than they can with all this bumbling about asking irrelevant questions of innocent people.'

'Aren't you afraid of letting an arson suspect into your
house?' Serena demanded, not commenting on Willow's apparent certainty that she could do the job better than the police.

'Don't be ridiculous.' Willow was quite unable to imagine
the woman at the other end of the telephone skulking about
setting fire to an uninhabited old hut on a patch of waste
ground miles from anywhere, let alone a government building
in a busy street in the middle of the capital.

Even if she had encouraged her sister to commit suicide, or
possibly even taken a more active role in her death, there was
not much she could do to Willow in broad daylight with Mrs
Rusham in the house as a witness, if not an actual protector.
Besides, Willow was curious to know more about the nephew.
If someone as astute as Chief Inspector Harness had been interviewing him for three hours, there must be something pretty
suspect about him.

'Why not come round and have some lunch with me and
talk?'

'What, now?'

'Yes.' Willow looked at the little gold carriage clock on the
mantelpiece. 'It's half-past twelve. It'll be lunchtime by the
time you get here.'

There was a pause before Serena said: 'Oh, why not? I'm
too furious to do any work. Thank you. I'll be with you in
about twenty minutes.'

Thinking that her estimate was optimistic, Willow went down to the kitchen to tell Mrs Rusham what she had done and to make sure there would be enough food for the unexpected guest. Not much to her surprise, Mrs Rusham looked positively insulted at the idea that she might not be able to cater for one extra at a few minutes' notice.

Willow thanked her and retreated to her writing room to call the minister at his Whitehall office. It was not until she heard the ringing tone that she realised she had been using her hands without thinking and that, clumsy though they were, and painful still, they did operate as she wanted.

The minister's staff were reluctant to put Willow through to his office, even though one of the more senior secretaries admitted that he was there.

'Then please tell him that I need to speak to him,' said Willow in a tone her own civil service staff would have recognised. It had its usual effect, and she was relieved to discover that love and terror for Tom had not destroyed all her old skills. Keeping busy, cramming more work into the day than seemed possible, was having its usual effect of keeping her emotions in check.

'Willow. Glad to hear you're up and about again,' said the minister a moment later. 'What can I do for you? I'm very busy this morning.'

'So I gather. I wanted to thank you for your flowers and also to say that we need to talk again before I can get any further with the report. This is obviously not a good time. Could we meet?'

'Is it really necessary?'

'Essential.'

'Ah,' said the minister, also responding to Willow's celebrated icy determination, 'in that case, how about the terrace of the House of Commons for a drink this evening?'

'I'm not very good at standing at the moment,' said Willow, wanting to make sure that they talked in a place where they could not be overheard. 'Couldn't I just come to your office—and rather earlier than drinks time? I've got a lot to do, too.'

'Very well.' The minister sounded taken aback to be treated

like an underling, but he did not appear to resent it. 'If you go to the House at four I'll be there then, and I could spare you a few minutes. Goodbye now.' He did not wait for Willow's reply.

'Ms Fydgett's downstairs,' said Mrs Rusham just as Willow replaced the telephone receiver.

'Good,' she said. 'Could you bring one of those bottles of Alsatian wine to the drawing room?'

'Certainly.'

Mrs Rusham moved aside so that Willow could go downstairs first. She found Serena standing in the middle of the elegant room, looking quite different from the composed, confident professional of their previous meeting. Her dark hair was loose and looked as though it had not been washed since they had last met, and her suit was almost as crumpled as Blackled's. There seemed to be absolutely no resemblance between her and the photograph of her sister. It occurred to Willow that one or both of them could have been adopted, which might have explained some of Serena's ambivalent feelings.

'Come and sit down. Have a glass of wine. You look as though you need something.'

Serena shook her head.

'Oh, come on. A drink will perk you up. I'm having one.'

'No, really. I never drink in the middle of the day.' Serena sat down on one of the silver-grey sofas, while Willow poured herself a glass of wine.

'So tell me what happened,' Willow said, watching Serena impatiently push a pink cushion out of her way. 'With the police, I mean.'

'First they badgered me for an alibi, and when I declined to give it to them they went and got hold of Rob, presumably to force me into talking to them. It's the most despicable piece of manipulation I can imagine. To use a child like that—and one in the sort of state Rob must be after Fiona's death. Outrageous!'

'Hold on for a minute,' said Willow, offering her a cheese-and-cayenne biscuit from the tray Mrs Rusham had provided. 'I can't keep up. Why wouldn't you give them your alibi?'

Serena looked furious, and shook her head at the biscuits. 'If you don't know without being told, you'll never understand,' she said.

'Explain to me in words of one syllable and then I probably will understand,' said Willow, putting the plate back on the tray. 'If I'm being particularly obtuse, I'm sorry. Most of my brain is still taken up with dealing with what's happened to my husband. Humour me and explain, won't you?'

The other woman shrugged. Her shoulders looked very broad under the black linen of her suit jacket. 'Oh, all right. My sister was outrageously bullied by the state. I can't do anything to help her now, but at least I can get back at them by refusing to let them bully me.'

Serena paused, as though she were listening to the echoes of what she had just said, and then added: 'I suppose that sounds childish, but that's just too bad. The police have no evidence whatsoever to connect me with the fire, and yet they came banging on my door at six-thirty in the morning, demanding information to which they have absolutely no right.'

'I can't believe they really had nothing.' Willow remembered the few things Tom had told her about some of his investigations. 'I can quite accept that whatever they had was wrong, but they must have had something they thought connected you with the fire.'

Serena shrugged. 'It was enough for them, apparently, that I am known to be angry with the man who died, and that I once defended an alleged arsonist.'

'Really?' Willow tried to disguise her interest. She could see why Harness and his team might have wanted a little more information before they eliminated Serena from their enquiries. 'How had he done it?'

'I successfully defended him.' Serena looked faintly amused for the first time that day. 'That means he was innocent.'

'Yes, I know it does.' Willow smiled back at her. Both of them were fully aware of what the other was thinking. 'We are on the same wavelength, you know, even if I don't understand about the alibi. Tell me how that fire was started.'

'The prosecution alleged that the underfloor wiring in my

client's warehouse had been tampered with. In fact, it had been damaged by mice. They had chewed through the insulation. That's one of the commonest causes of domestic fires, you know, and doubtless of those in commercial buildings too.'

'I didn't actually. What a lot you know!'

'Most barristers do.' Serena seemed to be relaxing. 'Just as they know their clients' rights and the lengths to which some police officers will go to get confessions. The men who came to my house seemed to think it extraordinary that I might choose not to co-operate with them. But even they could hardly arrest me without any evidence.'

Willow drank some more of the wine and sat down on the low hearth stool opposite the sofa where Serena was sitting. 'I'm sorry if this makes me sound unsympathetic, but I have to say that it seems a bit extraordinary to me, too,' she said, looking up from her deliberately lowly position. 'If you have an alibi, isn't it sensible just to give it and let them get on with the work they're paid to do?'

Serena hunched her shoulders and looked away from Willow's intent eyes. 'They treated me like a criminal and tried to persuade me that I had to go with them to the police station. I lost my temper, explained to them that unless they arrested me I wasn't going anywhere with them, and refused to say anything. That's all. I'm sorry I took it out on you. It wasn't fair.'

'Don't be silly. Come and have some lunch. It'll be ready by now.'

They walked through to the sunny dining room, where Mrs Rusham served them with cold Vichysoisse, fillets of subtle-tasting smoked eel with a chopped tomato salad in a gentle dressing, and a pink mousse that had been made with a mixture of mulberry, passionfruit and *crème fraiche*.

Willow and Serena ate slowly and talked their way back into friendship, ignoring the subjects of the fire, the police and Fiona. Willow thought it much more important to re-establish good relations than to ask Serena questions straight away.

'That was lovely,' Serena admitted when Mrs Rusham came to clear away the dishes. 'I feel much better—and a complete fool for having got so wound up. I must go back to chambers now, but thank you, Willow. You've been very kind.' She stood up.

'Nonsense,' said Willow firmly. 'And I haven't thanked you for the flowers yet. It was so good of you to take such trouble when we hardly knew each other.'

'Not at all. What happened to you was awful, and you were put at risk only because I...because I had protested about what happened to Fiona.'

As Serena spoke, Willow cursed herself for her overactive imagination and instinctively suspicious nature. If Serena had had anything at all to do with her sister's death, she was hardly likely to have stirred up interest in it by writing to protest about the Inland Revenue's treatment of Fiona. All she would have had to do was keep mum and soon everyone would have forgotten her sister.

'I'm all over the place at the moment,' Serena said. 'Half the time I don't know what I'm doing or saying or even what I ought to do. It's unprecedented. I've always been so sure of everything before.'

'Then we're alike in that as well,' said Willow. 'I loathe it too, but I can't help feeling that both of us will revert to competence again in the end. It's too deeply ingrained to be completely wiped away even by what's happened.'

Serena smiled. 'I hope so. You are all right really, aren't you? I mean, I can see that the burns must be agony, but there isn't any permanent damage, is there? I couldn't bear that. The consequences of what happened to Fiona just seem to go on and on, and I've been castigating myself for interfering. I ought to have done something before she died or kept my trap shut and not gone involving other people—like you.'

'I'm fine,' said Willow, almost convinced of Serena's honesty. 'And I don't hold you responsible for what happened to me in the fire. I'm determined to see that whoever was responsible gets his just deserts, but I know that it wasn't your fault.'

There was a pause before Serena said quite simply: 'Thank you for that. I won't forget it.'

When Serena had gone, Willow went back up to her writing room, trying to understand her. She was intelligent, appealing, and almost convincing, and yet her reasons for withholding her alibi from the police seemed so silly that they were hard to believe.

Tom had often said that if everyone connected with a case stopped trying to protect their own irrelevant secrets, the detection of crime would be a lot easier. Once he had been so angry that he had stomped out into the tiny garden in the pouring rain, muttering that if people wanted the police to deal with crime they couldn't expect to be allowed to withhold any information whatsoever, even if it was entirely innocent or seriously confidential.

Willow had spent so much effort for so long keeping her own secrets that she had disagreed with him then, but she was coming to see exactly what he meant. Serena's determination to protect her privacy—if that was what she was doing—was merely wasting time. The sooner the case was solved, the sooner everyone else could get back to normal.

The telephone rang just as Willow remembered that her life would never be normal again unless Tom regained consciousness. She stood up to reach for the receiver, cursing her hands again as she gripped too hard and the edge of the plastic pushed into one of the swollen blisters on her palm.

'Willow King.'

'Willow, it's Eve here,' said a voice that sounded full of warmth and pleasure.

'Oh, hello.'

'I think the book's wonderful,' said her agent at once. 'The best you've done by a long way.'

'Oh, good.'

'There's almost nothing that needs work, except for a looseness at the beginning of chapter nine.'

'Really? What's wrong with it?' Willow noticed that Eve's approval of the book was not having its usual effect on her. Normally she would be flooded with relief and exuberant delight. No one but Tom knew how much she had come to depend on Eve's judgment or how childishly depressed and angry she felt whenever it was withheld. She tried to sound more enthusiastic. 'I'm really glad you like it. But tell me about chapter nine.'

'It's nothing major, Willow,' said Eve, obviously sensing a lack of excitement in her client, 'and I don't think now's the time to go into it. You must still be feeling ghastly about Tom, and after what happened to you in that fire. I can't tell you how appalled I was by the news reports. How are you feeling?'

'Not so hot, as it were.' Willow managed a short laugh and then, thinking of Jason Tillter's repellant sense of humour, sobered up. 'But I'm functioning again. I was unbelievably lucky. Thank you for your flowers by the way. They're lovely.'

Willow looked hastily around the room, wishing that she could remember which of the bunches had come from Eve so that she could say something properly appreciative. Then, suddenly, she remembered. 'I took them to Tom. Yellow lilies have always been his absolute favourites. He can't see them, of course, yet, but... Sorry, I've got rather wobbly about all this.'

'I'm not surprised. But just remember, you've written a terrific book.'

'Thanks, Eve. I'll be a bit more enthusiastic about it when Tom's...' Her voice broke again and she hastily said goodbye, furious to have exacerbated her own weakness and misery.

I mustn't crack up, she thought, staring down at her bandaged hands. Work's the only thing that'll help. I must concentrate and not waste time anguishing about Tom. That won't help him. He's either going to live or not. Nothing I do can affect it. It's better if I don't even think about him. How can I persuade Serena Fydgett to co-operate with the police? Between us all, we must find out who killed Len Scoffer. And there's the report for the minister, too. Will he still want it, now that Scoffer's dead? Did Fiona Fydgett really kill herself or was someone else involved? Was that someone trying to kill me? Have I asked too many inconvenient questions about her?

Could it have been Serena after all? No, it couldn't. Unless

it was someone else who persuaded her to protest about the
Revenue, someone whose suspicions she did not want to
arouse by refusing. Any such person would have to have been
pretty influential.

Willow's mind went almost at once to Malcolm Penholt.

'No,' she said aloud. 'It's absurd. Byzantine layers of suspicion and conspiracy. It must be something much simpler.'

Perhaps the police were right, she thought, and it really was
Fiona's son who torched the building. He might have been
capable of it. The police had interrogated him for three hours,
and from everything she had ever heard from Tom and others,
they did not do that sort of thing for nothing.

'Am I going mad?' she said.

The telephone rang again, shocking her out of her disor-
dered thoughts. It was Black Jack, saying, 'You'll be glad to
hear we've got them, Will. The scrotes who shot Tom, and
they've nothing to do with any of your murder cases, nor the
fire.'

Willow leaned back against the squashy chair and let her
eyelids droop over her eyes.

'Are you still there, Will?'

'Yes. Just beginning to breathe again after the terror you
and Harness drilled into me the other day. D'you know if he
ever found out whether any of our four murderers are out of
prison?'

'None of them. All safely banged up for years to come.'

'I see. Well, it was kind of you to let me know. Good work.'

'I told you, you're family now. We take care of our own.
The papers have gone to the Crown Prosecution Service, and
we should hear from them pretty quickly.'

'Then it's not certain yet?'

'Virtually.'

'What's the evidence?'

'God, you sound suspicious! We've got the gun, matched
the bullets, got the right prints on the gun.'

'Have they confessed?'

'Not yet. But it's clear enough. Don't you fret. We know
we've got the right bunch.'

'But why did they shoot him?' asked Willow. 'He wasn't in uniform or anything. Did they know him?'

'Don't think so. It looks like the usual, I'm afraid, Will. Tom was just in the wrong place at the wrong time. He stumbled on a bunch of young men crazy with crack and high on the thrill of having a gun. I don't suppose they even knew he was a copper. They're not dealers, just petty crooks. We've checked the records, of course, and Tom had never arrested any of them. I suspect it was just bad luck that he was there.'

What a waste! Willow thought. What a hideous, cruel waste! Then she took herself to task. It was no worse for Tom to have been shot for nothing than it would have been if he had been on the track of a master criminal. He would have been shot just the same.

'Will, are you there?'

'Yes. Sorry. Nothing to say really, is there?'

'Not really, no. But I thought you'd like to know.'

'Yes, thanks. Jack, while you're on, d'you really think that the fire could have been caused by Robert Fydgett? He's only fifteen.'

'Unfortunately they get younger all the time. You ought to know that. But what makes you think Fydgett's a suspect?'

'His aunt told me. But it seems extraordinary. You can't have any evidence that he did it or you'd have arrested him.'

Black Jack sighed. 'Look, it's not my case. Nothing to do with me. All I've heard is that Fydgett was devoted to his mother in a rather creepy way and hated the men in her life. And there were plenty of those, I can tell you. He knows a lot about electricity. There's no alibi and he's altogether a bit dodgy: child of a single mother, low achiever at school although he's known to be bright, a trouble-maker. And he climbs like a cat. All in all, he fits the profile. No more than that, but if it'd been me, I'd have had to look into it. And then I gather that in the interview he exhibited all the classic signs of guilt.'

'What are they?' asked Willow, both interested and unconvinced. She could not help thinking that Black Jack must know a great deal more than he was admitting if he had told her that much.

'Body language. Very defensive: blushed a lot; held his arms across his chest whenever questions got tricky; turned sideways; lowered his chin. You know the score. And he got angry when he was cornered.'

'Oh. Still, I can't believe he had no alibi. He was at boarding school.'

'It's only a London boarding school,' said the superintendent impatiently. 'They think it's possible the arsonist set everything up the previous night with the timer or photo-electric cell or whatever. Fydgett's been known to abscond from school before and play the goat. He was caught putting the Welsh flag on the top of the school chapel's steeple one night at the end of last term, I understand.'

'That's hardly criminal, even if it is against the school rules.'

'No.'

'So what are you suggesting? That he climbed out of school, got to the tax office, climbed the walls, broke in and fiddled about with the wiring and no one even knew there'd been anyone there?' Willow's voice was full of incredulity and contempt. Blackled reacted to it at once just as she had hoped.

'It's not so unlikely, you know. After his mother died, the school gave him a bed in the sanitorium so that he'd have some privacy to cry over her if he wanted to. There was no one else there to say where he was at any time between lights out and the rising bell. He could easily have got out. It's not far to the Vauxhall Bridge Road. Scoffer's window overlooked the car park, and there's only other offices behind. There'd have been no one to see an intruder in the middle of the night. But I'm not suggesting anything at all. It's not my case—or yours, I may say. Leave it, Will. Harness is a good bloke. He and his team will crack it—and the less they're interrupted by irrelevancies, the sooner they'll do it.'

'Jack, I was almost killed in that fire. I need to know who did it and why. Can't you give me a bit more?'

'You know I can't. Shouldn't have told you even that much,

but I trust you. I must go now. I'll look in on old Tom tonight. Perhaps I'll see you then. 'Bye for now.'

'Goodbye.' Willow sighed as she put down the receiver again, but she could hardly blame Black Jack for not telling her everything. He had in fact told her much more than she had expected. She would just have to get the rest some other way.

ELEVEN

'YOU OUGHT TO LIE down and rest for half an hour,' said Mrs Rusham, bringing Willow a cup of coffee. 'You're not as strong as you think you are, and you're doing far too much. You haven't stopped since before I got here this morning, and it's your first full day out of bed.'

'The last thing I want is rest,' said Willow frankly. 'It just gives me too much time to worry. Work will keep me going better than any amount of sleep.'

Mrs Rusham raised her thick, dark eyebrows, but she went away without saying anything more.

Willow drank her coffee and tried to organise her mind for the meeting with George Profett. Not wanting to waste her time with him as she had wasted the first meeting with Serena, she set about trying to make sense of all the hints, suspicions, fears, and bits and pieces of information she had collected.

Normally she would have scribbled ideas, key words, and meaningless doodles on a large pad of lined paper until her ideas began to gel and she could draw herself up a systematic list of questions and things to do. As it was, the state of her hands made any sort of writing or even typing too uncomfortable to contemplate.

At the end of half an hour's concentrated thought, her ideas were beginning to sharpen. With her mind working almost normally again, she could see the absurdity of a lot of her earlier fears. No one who had wanted to harm her would have gone to all the trouble of attacking the Inland Revenue office. It would have been far more sensible for an arsonist to set fire to her home. She did not advertise her private address, but it was hardly secret, and anyone could have tipped a molotov cocktail through her letter box late at night with less risk of discovery and far greater certainty of success.

The relief from that anxiety did not lessen her determination to find out who had torched the office and why. Knowing that Blackled would tell her nothing more, Willow decided to talk to the Fire Brigade direct and heaved the heavy business telephone directory up on to her desk.

'Oh, hell!' she said when she discovered that there was no investigation department listed. None of the offices that were given numbers looked particularly suitable and so she decided that she would have to speak to Black Jack once again, however obstructive he was likely to be.

'Sorry, Jack,' she said when she eventually got through to his office. 'I quite forgot to ask you, but how do I get in touch with the Fire Brigade's investigators?'

There was a sigh down the line and a peculiar sound, which Willow eventually decided must be grinding teeth.

'Just leave this to the professionals, will you? You're not yourself at the moment. That's hardly surprising in the circumstances, but it really would help everyone if you'd keep out of the way. There is nothing you can do. I've told you as much as possible—more than I'd have told anyone else. You must leave it at that.'

'It's not that at all, Jack. I'd never have bothered you if it were. It's just that I've remembered that while I was working on the day of the fire one of my rings kept catching on the papers and so I took it off and put in on the desk beside me.' Willow hoped that she was sounding pathetic and feminine enough to arouse Black Jack's undoubted chivalry. 'I didn't remember until just now, but I must have left the ring there. And Tom gave it to me. I don't think I could bear to lose it, not now of all times.'

'Describe it to me, Will, and I'll tell the searchers.'

'Couldn't I just talk to the Fire Brigade themselves? That would be much simpler.'

'They're not dealing with it any more,' he said, sounding polite enough but as though he were holding on to his temper with difficulty. 'Look, the procedure's quite simple. When a body's discovered at a fire, a Fire Investigation Team is called in. It consists of the Sub Officer and the Station Officer. They look for evidence of an accelerant—you know what that is?'

'Petrol or something.'

''Sright. If they find it, they call us and hand over everything. It's a police matter now, nothing to do with the Fire
Brigade.'

'What evidence?' she said, forgetting that she was pretending to have lost a jewel.

'For god's sake, Willow! You know I can't tell you that.
It's under investigation. If you give me details of this ring of
yours, I'll tell them to look out for it.'

'Thanks, Jack. I'll write you a note about it so as not to
waste any more of your time now,' Willow said as sweetly as
she could. She did not think that he had believed in the existence of the ring.

There was still some time to kill before her meeting with
the minister and so she decided to use it up by walking to the
Houses of Parliament again. The air was still thick with dust
and a sweaty kind of heat, but simply being out in the open
without being afraid of watchers was a relief.

Green Park had a holiday air about it, with people lying on
the grass and strolling among the trees. Knowing that Black
Jack had Tom's aggressors safely in cells at Kingston, Willow
strolled slowly through the park and even found herself smiling at some of the half-dressed sunbathers.

It was cool within the vaulted halls of the Houses of Parliament and she managed to feel less irritated with their pom-
posity than usual. Up in his small but comfortable office over-
looking the river, the minister greeted her with apparently
genuine concern. As soon as she started to ask questions his
sympathetic expression changed.

'I can't tell you anything more,' he said with heavy emphasis on 'anything'.

Willow glared at him, regretting her spoiled moment of relaxation, and furious that he was still not being straight with
her. Tom's exasperation with people who kept secrets was
beginning to seem wholly reasonable. The minister's eyes did
not drop in front of hers as she thought they ought to have
done.

'You sent me to that office as your personal representative

to investigate a man who might or might not have caused Doctor Fydgett to kill herself. He is now dead and if I hadn't been very lucky, I'd be dead with him. Doesn't that suggest to you that there has been something pretty sinister going on?' Willow's voice trembled, but, as it was with anger and not misery, she did not mind.

'I think, if you'll forgive my saying so, Willow, that the events of the past week have made you look at things in a rather melodramatic light.'

'No,' she said, trying to bounce him into telling the whole truth. 'I won't forgive it, just as I can't forgive your not being frank with me in the first place. Don't you think what's happened to me gives me the right to all the information you have about Doctor Fydgett and about everyone in Kate Moughette's office?'

The minister looked at his surprisingly extravagant watch and then up at Willow again. His lips were very thin and his eyes cold. But he did not look at all ashamed.

'You certainly have every right to know why I wanted you to go there. As I have said before: I needed information about what happened, both in order to provide a basis for new legislation and in case questions should be asked about the cause of Doctor Fydgett's death. You must know that I am appalled at what you've had to suffer—and how inordinately relieved I am that your injuries are not worse.'

Willow watched him for a moment, trying to decide whether he was sincere. 'Did it ever occur to you that Fiona Fydgett's death might not have been suicide?' she asked bluntly. The minister's expression of astonishment was all Willow needed, but he gave her words too.

'Certainly not. It never crossed my mind—nor that of the coroner or anyone who knew her. I don't think you should worry about that.'

'I see,' said Willow, still trying to find out why the minister was so obstructive. She knew, without being able to say why, that he was concealing something from her. 'Have the police interviewed you yet about Scoffer's death?'

'They've been in touch with me to confirm your reasons for being at the Vauxhall Bridge Road office, yes.'

'And were they satisfied?'

'Naturally.' No old-school Tory grandee could have sounded more dignified.

'I don't believe it,' said Willow, trying to be offensive in order to provoke him into telling the truth. 'The police can be intensely irritating, but they're not generally stupid, at least not the sort who get to investigate arson and murder.'

The minister crossed his legs, leaned back in his chair and allowed his chin to sink into his chest. 'I really do think that, understandably, you have let yourself get worked up by all this. Why not take a few days off? I'm sure that when you've had a proper rest and recovered, you'll be able to see things in much better proportion. And the report can wait a few more days.'

'They know that you sent me there to make investigations,' Willow went on without listening to his advice. 'They know that the man I was investigating is now dead. They must have wanted to know more.'

The minister raised his shaggy eyebrows. 'But I understood that it's been sorted out. I suppose the verdict will be man-slaughter rather than murder, and, in view of his age and the strain he's been under since his mother died, he'll be treated mercifully. Perhaps even a suspended sentence and some psychiatric care. I certainly hope so. After all, he can't have known that either you or Scoffer would still be there at that hour.'

'Wait a minute,' said Willow, realising that the minister had more information on Rob Fydgett than she had managed to get. 'Are you really telling me that you believe them: that you think Fiona Fydgett's son set fire to the place?'

'Why, don't you?' asked the minister in a reasonable voice.

She stretched her legs, feeling them ache from the first exercise she had taken for days.

'Because it seems ludicrous to suspect a respectable school-boy of something so destructive,' she said, ignoring everything she had read about crimes that had been committed by boys during the past few years. 'And there's no real evidence as far as I've heard. All the police have is circumstantial. As far as I know there's nothing to put Fydgett at the scene of the fire, no fingerprints, no witness sightings, nothing. There's nothing more than a vague suspicion based on the fact that he loved his mother and might have wanted to take revenge on the man he believed responsible for her death.'

'I gather there's a bit more than that,' said the minister, 'otherwise they would hardly have brought him for questioning. But naturally I haven't been given any details. We have to leave it to the police and the courts.' He smiled kindly and, when she said nothing, added: 'Is that all you wanted, then?'

He brushed some stray blond hairs off his jacket. Willow assumed that they were his own. From where she was sitting they looked the right length and texture. But they were enough to raise a new suspicion in her mind.

What if George Profett had not only known Fiona Fydgett, but perhaps even been one of her lovers? What if his anxieties about her suicide were more personal than he had suggested? Regretfully Willow told herself that she was being absurd again.

'No,' she said aloud. 'I want an end to this shiftiness. I want to know exactly what it was you thought I'd find in Scoffer's office and how you thought I'd do it, working blind like that.'

As she saw the obstinate look return to the minister's thin face, Willow tried again. 'Please don't waste any more time. Yours or mine,' she said. She thought that she saw a softening in his eyes, as though he had decided to co-operate.

'Please,' she said again to urge him on.

'It's all rather delicate in the circumstances,' he said abruptly, swinging his chair round so that the only part of him Willow could see was an absurd little tuft of fair hair sticking out over the leather top.

'So there is something else. I thought so. Nothing that leads to arson can be too delicate to explain,' Willow said, holding on to her anger. 'There will only be more trouble if it doesn't get sorted out now.'

The minister swung back again, more slowly. Willow was surprised to see that his face was flushed. She did not think that he was aware that he had stuck his tongue between his teeth and was biting it.

'It is true that I had another motive in sending you there. It was of minor importance compared with the Fydgett case, but it is true that it existed. I had planned to keep it to myself, but I suppose you'd better hear it all now, if only to prevent you making unintentional mischief.'

'Thank you.'

'Some weeks ago, fairly soon after my appointment, I was contacted by Leonard Scoffer, who told me that he was worried about possible corruption in his office.'

'Why on earth didn't you tell me that in the first place?' Willow demanded, thinking immediately of Jason Tillter and his flashy suits and expensive silk ties. She also thought of the look of satisfaction he had been wearing when she first saw him after Len's death.

'Because everyone in authority agreed that there was no possibility that the allegation was justifiable. I merely wanted Scoffer to believe that I had sent someone to the office in order to stop him taking any more action.'

'But whom did he suspect?'

The minister looked even more uncomfortable and began to fiddle with the ornamental pen set at the further edge of his desk. It was a horrible contraption of vomit-green onyx and thin gold-coloured metal.

'That's what makes it all so delicate. He accused Kate Moughette of taking bribes in order to end investigations into taxpayers' affairs. I talked to Sir Roland Collins-Nestor, the Chairman, who had some extensive enquiries made and was able to assure me that there was no possibility of anything of the kind. Apparently the powers-that-be were well aware of Scoffer's dislike of Moughette and of his ideas about her.'

No wonder the atmosphere in the office was so full of aggression, thought Willow, wishing that she had brought a tape recorder with her. She did not want to miss—or forget—anything the minister might say.

'He'd already been on to them with his delusions. And I must stress again that they are certain that Scoffer was deluded. He was due to retire at the end of this year and it was thought that the problem would simply disappear with him. He'd made Moughette's job even more difficult than it would otherwise have been, and she's thought to have handled him well.'

'But you disagreed, didn't you?' suggested Willow, trying to keep all sounds of judgment out of her voice. 'Why?'

'It wasn't that I disagreed with their conclusions about Moughette's probity,' he said stiffly. 'I have no reason to doubt that at all. I simply thought they were over-confident about her containment of Scoffer. The very fact that he'd written to me suggested that he was not going to stop his campaign.'

'I wish you'd told me.'

'I couldn't. Slander, for one thing,' said the minister, looking at her with less defensiveness. 'As I say, I thought that your presence there might in itself keep him quiet. We don't want to rock any boats at the moment, and I was afraid that if he got no satisfaction from me he might go to the press.'

'There I think you underestimated his sense of duty,' said Willow in a judicious tone. 'He seemed to me to be devoted to the service. I don't think he'd ever have done anything to bring it into disrepute. But you do see what this means, don't you?'

The minister shook his head.

'You must tell the police. It widens their enquiries hugely. For one thing it puts Kate Moughette in the frame for the arson.'

'Don't be absurd.' The tone in which the minister spoke was surprisingly tolerant. It was not that of a man being given orders by someone well below him in the chain of command. Willow wondered why.

'I'm not,' she said. 'Apart from Scoffer and me, she was the last to leave the office. She did her best to get me to leave, too. She was virtually the only person who could have made him stay, and she could easily have stripped the wires that ran between their two rooms and put some accelerant down to catch the sparks.'

'Is that how it was done?'

'I don't know,' said Willow in frustration. 'I assumed you would. They won't tell me anything useful. And I know nothing whatsoever about electricity—or starting fires. Look, Minister, this is really serious. Will you ring Superintendent Blackled or shall I?'

'I don't know any Superintendent Blackled. I've been dealing with a man called Stephen Harness, who already knows everything that I know.'

'You mean you've told him about Kate Moughette?'

'Of course I have. What do you take me for?' Profett sounded amused rather than angry. 'Now, have you anything else to ask? If not, I really must be getting on.'

Willow clamped her teeth together, still frustrated and wishing that she could get a proper grip on her mind again. She shook her head. 'I'll draft my report as soon as I can get my fingers accurately on to the keys,' she said, looking at the bandages.

'Thank you. And please believe me when I say again how sorry I am at what has happened to you.'

'Oh, I do,' said Willow, hitching the strap of her bag higher on her shoulder. 'I'll leave you to it now. Goodbye, Minister.'

'Goodbye.'

As she walked to the door of his office, she could not help wondering whether he had yet been completely frank about his motives for sending her to the tax office.

George Profett might never have been anywhere near an image consultant, he might look unimpeachably honest, but he had fought his way into Parliament and on to the front bench, and to do that he must have made himself agreeable to voters, whips and colleagues. It was unlikely that all of them had shared all his views, and yet he had managed to persuade them that he was the best man for the job. Either he had fudged some of his beliefs or he was a super-salesman.

A taxi was depositing a quartet of American tourists outside the Palace of Westminster as she emerged, and she took it over from them, asking the driver to get her home as fast as possible. Looking at her swollen face and bandaged hands, he obviously assumed that she was ill and roared off into the middle of the traffic, frantically signalling and flashing his headlights at anyone who got in the way. Willow, who had wanted to get home quickly, but not quite that quickly, had to hang on to the strap above the door during some of his more ferocious manoeuvres, and closed her eyes as the taxi almost crashed into the side of an enormous lorry.

With her mind playing around Scoffer's allegations of corruption, the first thing she did when she got back into the house was to search the Yellow Pages for a list of private detectives. Checking that there was still time before offices closed for the day, she tried one of the agencies in the list.

The woman she spoke to sounded quite untroubled by the fact that Willow wanted private financial information about a group of individuals but the price she quoted for providing it was enormous. Willow thanked her and tried another agency.

That turned out to be a one-man band, and the man in question, whose name was Brian Gaskarth, quoted her a much more reasonable fee. Willow accepted it at once.

'It's all rather urgent,' she said when Gaskarth had repeated all the names she gave him, checking that he had got the spelling right. 'How soon can you get it for me?'

'Twenty-four hours probably,' he said, making no comment on any of the names. 'Perhaps less.'

'Great. D'you have police sources as well?'

'A few. Why?'

'I'd like to find out what evidence they have on a suspect they've been interviewing about…'

'That's not the kind of information I can provide,' said the man at once. His unaccented voice did not sound at all shocked or angry, merely firm. 'Criminal records? Yes. Car ownership? Yes. But not ongoing investigations. I don't say it's impossible, but it's not part of the service I offer.'

'Pity. Never mind. Get me the financial stuff and I'll be happy. D'you need paying in advance?'

'Cash when I bring the reports would be fine.'

'Cash?' repeated Willow, thinking of his tax position.

'It's simpler,' he said, 'than waiting for cheques to clear. Not all my clients are exactly…good risks.'

Deciding that she could hardly be committing an offence by paying in cash since it was up to him to account for everything he earned and pay the tax on it, Willow agreed. Then she suddenly remembered the minister's watch and his shiftiness, and added his name to the list. Brian Gaskarth accepted it without a murmur.

Willow thanked him again, cut the connection, rang the temporary tax office and asked for Cara Saks.

'Cara, it's Willow here. I'm not sure if I'm going to be up to getting to Croydon for the funeral on Thursday. Could you give me the Scoffers' address so that I can send some flowers?'

'Of course,' said Cara at once, making Willow fear for her future. The mixture of naivety, indiscretion and fear seemed to make her a most unsuitable candidate for senior management, even though they all made her an appealing human being in an office inhabited by the likes of Jason Tillter and Len Scoffer. Cara dictated the address.

'Thanks,' said Willow. 'How's it going with the reconstruction of the files?'

'Not too badly. And we have had some luck. A whole heap of files has just been sent over by the police. Some of them are fairly hard to read because they got quite wet, but they're not bad enough to go to the conservators. We're working on them now. And the conservation people are… Oh, here's Kate. I'd better go.'

'Sure. Good luck. I'll see you in due course.'

Willow rang Directory Enquiries and got the telephone number for Len Scoffer's house without difficulty. When she dialled it, she was answered by a quiet female voice.

'I wondered if I could speak to Mrs Scoffer? I worked with her husband. My name's Willow King.'

'I'll see. Please wait.'

'How dare you?' said an angry voice a moment later. Willow held the receiver a little further from her ear.

'Is that Mrs Scoffer?' she asked, trying to make herself sound timid. She was surprised that Len should have told his wife anything about her.

'How dare you ring me?' she said before Willow could even begin to offer condolences. 'If it hadn't been for you, he'd never have been there at that time of night.'

'I don't understand.'

'Well, you ought to. If you hadn't been poking about, causing trouble, stirring up his staff against him, ransacking his office after he'd left the building, he'd never have had to make sure you weren't alone in it again. He'd have been home long before the fire even started. It's your fault.'

'But I wasn't stirring anybody up,' said Willow, shaken out of her own anger. 'And I never went near his office when he wasn't there.'

'If it hadn't been for you he wouldn't have died. You got out all right. Oh, yes, I read all about that. You're fine. But Len's dead. I hope you remember that for the rest of your life.'

The protests did not ring altogether true, but Willow told herself that lots of people found it hard to express strong emotion convincingly, and that Mrs Scoffer might well be parroting something she had read or heard because she could not find words of her own.

'It's you who should have burned to death,' she went on very quietly just before she rang off, and that sounded much more convincing.

Sickened by the injustice of the accusations, Willow sat back in her chair as she painfully put down the telephone receiver. She found herself thinking up excuses for Mrs Scoffer, who, after all, knew her only through Len's exaggerated diatribes, but no rationalisation could remove the nausea she felt. Memories of the fire welled up in her mind and it seemed vile that anyone, however unhappy, could wish her dead in it. She felt like ringing Mrs Scoffer again to describe just what it had been like and how much responsibility Len had borne for her presence in the building in the first place.

But she knew it would not help. And whatever Len might have done, he had not deserved his death.

Much later in the evening, when Willow recovered some of her equilibrium, she went into the pristine kitchen and found the gazpacho and cold veal that Mrs Rusham had left for her. The sauce that accompanied the veal was a kind of mayonnaise, flavoured with capers and the wine and herbs she had smelled in the kitchen that morning, and it was delicious. Even so, she could not eat much of it and eventually put the remains in the bin and returned to the drawing room, switching on the television.

For nearly an hour she pretended to be absorbed in a documentary about the health service, and then watched the news, hoping that there might be something about the police investigation of Scoffer's death. There was not, but she was able to watch a short clip of George Profett speaking on human rights abuses during a debate that had taken place in the House of Commons that afternoon. He came over quite well, she thought, and looked good, too: earnest and well-meaning and thoroughly intelligent.

'Perhaps he really is honest,' she said aloud.

The thought of lying sleepless in bed throughout another long sultry night filled her with horror, and so she went to the hospital, where she sat at Tom's side until after one o'clock.

TWELVE

THE NEXT MORNING'S post brought Willow a collection of bills and more letters of sympathy over Tom's condition and her own experiences in the fire. There was nothing from the private detective, which disappointed her until she remembered that he had had only about thirteen of the twenty-four hours he had said he would need, most of them at dead of night.

Reading the letters, she drank the superb coffee Mrs Rusham had made and ate a little of the grilled bacon. They had nothing to say to each other that could be safely said, and so they kept their own counsel.

As soon as she had finished breakfast, Willow retreated into her lettuce-green writing room to work. She tried to ring Serena Fydgett but was told that she was not in chambers.

'Are you expecting her?' Willow asked the clerk.

'Not today,' he said politely enough.

'I'm anxious to get in touch with her. She came to see me yesterday and there's more we have to discuss. I never asked her for her home telephone number and now I find it's ex-directory.'

'I...' began the clerk, but Willow hurried on.

'I'm not asking you to give it to me, but I'd be grateful if you would ring her and tell her that I need to speak to her. I shall be on this number for the rest of the day.' When the clerk agreed to do as she asked, she dictated her number and said goodbye.

Brian Gaskarth telephoned soon after that and asked when it would be convenient for him to bring round his report. Delighted with his quickness, Willow invited him to come straight away and waited in some curiosity to see what he would be like.

When he came he was a surprise—tall and grey-haired, looking more like an experienced salesman than anything else.

As he opened his Samsonite briefcase, Willow almost expected him to get out a bunch of glossy brochures and explain
to her how he could get her huge discounts on a fitted kitchen
or some double-glazing. Instead he took out a transparent plastic folder, from which he offered her several sheets of paper,
neatly typed.

Glancing through them as quickly as she could, Willow discovered that he had provided her with precise details of the
income, debts and credit references of Kate Moughette, Jason
Tillter, Len Scoffer, and the minister, together with opinions
about their honesty from their respective banks.

'That's remarkably impressive,' she said, glad of the information but uncomfortable, too. She wondered how many people had the same kind of data about her and almost laughed
at the naivety that had once led her to believe that she could
keep her identity as Cressida Woodruffe secret from all those
who had known her as Willow King.

'How did you get it all so quickly?'

Gaskarth shrugged and then murmured something indistinct
about fax machines, modems and new technology, adding
more clearly: 'You'll find details of their standing orders, direct debits, and major spends attached to the covering sheets.'
He seemed quite unaware of the turmoil of feelings he had
aroused in his newest client.

'Then I think that's it then, for the moment. Perhaps I can
call on you if I need anything else?'

'Delighted. Here's my account.'

The bill seemed surprisingly modest. Remembering that he
wanted cash, Willow frowned.

'Is there something wrong?'

'No. It's just that you've been so astonishingly quick that I
haven't got any cash out of the bank yet. I know it's just what
we agreed, but I haven't got anything like enough on me. Is
a cheque any good to you, or would you rather come with me
to the bank while I get cash?'

Mr Gaskarth looked around the room, as though he were
pricing the furniture and paintings, and then grinned. 'I'll take
a cheque from you, Mrs Worth.'

'Great,' said Willow and wrote one out, meticulously noting all the relevant details on the counterfoil and deducting the sum from her running total.

When he had gone, she studied the reports more carefully, trying to find any evidence of the corruption Len Scoffer had suspected. Both Kate and Jason received money from sources other than their salary, but, reading further down the reports, Willow discovered that the odd sums were payments by wholly reputable magazines and newspapers for published articles.

Kate's greatest expenditure after the mortgage on her Pimlico flat was her monthly Access account. Willow was amused to see that her guess about Kate's dry-cleaning bills had been right. They were huge in comparison with her total expenditure. On the other hand she did not spend anything in any of the well known clothes shops, which did seem surprising.

Willow looked at the list of cheque payees more closely, identifying each one with ease except for a company called Frohberg, which recurred nearly every other month. Looking them up in the telephone directory, Willow saw that they supplied 'couture fabrics' and began to understand.

If her clothes were made for her, it was not surprising that they were so well fitted. On the other hand, it was still surprising that she had quite so many custom-made suits.

Her direct debits were unexciting, as were Jason's. But there were regular payments in two of the other lists that gave Willow a shock. Len Scoffer transferred sixty pounds into his wife's account on the second of every month, presumably for housekeeping. Willow wondered how much Mrs Scoffer had had to buy with that. If it were only food for the two of them, then it might be enough, but if she had no other income and was expected to buy her clothes or pay the household bills, it would be outrageously little in comparison with her husband's earnings.

Turning back to the list of regular payments that had been made from Scoffer's account over the past year, Willow could see none to the telephone, electricity or gas companies, although there were regular amounts to his local council, presumably for the council tax, and the water company.

Of all the targets of her investigation, Scoffer saved the most. Jason Tillter made no investments at all and had a large overdraft. Kate paid one hundred pounds a month into an investment trust but otherwise spent everything she earned. Neither Scoffer nor Jason made any cheque payments to a charity, although Kate subscribed small amounts to both Mind and Crisis, and the minister made a large, regular donation to Amnesty International.

But the most interesting item in the entire bundle of paper was a monthly standing order for three hundred pounds paid by the minister to a Miss Andrea Salderton. Willow read through everything the detective had given her before ringing his office.

'Miss Andrea Salderton?' he said as soon as Willow had given him her name. 'Interesting, isn't it?'

'Yes, but if you realised that, why didn't you look into it?'

'No pay, no look,' said the detective, laughing. 'Besides, how was I to know you'd find it as tantalising as I do? You didn't give me any idea what it was you were looking for.'

'Okay,' said Willow, irritated by his jocularity but needing his skills and contacts. 'I want to know who she is, where she lives, what she does for a living, why he pays her.' She stopped talking, suddenly aware of yet another reason why the minister might have wanted Scoffer's tactics investigated. 'And which her local tax office is.'

'Can do. Health records of any interest?'

'No, I don't think so. Well, yes, actually they might help. And anything else you can turn up quickly.'

'I'll see what I can do. If it looks as though it's getting very expensive, I'll let you know. Goodbye, Mrs Worth.'

Putting down the telephone, Willow tried to remember how she had introduced herself. It was most unlikely to have been as 'Mrs Thomas Worth'; she never called herself that. Presumably Gaskarth had run a check on her too. It was an unpleasant thought and she had a moment's sympathy for Miss Andrea Salderton, whoever she might be.

The telephone rang again. Willow picked it up to discover Serena Fydgett on the other end.

'I thought it was urgent that we speak,' she said irritably. 'I've been obediently trying to ring you for the past half-hour but you've been constantly engaged.'

'Sorry. The hospital rang me. I had to talk to them,' said Willow, lying in an attempt to placate the other woman, who was clearly furious about something. 'I wanted to ask whether I could come and talk to you today—and perhaps to your nephew as well, if he's still with you?'

'Why?' The single word emerged from the telephone like an angry bark.

'It's just that I'm trying to sort out my own thoughts on who might have started the fire, and I'd like to check one or two things out with you both.'

'You're beginning to sound like the police, Willow.'

'I'm sorry. I didn't mean to. You must know I don't think you had anything to do with the arson. It's just that I need to get my mind clear about what the police are up to and why. They won't tell me, despite the fact that I'm involved. If I could talk to Robert about his interrogation, that would help. I...' Willow made herself sound pathetic. 'I need to know what's going on. That's why I was in a bit of a panic when I spoke to your clerk and told him how urgent it was that we speak.'

'Oh, I see. All right. Why not? Provided you promise to be careful with Robert. When d'you want to come?'

'Well, now, really. If he's there and it's not inconvenient to you. Where are you?'

Serena gave her an address in Stockwell. Willow pressed the fingers of each hand into the palms of the other and then bent the fingers to and fro, trying to decide whether she could bear to drive or not. She did not like taking minicabs from firms she did not know, and the thought of trying to find a taxi in Stockwell when she had finished with the Fydgetts decided her. She took her car. After all, it had power steering and she never had to grip the wheel.

The journey was not too bad and she found Serena's address without difficulty. But she was surprised. In the shadow of a tangle of horrible modern tower blocks was a lovely circle of big, early nineteenth-century houses, marred only by the scrubby fenced lawn in the centre, which seemed to have more dog excrement than grass within its low railings. Parking outside Serena's house, Willow switched on the car's alarm and locked the doors carefully.

'I never knew this was here,' said Willow as Serena opened the door. 'And I lived down the road in Clapham for nearly twenty years. It's charming.'

'I must say I like it, although there are drawbacks. I've had to put in an alarm that's wired directly to the police station.'

'Oh?' said Willow, glad that she had protected her gleaming car as best she could. 'Like that, is it? Have you been burgled often?'

'Nine times in my first nine years; but not since I got the alarm. But you haven't come to talk about crime prevention. Rob and I are just having some tea in the kitchen. Coming?'

Willow received a pleasing but blurred impression of wooden cupboards, rustic terracotta tiles and copper pans. She concentrated on the boy who was perched on the edge of the table, both hands clasped round a scarlet-and-gold mug.

'This is my nephew, Robert Fydgett. Rob, this is Willow King, a friend of mine. I told you about her. She was in that fire.'

Still gripping his mug and making no move to stand up, the boy nodded. Willow saw that he was already about six foot tall, but gangly. Yellow-tipped spots protruded through the sparse black stubble on his chin and spread across his large nose and forehead. His wide mouth hung slightly open and he looked sullen as well as gormless. One day, when he had got used to his height, filled out and grown into his features, he would probably be very attractive, but that time seemed years away.

Despite her suspicions and her anger, Willow ached for him. 'How are you?' she asked, smiling.

'Okay,' he said in a sepulchrally deep voice.

'I'm doing all right now,' Willow answered, as though he had returned her greeting. Holding up her bandaged hands, she added: 'These were really the worst and they're miles better. I was saved by a climber, you know.'

'Yeah,' he said, flushing violently. 'I read in the paper. Jonathan Fergusson-Miller, wasn't it? He's cool.'

'Didn't he do something pretty spectacular in the Himalayas last year?'

'That's right,' said the boy, beginning to look more relaxed. 'Kangchenjunga.'

'Oh, I love that,' said Willow, turning to Serena. 'You know, from the *Swallows and Amazons*. Wasn't that what they called one of the hills above the lake?'

'I think they call them fells up there in the Lake District,' said Serena drily. 'Tea, Willow, or would you rather have coffee?'

'Coffee, please.' It was clear that Serena was not going to leave her nephew unprotected. Willow could hardly blame her for that, but it was inconvenient.

'Robert, I can imagine that you've had a hellish time with the police, and, unlike them, I don't for one minute think that you started the fire.'

'Why?' He sounded surprised.

'I can't imagine why you should do anything so stupid.' Willow smiled at him again, with as much warmth as she could manage. 'Did they tell you why they suspect you?'

'They banged on about me climbing out of school,' he said, still blushing.

'You do sometimes, don't you?'

'Sure.' He smiled, but his lips quivered and he clamped them shut again. His eyes slid sideways and he added casually, 'Good practice for when I get to real mountains.'

'When did you last climb out?'

There was a long pause. He looked down into his mug and then at his feet, and finally at his aunt who stood holding the boiling kettle and staring at him.

'Rob?' she said.

'At night?' he asked, looking back at Willow.

'Any time,' she said at once. Serena poured water on to the coffee grounds in a glass jug and brought it to the table with a clean mug. She sat down before her nephew had answered. Willow pulled out a chair, too. He stood, looking unhappy, belligerent and, she thought, ashamed.

'Don't worry about it,' said Willow, 'just tell me.'

He shook his head and looked up at the ceiling. Suspecting tears, Willow looked at his aunt and jerked her head towards the door. Serena shook her head slowly, mouthing the word: 'No.'

'What is it, Robert?' Willow asked very gently.

He breathed deeply and shook his head.

'Was it on the night of the fire, or the night before that?' Willow asked when it was clear that they were going to get nothing out of him without some more pressure. His face cleared at once.

'Oh, no!'

'Then what's the trouble?'

He shook his head again and walked to the sink, where he poured the contents of his mug down the drain. Refilling it with cold water from the tap, he drank it down, gulping noisily, and then refilled the mug again.

'Serena,' said Willow quietly, forgetting the details of their earlier conversation, 'were you with Rob when the police talked to him?'

'No, but I got a lot of the details out of the headmaster before I took Rob out of school for the duration.'

'Did they ask that?'

She shook her dark head. After a while Robert came back to the table.

'Do we have to do this?' he muttered.

'Not if you can't bear it. And I can understand how you must be feeling,' said Willow, looking at him directly and recognising all the hostility Serena had described at their first meeting. She thought that she saw not only fury but also violent hatred in his brown eyes. He said nothing. She tried again.

'You know I really do understand what it's like to—'

He slammed both his fists down on the table, making the two women jump.

'No one could understand,' he said and ran clumsily out of the room.

There was silence until Serena blew out a long breath and said, 'Perhaps I ought to thank you for getting through to him. It's the first time I've seen any sign of tears, and he ought to be crying. Good God! What's he doing now?'

They both heard a tremendous cracking, tearing sound followed by the rush of pouring water.

'Aunt S!' yelled Robert from the floor above. 'The place is exploding!'

'Get down here at once,' she shouted back, running to the door. 'What's happened?'

'The ceiling's down. There's water everywhere. I don't fancy the stairs.'

Willow followed Serena through the door into the hall. They stood there together staring upwards in horror as a huge rolling wave of water came at them down the stairs, spilling out of the banisters.

'What the hell is it?' Willow said, moving back.

'It must be the cold water tank in the roof. Rob? Are you all right?'

'Fine. It's all coming down the stairs. Or most of it.'

'A plumber!' exclaimed Serena. 'I wish I knew a good one. The last I tried was a cowboy who charged me hundreds for a simple unfreezing job. Willow, do you…?'

'Actually, yes,' Willow said, returning to the kitchen for her shoulder bag. Inside it was the black notebook in which she had been writing notes for her report. Among them was the name and address of the successful plumber whose tax affairs had so exercised Len Scoffer. 'Shall I ring him?'

'Please.'

As Willow turned away the water reached the bottom step, splashing up her legs and skirt and finding its way across the hall floor and in through the open doorways. Serena ran to the front door, yanking it open. Very little water even reached it. All the floors seemed to slope the other way. Willow shouted at Serena to open the door to the garden and thought of towels, old newspapers, blotting paper. None of them could have made any impression on the quantity of water pooling on the ground floor of the beautiful house.

The sickly, horrible smell of wet wool was already rising from the carpets, and the water was marking everything it touched. Wading through it towards the telephone, Willow heard Serena swear.

A moment later she was connected to the plumber.

'You just caught me,' said a cheerful voice. 'Between jobs. What can I do for you?'

'There's been a most frightful flood,' said Willow, not minding that she sounded hysterical. 'We think it must be the water tank in the roof.'

'Come down the stairs, did it? Often does.'

'But why?'

'Water always takes the line of least resistance,' he said. 'Just like me, love. Still coming, I take it?'

'Yes,' said Willow, who could hear it rushing down from the smashed ceiling.

'It'll be the ballcock, see. Nothing to push it up and stop the water flowing in from the mains. I'll be round and deal with that at least. And then we'll have a look-see. Do you know where the electricity mains are?'

'No. Why?'

'You never know where the water'll get to and if there's any dicky wiring, the whole place'll go up. You need to turn it off at the mains.'

'All right, I'll do that,' said Willow, finding that her brain was beginning to work again. 'I mean, it's not my house. I'll get it done at once. Please hurry.'

Serena knew where the main fuse box was and went to push the heavy red switch upwards.

'What about the freezer?' said Willow. 'Oh God, and the burglar alarm? You don't want the police to come racing round here in defence of your silver cupboard.'

'The alarm has its own batteries. The fitter said they last for twelve hours,' said Serena, 'but you're right. I'll ring the police in case anything goes wrong. Rob? Are you all right?

You'd better come down. We've got a plumber coming. Rob?' She sounded anxious. 'Where are you?'

'I'm in the roof,' came his distant voice. 'I think I can get the ballcock tied up so that I can stop the water coming into the tank.'

The two women looked at each other in astonishment.

'How wonderful!' said Willow, meaning both that the water would stop and that Robert would have been able to do something useful. She remembered his school project on supplying utilities to private houses.

'There must be hundreds of gallons,' said Serena in despair, looking around her ruined stairs and hall. Willow thought of the dangers of soaked joists and falling ceilings and rot of all kinds and shuddered for her. Feeling her hands smarting, she looked down and saw that something was seeping through the bandages. Sniffing one hand after the other, she smelled nothing but the antiseptic scent of the ointment.

'Hadn't you better get something done about those?' said Serena. 'It looks as though the blisters have burst.'

'I'll call in at the clinic on my way home,' Willow said, shaking her hands as though that could get rid of the new pain. 'But I don't want to leave you to face the plumber alone.'

'I think I can probably manage that,' Serena said with a touch of sarcasm. 'If your hands need dressing you'd better get them seen to.'

'They'll be okay,' said Willow, aware that they were still oozing. 'What will you and Rob do? You can hardly live in the house in this state.'

'I don't see why not. And I'd hate to leave it unmanned. We'll see what the plumber has to say. Rob, you are marvellous,' she added as her nephew appeared, looking wet and grimy. 'Where did you learn to deal with ballcocks?'

'Someone had to be a bit handy at home. Mum was the most cackhanded... Sorry,' he said and rushed into the kitchen. The sound of running water and a lot of splashing reached the two women, who waited outside for him to sort himself out.

The plumber arrived in a battered white van five minutes

later. He nodded to Serena, took one look at the water all
around and called his apprentice. Together, with a heavy-
looking extending ladder, they ran up the dripping stairs. Serena followed them. Willow waited at the foot of the staircase.

THIRTEEN

BOTH THE FYDGETTS moved into Willow's house that Tuesday afternoon, as soon as the plumber and a local builder Serena knew had made the house secure against further flooding and any passing thief. Serena had telephoned her insurance company as soon as the immediate mopping up had been completed, and the man she spoke to had told her that a loss adjustor must see the damage before the company would be able to settle any claim she might make. It was clear to everyone that the house would not be habitable until the work was done. Serena had muttered something about moving into Fiona's house in Chelsea.

Rob's instinctive grimace of horror had told Willow how much he hated the idea and she had rushed in with her invitation. It was only later that she rationalised her impetuosity with the thought that she still needed to know a lot more about them both. The risk she was taking did not occur to her until later still.

Serena had demurred at first, talking politely about the trouble she and Rob would cause, but Willow explained that Mrs Rusham would love to have more people to look after and that she, herself, would be glad of the company while Tom was in hospital. As she said that she realised with surprise that it was true. Her unintended sincerity had obviously got through to Serena, who eventually accepted the invitation.

Mrs Rusham had not been at all put out by the prospect of having two extra people in the house for an unspecified length of time, and had announced that Ms Fydgett would have the spare room and her nephew the sofabed in Mr Tom's study. Disliking the idea, Willow had eventually admitted that it was the only possible place for him to sleep and went to lock away her husband's papers while Mrs Rusham made up the bed in the spare room.

Tom was a tidy man and so there had been little for Willow to do. She found the keys to his desk hanging in their usual place on the window frame, unlocked the top drawer to put his few loose papers in and was confronted with a packet of letters topped with a photograph of herself, which she had never seen before.

It must, she had decided, have been one of a batch he had taken on one of their holidays. She hated almost all the photographs anyone had ever taken of her, but this one was really not too bad. Tom had caught an aspect of her that she had always thought was completely private, even from him. Sitting under a canopy of vines with her elbows on a marble table, she was ostensibly reading, but in fact her eyes were unfocused, staring well beyond the book. Sunlight was dappling through the leaves on her red hair and she looked quite unprotected.

'I'm giving him the red towels,' Mrs Rusham said from the doorway. 'Is that all right?'

'Whatever you say, Mrs Rusham,' said Willow, wiping her eyes as unobtrusively as possible. She had turned to see her housekeeper standing with a pile of linen and a thick duvet in her arms. 'He's going to be a bit hot under that, isn't he?'

'He can kick it off or turn it sideways.'

'So he can. Do you need any help?'

Mrs Rusham had looked so surprised that Willow nearly blushed for her past behaviour.

'I don't think your hands are up to pulling up mattresses.'

'Nor they are. As always, you're quite right. There's the telephone. I'll go and deal with that while you're busy in here.'

WHEN THE FYDGETTS arrived late in the afternoon, Mrs Rusham asked Robert to help her carry the suitcases upstairs. Watching them go, Serena said, 'We must sort out something about money. I can't possibly sponge off you.'

'Don't be silly. It'll be a positive help having you here so that I don't prowl about the house thinking of Tom all the time.'

'No, no. I must. I...'

Willow, who had recovered some of her carapace of pretended toughness, looked at Serena and took a chance. 'If you
really want to repay me, you could always give the police your
alibi for the fire.'

Serena frowned and asked in a withdrawn voice: 'Was that
why you invited us here?'

'Certainly not,' said Willow. 'You were in need, and I've
got the space, and the help to make it easy. But you seem to
want to hand over a quid pro quo. Your alibi would help,
whereas a few pounds of rent would only complicate my tax
position.'

'Actually they wouldn't,' said Serena, laughing. 'Don't you
know that you're now allowed a certain amount free of tax
for renting a room in your own home?'

'Even so, no amount of rent—tax-free or otherwise—is going to do nearly as much for me as knowing that the arsonist
is in gaol.' Willow hoped that Serena's amusement meant that
she was going to be co-operative. 'And your exercising your
right to silence is holding up the police investigation. I can—
just—understand why you've been doing it, but quite frankly
I think it's irresponsible—and it's prolonging all my terrors of
another fire.'

Serena turned away. 'Is there somewhere I can wash?' she
asked.

'Yes, of course,' said Willow, concealing her impatience.
'There's a bathroom next to your bedroom. I'll take you up.'

Showing her guest up to the spare bedroom, which was
furnished with an old blue silk Chinese carpet, Chinese Chip-
pendale furniture and a row of blue-and-white porcelain jars
on the chimneypiece, Willow wanted to shake her. Instead,
she smiled politely and said that Mrs Rusham would have tea
ready in the drawing room within about ten minutes.

As she went downstairs again, asking herself whether she
had made a stupid mistake—or two of them—Willow heard
the sound of Mrs Rusham's voice through the kitchen door,
saying: 'I've seen a lot worse, you know. What d'you use on
them?'

There was an indistinct, deep-toned mumble, which must

have come from Rob. Willow paused, eavesdropping shame-
lessly.

'I don't much fancy those elaborate lotions,' Mrs Rusham
said when the mumble stopped. 'If I were you, I'd stick to
good old-fashioned soap and water. There are some sorts of
soap that don't have any perfume or colouring and are specially made for faces. I'll pick up a tablet when I'm shopping
next. If you use that, rinse it off well and eat plenty of veg-
etables, they should start to clear up.'

There was another buzz of sound from Rob. Willow leaned
over the banisters, and made out some of the words: '...called
them "shag spots", and said that I must have been, you know,
um...to get such bad ones.'

Mrs Rusham's clear tones were unmistakable as she said
indignantly: 'That sounds most unfair and silly. Spots are a
product of your age and what your hormones are doing to your
whole body. There's nothing you could have done to prevent
them. But soap and water will soon dry them up. Don't you
worry yourself. There's lots more in the world to trouble you
than a few pimples. And take care shaving. Nicking the top
off just doesn't help, does it?'

Touched by Mrs Rusham's robust care for the boy, and the
fact that he was so worried about his spots, Willow walked as
quietly as possible to the drawing room to wait for Serena.
She came in only a few minutes later, looking less tense. Mrs
Rusham followed her almost at once, carrying a tray loaded
with small neat sandwiches, minute strawberry tarts and part
of a Dundee cake.

'Should you mind if Robert has his tea in the kitchen with
me? I think he feels a bit daunted by all this.' She waved her
hand towards the antique furniture, the paintings, the elegant
silver-grey sofas with their load of multi-coloured silk cush-
ions, and all the vases full of exquisitely arranged flowers.

'Not at all, Mrs Rusham,' said Serena. 'I hope he's not in
your way.'

'On the contrary. He's going to peel the potatoes for dinner.
He'll be a big help to me.'

When Mrs Rusham had gone back to her new charge, Serena said, 'Are you sure that's all right?'

'It seems ideal,' said Willow. 'They were talking about spots when I came downstairs and it sounded as though they were getting on like a house on fire. Oh God! Sorry. I can't stop those sorts of images popping out. I'd have thought that if Mrs R. can get through to him, it might help.'

'It certainly wouldn't hurt if he opened up to someone.'

Willow looked at her without saying anything.

'I know, I know,' said Serena. 'You think the same about me. But why the hell should I tell the police all about my private life? There are a lot of perfectly good reasons why I don't want to pass on what I was doing that evening.'

'But it won't go any further than them.'

Serena raised an eyebrow in the kind of elegant gesture Willow had always envied. 'You don't really believe that, do you?'

'Actually, yes, I do.'

'Well, it takes all sorts.'

'Look, what about if you just told me and I told them I knew where you'd been and made them leave it at that?' Willow kicked herself for not thinking up something a little more convincing than that.

'Don't be naive. However much you think they trust you because you're a colleague's wife, they're hardly likely to accept my alibi on your *ipse dixit.*'

Willow slowly shook her head, more in sorrow at Serena's lawyerly tendency to slide into Latin than in anything else.

'I was with the man in my life. He's married. He has a public position. He's—'

'Not the Minister for Rights and Charters?' said Willow, wondering whether she had at last stumbled on the answer to all her questions. Then she remembered the mysterious Miss Andrea Salderton and quickly said, 'Sorry. Silly of me.'

'No, not the minister,' said Serena coldly, without giving Willow any help.

'Is his the sort of public position that would be respected by the police?'

'I doubt it, but anyway that still wouldn't mean that I'd trust them with the information.'

'No, but couldn't he speak to Chief Inspector Harness direct?' suggested Willow, assuming that Serena's lover must be a High Court judge at least, if not a Lord of Appeal. 'Then you'd be wiped off the list of suspects. They'd get a move on and find out who really did it. They'd lay off Rob. And we could all relax.'

'That does make sense of a sort,' said Serena after a long pause. She smiled and suddenly looked much more human. 'But, you see, quite apart from his wife, I'm particularly anxious that Rob shouldn't get to hear about my…um, romance. I've got a feeling that some of Fiona's more florid affairs have worried him a lot. I sort of needled him about them one weekend when I was in a bit of a state about her, and he blew up at me.'

Her face twisted and for no very good reason Willow suddenly felt a rush of affection for her. Then she began to consider the implications of what Serena had just said and asked herself what kind of 'state' she had meant. Had she been miserable about Fiona's death that weekend, or was it something else? Could she have been feeling guilty? Or even jealous of one particular conquest? Was it possible that the lovely and apparently promiscuous Fiona had pinched her sister's own lover?

You've no evidence for any such thing, said a stern voice in Willow's mind. It was almost as though Tom himself had spoken. Then a real voice distracted her as Serena said, 'You see, I don't want him growing up thinking that all women carry on as Fiona did.'

Willow nodded as though she understood and poured out two cups of tea. 'As I said, you're a good aunt. Have some of Mrs Rusham's sandwiches. They're usually pretty good. What do you mean by "blew up"?'

Serena took a crab sandwich and sat holding it. Her eyes looked unhappy, almost ashamed. 'Oh, he shouted a bit, you know the sort of thing. Just made it clear that he'd loathed it when she thrust the affairs in his face. The sort of thing any fifteen-year-old might feel. I used to be vilely embarrassed by my parents at that age and they never did anything remotely indiscreet. Weren't you?'

Willow, whose parents were so detached that she could not remember feeling anything for or about them, shook her head. Veering away from her suspicions of Serena, she was forced back into wondering how far Rob's loathing of his mother's love affairs might have made him go. If he had harmed her in some way, might not his guilt have made him want to atone by taking revenge on someone else who had hurt her? Len Scoffer, for example?

'You're right,' said Serena apparently unaware of Willow's racing thoughts. 'This is a wonderful sandwich.'

They changed the subject then, and talked of nothing but trivialities, both of them obviously keeping at least half their minds on their own thoughts, until Serena asked: 'What were you saying to the plumber just before he left?'

'I wondered if you'd heard,' said Willow, feeling her cheeks warming up. She hoped they were not as flushed as they felt. 'Like your sister, he was a victim of Len Scoffer. That's how I had his name and address so handy. I want to find out how he was treated—from his point of view—before I write my report for the minister.'

'Did he tell you anything useful?'

'No, but sodden as he was, he clearly did not feel much like chatting. We've an appointment tomorrow morning at his place of work.'

'Ah.'

'Talking of appointments,' said Willow, looking down at her watch, 'I haven't been to see Tom yet today.'

'Oh lord! You haven't had your hands redressed either.'

'Nor I have. They've stopped oozing though, and they don't hurt nearly as much as they did.'

'God, I do feel conscience-stricken! Rob and I have hi-jacked your whole day. Shall I drive you to the hospital?'

'I'll be fine. Driving doesn't seem to hurt them too much. I'll nip off now and do both at once. See you for dinner. Mrs

Rusham never stays to serve it. She just leaves something in the fridge or oven, so we can have it at any time. Okay?'

'Wonderful! I wish I had someone like her in my life.'

'There isn't anyone else like her,' said Willow, smiling over her shoulder as she opened the drawing room door. 'She's unique.'

THE FOLLOWING MORNING Willow woke up ashamed of her suspicions of Serena and Rob. She decided that, along with vagueness and an inability to concentrate, the combination of Tom's condition and the fire had left her prey to wholly irrational anxieties. She mentally apologised to them both, got up, dressed and left the house at seven in order to be at Joe Wraggeley's office before he started his working day.

He had taken over a defunct panel-beater's premises in the depths of Battersea and converted it. There were two white vans parked inside a pair of high iron gates, which he was unlocking just as Willow drove up. He waved her in and pointed to a neatly marked space beyond the vans.

'Morning,' he said, wiping his hands down the thighs of his overalls as she got out of the car. 'Somehow I didn't think you'd make it this early.'

'God forbid that I should keep you from fee-paying customers,' answered Willow cheerfully, locking her car.

He led her into his office, proudly pointing out his computer.

'They did me a good turn in the end, those tax buggers,' he said. 'It's all on there now. Second-hand, you know, but it works a treat. Took a bit of getting used to, but it seems to impress the punters to have typed estimates with reference numbers and bills and that. And the work's rolling in; I'm even having to register for VAT now. I've got a brew going. Like a cup?'

'Okay, thanks. You sound remarkably charitable for a man whose business was practically turned upside down on Scoffer's orders,' said Willow watching Wraggeley pouring the thick brown tea into two chipped mugs.

'Ooh, I was hopping mad at the time, I can tell you. But

I've mostly got over it now. I'll be free and clear of debts within the year. The only thing that still riles me is that they question every bloody thing I spend.'

'I don't understand.'

'Look, they think I earn more than I declare, right?'

Willow signified that she understood him so far.

'Right. So they check through everything I've been doing, see? Take the wife on holiday? They want to see the air tickets, hotel bills, meals, drinks, bus tickets, everything—all to see if I could've afforded it on what I said I earned. Then they ask things like don't I ever buy presents for anyone? How can I buy presents, they say, if I only earn what I put on the bleeding form? And they check through everything I claim as an expense—go through it all with a tooth-comb. Not that I mind that in principle, of course.'

Willow raised her eyebrows at his bizarre idea that there could be a comb for teeth. He grinned at her, and went on: 'If I'd known... Well, be that as it may. What I don't appreciate is having to send them so many bits of bloody paper. Luckily the wife's turning into quite a good little book-keeper and she seems to like doing it. The kids are all gone now and she has nothing else to do.'

Willow wondered how well he knew his wife, but she said nothing.

'What I don't get is what it is you're after,' said the plumber, watching her with his head on one side.

'Didn't I explain that? I'm preparing a report on how Scoffer carried out his investigations. As I say, you seem remarkably charitable. Do you think he treated you fairly?'

'Since you ask me, love, no, I don't. But in the end, when he told me what they could do to me year after year till I snuff it, if they wanted, I took the line of least resistance. It was cheaper that way all in all, and I couldn't face the hassle. I hate forms and argy-bargy, and the last thing I want to do is go to court or have the bailiffs round. So I paid up. Luckily there was no effing VAT involved then.'

'Oh, why was that?'

'I was well under the turnover limit, wasn't I?'

'I see. Well, that was lucky. You'd have been in a real mess otherwise.'

'Telling me. I've a mate who got caught up with that mob, and what he told me would make your hair curl. Still, you don't want to hear about them. Horror stories about old Scoffer, eh? He's dead, i'n'e? Sure you still need to know?'

'Yup,' said Willow, taking out her black notebook. 'Give me a list.'

'Tea a mite strong, is it?' he said, noticing how little she had drunk.

'It's fine. But I know you're in a hurry.'

'Okay. He was a bloody-minded bugger, y'know. Sorry. Bastard.'

'Bugger's fine,' said Willow with a smile.

'And he lied. That's what really got up my nose,' said Wraggeley, scowling at his memories.

'What do you mean lied?'

He looked at her, took a moment to focus on the present and then smiled. 'Well, we'd have one of those meetings and he'd say something then that he'd deny when I quoted it back at him later.'

'What sort of thing?'

Wraggeley shrugged and picked at his left ear with his little finger, examining the nail when he had withdrawn it. Willow could see a gout of sticky brownish wax.

'One day I told him he was daft to think I owed so much— or could pay it. I'd never seen so much money together in my life. I told him he'd no right to pick a figure like that out of the air. He said he hadn't done that; he'd used the best of his judgment.'

'Didn't you agree?'

'Quite frankly I told him what he could do with his effing judgment and then he lost his temper and told me that if, in his judgment, the figure should be doubled then it would be. Later, when I'd thought about it and talked to the wife, I rang him back and told him what I thought of his threats. He slagged me off and said he'd never threatened me at all. See

questions about your private life,' said Willow as gently as she could. 'After all, we've worked in close proximity for several years now.'

'Yes, I know you're not the prying kind.' Mrs Rusham nodded and disappeared back to the kitchen. Willow ate the omelette and drank the delectable coffee, leafing through her letters in a hopeless attempt to stop thinking about Mrs Rusham's uncharacteristic behaviour.

There was nothing of much interest to divert Willow's mind, except for a scribbled note from Chief Inspector Harness. Peering at the clenched handwriting, she eventually made out the words:

> *Dear Mrs Worth,*
> *I see I owe you thanks and an apology. Ms Fydgett's alibi has been on to me and we've been able to eliminate her. Good of you to take the trouble. Hope the news of your husband is better soon. In haste,*
>
> *Stephen Harness*

She finished her coffee and was about to go into her writing room to ring him up when Mrs Rusham came through from the kitchen. Her face was unbecomingly flushed, the usually pale cheeks mottled dark red.

'You always have two cups of coffee,' she said gruffly. Willow obediently turned back from the door.

'Yes, I know. Thank you. You do make delectable coffee. I'll take it with me to the study.'

Mrs Rusham opened her mouth, shut it, looked down at her shoes and then deliberately said, 'I had a son once. Richard. He'd have been thirty this September. He was killed on his motorbike on his seventeenth birthday. I've always liked boys, you see.' She shook her head angrily and did not wait for Willow's comment, which was lucky because she did not have one ready.

That explains a lot, Willow thought as she walked slowly, cup in hand, to her study. Poor Mrs Rusham. To bear a child and watch him grow, nurse him through babyhood all the way to adolescence, see him on the verge of adulthood, only for him to die for something so stupid, so unnecessary as a road accident… No wonder she's never talked about herself or her family. No wonder I've treated her like a robot. That must have been what she wanted, too. And no wonder that we've always got on so well, however limited the way we've done it. Will it change now? What with that revelation and the feelings she couldn't hide when Tom was shot…

Willow stopped her internal conversation with herself. Her mind was suddenly full of Tom. There was no more room for Mrs Rusham or her dead son or her unhappiness. Willow leaned forwards until her head touched the desk. She tried to force away the mental pictures of life without him.

It was several minutes before she could regain control of herself, but eventually she managed it and pushed all her anxieties and her own feelings to the back of her mind. Then, in an attempt to do something useful, she tried to ring up Chief Inspector Harness. She was told that he was unavailable.

'What a pity,' she said to the officer at the other end of the line. 'He's written me a note. Um. I wonder…will he be in later?'

'Yes, I expect so.'

'Could you ask him to give me a ring? I'll be here,' she broke off, looking down at her watch. 'I've probably got to go out over lunchtime, but I'll be here until about twelve and then again after, say, three.'

'I'll tell him. What's the number?'

Willow gave it and then cut the connection, flexing her fingers. There was no doubt that the burned skin was healing at last and it did not feel as though she had lost any of the movement in her hands. She thought that she might even be able to operate the keys of her word processor and turned it on.

Finding that although she was still clumsy she could type, she started to rough out her report for the minister. As she worked, she came up against all sorts of gaps in her knowledge and told herself that even if her fingers were on the way to recovery her brain was still not operating at full throttle. The telephone rang before she could lose her temper with herself.

'Mrs Worth. Stephen Harness here. What can I do for you?'

'Well, I really just wanted to thank you for taking the trouble to write.'

'Good of you. I am in a bit of a hurry, so if that's all…'

'It isn't quite,' said Willow, smiling at his Tom-like efficiency. 'Look, now that you've eliminated Serena Fydgett, I take it that you've lost interest in her nephew as well…?'

'I hear you've got him staying in your house,' said Harness, sounding more like the man who had questioned her straight after the fire. 'What gives, Mrs Worth?'

'Nothing. I've got them both here because her house was flooded after the cold water tank exploded while I was there. It was the least I could do, and I must admit that I thought it might be useful to get to know them both better. The boy's in school again during the day, but I'm worried about him and the effect that your questioning might be having.'

'Not you too! I've had half the establishment on the phone bending my ear about that boy.'

'Maybe, but there is no evidence against him, is there? Come on: it can hardly harm whatever case you're building to tell me that.'

'All right,' he said after a sigh-filled pause. 'I see what the superintendent meant. No, there's no actual evidence against Fydgett, but he's hiding something and we need to find out what it is.' Harness laughed. 'Perhaps you could work another of your little miracles for us, or…'

'Or what?'

There was a pause before Harness answered, sounding reluctant. 'I wouldn't be doing my bit by your husband if I didn't warn you. I'm not sure that it's altogether wise to have a boy like that in your house.'

'You can't think he's likely to set fire to my house,' said Willow, disliking the way he had activated her own suppressed fears, 'whatever you think he did to his mother's tormentor.'

'Maybe not,' said Harness slowly. 'But he's either a destructive little beggar or at the very least accident prone.'

'I don't understand.' Willow felt surprisingly cold, considering the heavy sultriness of the weather.

'Don't you? Look what you've just told me. How many houses do you know that are flooded by their cold water tanks exploding?'

'None,' said Willow, annoyed with herself, 'but the plumber had clearly seen it more than once before. You're not really suggesting that the boy engineered the flood are you?' As she spoke she remembered her surprise that he knew all about ballcocks and indeed that he was agile enough to get up into the roof space while water was still flooding down through the broken trap door.

'It's a ludicrous proposition,' she added in an attempt to persuade herself.

'Perhaps.'

'What else has happened in buildings where he's been?'

'Mrs Worth, I really am very busy. I have to go.'

'Fine,' said Willow and banged down the receiver in a rage. It was short-lived and had been born, she knew perfectly well, from anxiety.

Trying to dismiss Harness's warnings, she concentrated on what else she needed to find out. The most comforting thing would be that Scoffer, and he alone, had been the target of whoever had set fire to the offices and that it had had nothing whatever to do with Fiona Fydgett, her tax affairs or her death. To establish that, Willow thought, she needed to confirm her picture of him and the way he had operated.

Having rung the temporary tax office, she asked to speak to Kate Moughette.

'Yes, Willow, what is it?' asked Kate with her old briskness.

'I'm almost there with my report, but there are some more things that I do need to ask you. Have you any time for me to come and talk today?'

'Nope,' said Kate. 'I'm hellishly pushed.' There was a pause and then in a reluctant voice, she added: 'But if it would help you finish what you've got to do here and leave us to get on with our work, I could give you a lift to Croydon tomorrow afternoon. We could talk then.'

'Croydon?'

'Yes. Len's funeral. You said you wanted to come. Have you changed your mind?'

'Ah,' said Willow, thinking of Mrs Scoffer's fury. Well, she would hardly recognise a woman she had never seen. 'No, indeed. That would be fine. What time?'

'Where d'you live?'

Willow gave her the address.

'Why don't I pick you up at two? It'll be a slow crawl down the South Circular, but that can't be helped and I don't want to find myself stranded down there if there are no trains when I want to get back.'

'I couldn't agree more,' said Willow. 'I'll see you then. That's very good of you. Oh, before you go, could you transfer me to Cara Saks's phone? I need to talk to her, too.'

'Must you? She's distracted enough from her work as it is and even more useless than normal.'

'Honestly, I think I must,' said Willow.

'Well, I can hardly stop you, but I should point out that she was petrified of Len. Please don't take her exaggerations too seriously, and don't keep her away from her desk during working hours.'

'Very well,' said Willow.

There was a click and then a moment later she recognised Cara's voice at the other end of the line. 'Is that you, Willow? Did you want me?'

'Yes. I've nearly finished the first draft of my report to the minister but there are some things I need to ask you. Kate says you're frantically busy, but perhaps we could meet over a sandwich at lunchtime.'

'Why not? Actually, I'm not all that busy at the moment. We're fairly stuck until the document conservators produce some more results. It does look as though some of the investigation files are going to come out all right, and it'll be all hands to the pump then, but there's not a lot I can do yet.'

'That's great,' said Willow. 'I'll loiter outside your office at one then, shall I?'

As she put down the telephone receiver, Willow suddenly

remembered that there had been no payments to a dressmaker in the details of Kate's finances. She had spent plenty on couture fabrics, but nothing on fees to anyone to make them up. For a second it occurred to Willow that Kate might make her own clothes, and then she dismissed the idea. The suits looked far too professionally cut and sewn.

Remembering Scoffer's suspicions, Willow toyed with the idea that Kate could have been paying some dressmaker in cash, perhaps even cash from bribes she had been handed by anxious taxpayers like the architect, whose case had been settled without penalties.

'It's not possible,' she said loudly. 'An intelligent woman like that, dealing with tax investigations all the time? She'd have to be barmy to think she could get away with it.'

FOURTEEN

THE SANDWICH BAR Cara had chosen for their lunch had a few tables at the back, but the atmosphere inside was so stuffy that Willow suggested they should take their sandwiches and find somewhere to sit outside.

'I don't think there is anywhere,' said Cara, 'at least nothing very nice. It's quite rough until you get to the National Theatre, and that's miles.'

'Dowting's has quite a nice garden with benches. That's only five minutes' walk from here. Come on.'

Cara followed her and they found several empty benches among the scented rose bushes.

'I never thought of doing this,' she said, 'but it is the nicest place for miles. Don't you think they might mind? It must be meant for patients.'

'Not many of them are in a fit state to sit about in gardens,' said Willow, thinking of Tom lying silent and unknowing up in his dim room. 'No one convalesces in hospital these days, even if they did when the garden was planned. I shouldn't have thought anyone would mind, but if they do, I'm on my way to visit my husband, so I count, and you can come on my ticket, as it were.'

'Of course,' said Cara, flushing. 'How is he?'

'So so.'

'I'm sure he'll be all right.' Cara laid a hand on Willow's arm. 'I'm sure of it.'

All Willow's mental toughness told her that since Cara had no private line to the deity she could not possibly know what was going to happen to Tom, but she took the reassurance in the spirit in which it had been offered.

'Thank you. Now, tell me about Len. I know he could be a bastard in the office, but what was he like with taxpayers?'

'A bastard with them, too,' said Cara with a confiding smile.

'I used to think that he actually enjoyed bullying them, particularly the ones he thought were cocky or even just extravagant. He hated that and nearly always thought it was a sign of dishonesty. I sometimes wondered what there could be in him that made him want to make other people even more miserable than he must have been.' She paused and then added in a rush, 'It wasn't unknown for them to burst into tears in meetings with him, even the men.'

'Is that what upset you so much?'

'How d'you mean?' Cara frowned. With her head on one side and her lips pursed she looked like a small, cross bird.

'He told me on my first day that you tended to get upset in meetings and sometimes broke down.'

'That's not fair.' Cara straightened her head and not only looked but also sounded tougher. 'It only happened once. Len was really going at an electrician, a big, tough man with tattoos even, who looked as though he could take on the whole world. Len started needling him and he obviously got right under the man's skin because he broke down and started to cry. It was horrible, seeing someone broken like that. Okay, so he'd been fiddling his taxes in a small way and there was a significant payment still outstanding from last year. Len was right to challenge him—of course he was—and right to tell him that we'd pursue him for the last penny, but he didn't have to be such a bully.'

'What was it he said?'

'I can't remember. I was… It made me feel sick, you know. I couldn't bear it. I suppose it just reminded me of all the times he'd had a go at me. My knees went wobbly, I felt hollow, my head buzzed and I was terrified that…well, that I'd have to rush to the toilet.' Cara blushed.

'It sounds most unpleasant.'

'It was. Kate can do it to me too, sometimes. You know, one of the reasons why I chose the civil service was because I thought there'd be less pressure than in one of the big accountancy firms, even though they pay better. But perhaps Jason's right.'

'I don't follow you,' said Willow, thinking that for a woman of twenty-eight, Cara was exceptionally thin skinned.

'That's what Jason wants: a job in private practice. He often says it's the only kind of work that's worthy of our talents; that we're wasting ourselves harassing small businessmen for derisory salaries.'

'There's always the index-linked pension. Would Jason be able to transfer, do you think?' asked Willow, realising that his ambitions probably explained why he spent so much on City suits and Jermyn-Street shirts.

'Well, he might, but you see he's determined to get in at a high level.'

'Don't you think that's possible?' asked Willow, watching a fat pigeon waddling among the flowers, pecking at juicy-looking aphids. 'Isn't he clever enough?'

'It's not that. He's got a mind like a razor; and he's got the confidence, too. I suppose he might just make it, even though no one I've ever heard of has gone in as high as he's planning. No, Jason's main problem is that his attention span is shorter than a baby's. He gets bored very quickly and then starts stirring up trouble in the office. That's bound to be on his references and it would have to count against him, I'd have thought, even in private practice.'

Willow looked at Cara, wondering whether she had deliberately planted that piece of information or whether her desire to please was such that it had merely slipped out. It was hard to assess exactly how naive she really was.

'What kind of trouble?' Willow asked, trying to find out.

Cara wrinkled her pretty nose and pursed her lips again. 'He knew how easy it was to get Len going about things and so he'd wind him up; you know, give him hints that someone was fiddling something, like poor Doctor Fydgett, and then watch laughing as Len floundered around trying to get proof of something that had never existed.'

'I don't quite understand,' said Willow. 'What things got Len going?'

'Oh, dishonesty of any kind. He was a real stickler, you know. That's one reason why everyone hated him so much.'

Seeing that Willow was still looking puzzled, Cara explained. 'If he caught one of the typists doing a letter of her own, say, or nicking an envelope, or someone taking too long at lunch, that sort of thing, he'd haul them into his office and give them a real dressing down. ''We're government servants,'' he used to say. ''Paid by the taxpayer. We have to be more honest than anyone else.'' The law was his god, really, and it amused Jason to wind him up, like on the Fydgett case. It was childish and destructive, but in a way it provided a safely valve for the rest of us. And it was bonding—you know, all of us together hating Len and laughing at him, sort of thing.'

While Cara folded her sandwich papers neatly and took them to the nearest litter bin, Willow thought of Len's alleged habit of threatening taxpayers and the suggestion that his file notes might not have accurately reflected the details of what had been said in meetings.

'Was it the letter or the spirit of the law that meant so much to him?' she asked when Cara came back to the bench.

'That's bright,' she said, sounding surprised enough to be rude. 'I hadn't realised you'd seen enough of him to get on to that. I think he would always stick to the letter, but the spirit might get a bit bent sometimes, if you see what I mean.'

'Hm, thank you, Cara. You've helped a lot.'

'Great.' She looked at her watch and then stood up in a hurry. 'I must go or Kate will be furious. She's twitchy at the moment and needs to see us all working every minute of the day. I gather I'll be seeing you tomorrow at the funeral after all.'

'What?' said Willow, forgetting the excuse she had used to get Cara to give her Mrs Scoffer's telephone number. 'Oh, yes, probably. Kate's going to give me a lift.'

Cara smiled and turned away, muttering something that sounded like, 'Well, lucky old you.'

'Before you go,' said Willow. Cara looked back enquiringly.

'You said that Jason wound Len up about the Fydgett case. What did he actually do?'

Cara smiled and shrugged and looked prettily reluctant.

Willow pressed her with a brisk 'Come on, out with it.'

'It was fairly simple, really. He overheard Len talking about Fydgett one day and he said: "Up to her old tricks again, is she? It wouldn't surprise me. I was at an auction the other day." Len asked him what he meant, but Jason wouldn't tell him. "Only hearsay, old boy, but it sounds as though someone's been selling pictures secretly and pretty well this last year."'

'Had he made that up?'

Cara shrugged. The points of her collarbone stuck up above the scooped neck of her T-shirt. Willow thought that there was a calculating look in her eyes, but it could merely have been the way the dazzling sun caught them.

'I asked him that after we heard she was dead, and he said that he hadn't told any lies. He had actually been in an auction room recently, and people are always selling pictures secretly and well. And that in any case, Fydgett was bound to have been doing it because she always did sell one or two a year even if she did declare them for CGT. And then he added that "poor old Len hasn't had any fun for ages" and needed a nice rage to get him going properly.'

'I see. Thank you, Cara.' Willow watched her go, wondering just exactly who had been stirring up trouble.

KATE ARRIVED at the mews the following day at noon. She looked unfamiliar in her black linen dress, the first dark thing that Willow had ever seen her wear. With its discreet buttons, square-cut neck, which only just revealed her collarbone, and roomy sleeves to just above the elbow, it could hardly have been more funereal and yet it must have been wonderfully cool to wear.

Willow herself was feeling hot and uncomfortable in a black suit; her only dark dresses were either designed for winter or the evening. She took off the unbuttoned jacket before she got into Kate's red Astra, wincing as the material rubbed through the bandages on her hands, and laid it on the back seat.

'I wish I were Chinese.'

'Why on earth?' asked Kate, looking over her right shoulder as she eased her heavy car out of its parking space.

'They wear white in mourning.'

'Ah, I see. Yes, black is horribly stuffy on a day like this.'

'Not yours. It's great. I'm not sure I've ever seen a dress quite like it. Where did you get it?' Willow was genuinely admiring, but she was also glad of the opportunity to flatter Kate.

'I made it. I make all my clothes.' Kate sounded defensive.

'What, not the suits as well?'

'Yes, the suits as well.'

'Goodness, I am impressed,' said Willow, glad to have one minor mystery cleared up. 'D'you know, I'd never have suspected it?'

'Why?' Kate looked at her for a second. Willow was surprised to see hostility in her small dark eyes. 'You surely can't be like my step-sister, who thinks a career makes one unfeminine.'

'Certainly not.' Willow laughed. 'Nor that dressmaking is a gender-specific skill.'

'That's all right then.' said Kate with considerable emphasis, as though Willow had unexpectedly produced the correct password. 'Look, what is it that you want me to tell you? Let's get that out of the way.'

'I've got a list of questions in my bag,' said Willow without even reaching for it. 'But the first and most important one is what was the information that Len Scoffer told Fiona Fydgett he had about income that she'd concealed?'

'Oh God!' said Kate, putting the back of her hand against her forehead as though her persistent headache was still with her. She lifted her foot off the accelerator for a moment, causing the driver behind, whose car was only three inches from her back bumper, to hoot furiously. 'Look, it's just one of those hideously unfortunate things.'

'Which hideously unfortunate things?'

Kate shrugged and put her hand back on the steering wheel. 'As you probably know, banks and building societies pass on to us information about the interest earned on all their customers' accounts.'

'Yes, I knew that.'

'Fydgett's bank gave us figures for the interest on her two accounts. The first coincided with the information on her tax return. The second did not. In fact, to have earned that amount of interest she would have had to have received a large injection of capital. We took it—Len took it—that she'd done another big picture deal and tried to keep it secret because it would have been the third that year.'

She paused as she overtook a lorry parked on a double yellow line.

'Why would that have mattered?' asked Willow.

'When the commissioners ruled that her picture profits were capital gains after all, she had had only two sales in the year. Len thought that she must have believed three deals would put the picture sales into the category of business profits after all, and that she'd concealed the biggest for that reason.'

'That was all? Didn't he have any evidence of a big deal? If she'd made a really crunchy amount, surely she would have had to have sold the painting through one of the big auction houses, and then there'd be a record. Did he check?'

'In some ways a private sale would have been more likely,' said Kate, as she braked at a set of traffic lights that was just turning amber. Once again there was a loud hooting from behind, combined with the sinister sliding shriek of rubber skidding on tarmac.

The sound shocked Willow out of her musings about the possibly murderous fury someone might feel at seeing reports of a painting, for which they had earned only a hundred pounds, being sold on for ten or twenty times that amount by the woman to whom they had sold it. She turned to look out of the rear windscreen.

The car behind was a big, navy-blue BMW and its brakes must have been recently serviced for the driver had just managed to stop without crashing into the back of the Astra. He was a thin-looking man in his forties with a dark, sneering face, and he was tapping at his steering wheel. Kate only glanced in her mirror and allowed herself a scornful smile.

'Pillock!'

As the lights changed she drove smoothly across the junction, checking her mirror more frequently than usual. As soon as the road widened at all, the BMW driver accelerated violently and whipped past them. The driver tapped his forehead as he passed, staring at Kate. She merely shook her head.

'Well?' said Willow after they had driven in silence for three crowded miles. 'Did you ever discover whether there had been a private deal?'

'No. In fact, the bank had made a mistake. I'm not sure how it happened. Presumably the computer malfunctioned or someone entered a wrong account number at some stage. The sum we were given for interest on the long-term account was in fact the total money she had in the account. It wasn't our mistake at all, but it was most unfortunate.'

'But didn't you ever consider that the bank might have been wrong?' Willow hoped that she did not sound as outraged as she felt.

'You don't understand.' Kate sounded unhappy but not apologetic. 'We get that sort of information all the time. Have you any idea how many interest-bearing accounts there are in this country? We get details of them all. We can't go checking every single one. Not only we, but also the banks would grind to a halt.'

'But in a case where the taxpayer repeatedly denied any dishonesty,' protested Willow, 'surely any reasonable person would have thought there might have been a mistake.'

'In an ideal world, yes. Len ought to have made some more enquiries. But, look at it his way: the picture dealing had been a thorn in his flesh for years. Fydgett not only denied having done any more deals to make the money he believed she had, but she also refused to supply any proof. If she had complied with Len's request for her books and statements at the beginning, the whole problem would have been cleared up months ago. As it was, he was certain that she was lying. Seen from his point of view the whole thing is perfectly understandable.'

Willow looked at Kate, for the first time seeing the strength of her chin, which was only noticeable in profile, and the sharpness of her small nose. 'Well,' she said drily after a while, 'I can only say that it's admirable that you defend your staff so forcibly. What did you really think of Len? Between us, off the record, going no further, and all the rest of it.'

Kate sighed, slowed as the car approached a roundabout and swung neatly round it. The impatient BMW was caught in the next traffic jam, still only one car ahead of them.

'He was a tricky man to work with,' Kate said, biting her lip. 'I don't know how much you've been told...?'

'Not a vast amount, but I understand that he resented working for a woman so much younger than himself.'

'I don't think my age had much to do with it. He would have resented any woman, and probably most men, too. He hated being told what to do by anyone, and he despised a lot of my decisions.'

Before Willow could ask for any details, Kate hurried on: 'He didn't believe in conciliation of any kind. Belligerent confrontation was more his style, and he could never accept that while it might make him feel tougher, it was unlikely to increase the tax take. I used sometimes to try to make him see that a considerable proportion of taxpayers are muddled and frightened rather than dishonest, and that if gently treated they will co-operate and our record of collection will improve.'

'Belligerent confrontation is certainly the impression I've got from the files I've read,' said Willow, surprised into admiration. Kate seemed to sense it for she flashed a glance at Willow and smiled. 'It must have made him a difficult colleague.'

'It did; that along with some of his other beliefs. The concept of *de minimis,* for instance, meant nothing to him at all. D'you know, he once raised an assessment for twenty-five pence?'

'That's loopy,' said Willow. 'I've heard of that sort of thing and assumed the stories were apocryphal. The postage alone would have cost that much, let alone the paper, the explanatory booklets, the computer time, his time… What a ridiculous waste!'

'You're telling me.'

'Tell me something, Kate.'

'What?'

'What did you mean about Len's despising your decisions? What kind of decisions?'

'Well, you've seen the files,' said Kate, apparently concentrating on the traffic ahead. 'The architect whose accountant advised him so badly. Len thought it iniquitous that I wasn't pursuing him for every penalty in the book. Try as I might to explain my reasons, he would not accept them. I… Oh, what's the use? The man's dead. I can't help feeling relieved and I wish that I didn't. But one must be honest.'

'Yes.' Willow could hear the dryness of her own voice and hurried to disguise it. 'Is that why you gave him a free ride on the Fydgett case?'

'He was too senior to have me breathing down his neck all the time,' said Kate, sounding resigned. 'His files were his own to deal with as he chose unless there was a complaint. I had nothing whatever to do with the Fydgett case until the Chairman wrote to me, because she had never complained at all. I can't think why not, if she was so upset about it all. That's why I don't believe her suicide was anything to do with the way Len behaved.' Kate shrugged and then went on. 'Anyway, as soon as I'd been brought in I instituted enquiries, discovered that the bank had made the error and satisfied myself that, even if Len had been a bit heavy-handed, at least he had followed the law. Then you appeared.'

'Yes, I'm sorry that I added to your burdens. But do you really think that Len acted properly? I mean, even in his suggestion that if she didn't agree to pay up, went to the commissioners and got away with it again, he would simply have investigated her every year until she died.'

Kate groaned. Willow suddenly noticed the name of the street they were passing and recognised it as the one in which the Scoffers lived.

'That's a matter of perception,' said Kate. 'He wouldn't have put it like that, whatever the woman thought she heard.'

'But he was a bully, wasn't he?' Willow said quickly, making plans.

'Yes, he was certainly that. And, oh, put it like this: in his private, internal narrative he was the only honest person around. Everyone else was careless at best, criminal at worst, and dishonest in any case. Look, here we are. That's the church over there. I'll park here. You don't mind walking the last bit to avoid the one-way, do you?'

'Not at all,' said Willow, half-amused by Kate's reference to Len's private narrative. She was tempted to ask whether Len had ever found his inner child. 'Look here, Kate, I think I'm going to have to bottle out of this after all.'

'What on earth do you mean?'

'I had a bit of a run-in with Mrs Scoffer on the telephone. I know she's no reason to know what I look like, but if someone told her who I am, she might feel that I'm rubbing her nose in it a bit. You know—that I survived and Len didn't. I... It may be sentimental of me, but I'd rather not do that. I'll hang about for a while and perhaps go back by train.'

'Are you sure? You could always have a coffee or something and then come back to the car. I'm not planning to eat the funeral baked meats, you know, and I don't suppose the service will take more than an hour, if as much.'

'Okay. But if I'm not here, don't wait for me.'

'Right.' Kate turned away and crossed the road towards the forbidding grey church.

Willow waited until she had gone in before turning back the way they had come. Five minutes' fast walking brought her to the end of the street of matching semi-detached houses where the Scoffers lived.

FIFTEEN

A FUNERAL, as all burglars know, is one of the few times when a family home is certain to be empty. Willow made her way along the row of houses until she came to the Scoffers'.

It had been carefully, if insensitively, maintained. The original sash windows had been replaced with modern double-glazing and the slate roof had been renewed with red tiles, which clashed with the pinker colour of the bricks. The windows gleamed with recent washing and even the doorstep looked as though it had been scrubbed that morning.

Two black plastic dustbins stood neatly aligned on the bare concrete in the centre of the small front garden. Willow was amused to see that both had their lids firmly attached with wire clips. From her years in the Clapham flat, she knew how difficult it was to persuade the refuse collectors to return the lids with the emptied bins.

A row of regimented petunias edged the narrow flower beds. They were arranged by colour, one white, then a red, then two whites and then a pink, another white, another red and so on. Inside the row were neat, humpy green plants speckled with small yellow flowers, which Willow could not identify. There was no ease or generosity or spontaneity in the garden, and it seemed typical of Len's obsession with rules, obedience, and symmetry.

Shuddering despite the damp heat, she rang the front door bell. No one came and so, checking that none of the neighbouring net curtains had been twitched aside, Willow walked down the dark passage between the Scoffers' house and their neighbours', hoping to find an easy way in.

There were two gates, about five feet high, set at an angle to each other at the end of the passage. She pushed at the one that seemed to lead to the Scoffers' garden. It did not give at all.

Thinking of her tights and short straight skirt as much as her bandaged hands, Willow was reluctant to try to climb over the gate. She reached up so that she could tip her right hand over the top and felt around for a bolt. There was one only a few inches from the top of the gate, and she pushed it back. There might have been another at the bottom, which would have been impossible to undo from the wrong side, but she was in luck and the gate gave way.

The back garden was as tidy as the front of the house. There was a small lawn, very deep green and evenly mown, with tall, bright but ill-matched bedding plants arranged in rows all round it. A small, gleaming lean-to greenhouse, which seemed to contain nothing but tomato plants, stood next to a locked shed, presumably housing the mower and tools. An empty washing line had been slung between two sturdy-looking fence posts.

Hoping that the ease with which she had gained entry to the garden was not a fluke, Willow pushed at the handle of the back door. It yielded at once and she pushed the door open. Immensely grateful for Mrs Scoffer's surprising carelessness, Willow called out: 'Hello. Anyone there?'

There was no answer. Inside the kitchen, Willow felt even more sympathy for the widow. The room must have been arranged before fitted units became affordable. There was an old but impeccably white pottery sink between two wooden draining boards, which were pale with scrubbing. A large, formica-topped table with slanting metal legs provided most of the working surface, and the cooker was a small gas stove, perched up on legs, of a kind that Willow had not seen since she last watched a film set during the Second World War. The only modern thing was the fridge, which at least looked as though it might have been bought in the last ten years. There were two tall, narrow, dresser-like cupboards, free-standing and painted pea green.

The top of the cream-coloured table was covered with piles of cups and saucers and plates of sandwiches draped with damp tea-cloths. Other plates held neat squares of fruit cake, covered in cling film, and empty jugs stood next to a sugar bowl. It was clear that Mrs Scoffer was expecting to return to the house for tea with several of the other mourners.

Checking that there was still time before the likely end of the service, Willow left the kitchen to explore, not at all sure what she expected to find but obscurely certain that she would not be doing her duty if she did not look.

The front room was bare of everything but a velvet-covered three-piece suite and two highly varnished revolving book cases filled with hard-backed books that did not look as though they had ever been opened, let alone read. The whole room smelled of furniture polish, mothballs and stale air, as though it were hardly ever used. Behind it was a smaller room with a big television and video as well as a square oak dining table and matching chairs with grey-velvet seats. Everything was completely dust-free. There were no pictures; the few books were neatly stacked in their shelves, apparently arranged by size rather than author, title or genre; and there was no sign of any alcohol at all.

Upstairs Willow found the main bedroom with narrow twin beds covered in mushroom-coloured candlewick, and a highly polished, mahogany-veneered dressing table on spindly legs near a matching wardrobe with a mirrored door. Once again there was a powerful smell of mothballs.

Risking a glance between the net curtains, Willow was shocked to see a large dark-blue BMW parked about three houses further along the street. She did not recognise the registration number, but she had not even looked at the number plate of the car that had almost crashed into Kate's. With a sinking feeling in the pit of her stomach, Willow wondered whether someone might be watching her after all.

Letting the curtain drop, she backed out of the room and went on to check the rest of the house as quickly as she could. The next room was obviously a spare bedroom. The bed was flat, covered with another candlewick bedspread, and all the rest of the furniture was draped in old-fashioned dust sheets. Apart from the bathroom, there was only one other. It looked as though Len had used it as a study.

Willow went at once to a filing cabinet that stood beside

the window and pulled at the top drawer. It was locked. Cursing herself for not having learned how to pick locks, Willow turned instead to the desk. All she found were neat sheaves of receipted bills and a series of account books. Even though she already knew all there was to know about Scoffer's finances, she opened one and looked down at the tidy entries.

They were all concerned with household expenditure. Turning the pages, Willow saw that month after month the totals were within a pound or two of the sixty he allowed his wife. It seemed that as well as the food and the heat and light she had to pay for her own clothes, small presents, and anything spent on the house or garden. The only thing approaching frivolity was her subscription to a local bowls club.

From the evidence of the account books, her existence seemed appallingly bleak.

'Well, at least she'll be a rich widow,' said Willow aloud, putting the books back where she had found them.

The wastepaper basket was annoyingly empty and there seemed to be nothing else in the room that looked at all promising, except for the filing cabinet. Willow could not imagine what he kept locked up in it, and felt that she had to find out.

Spurred on by frustration, she suddenly remembered reading in a novel that filing cabinet locks are not at all difficult to deal with. The cabinet merely needs to be tipped back and the steel bar holding the drawers shut can be pushed up to release them. There was no need to pick the lock at all. The only difficulty would be lifting the cabinet.

Willow dealt with that by putting her shoulder to the top of the cabinet and pushing. The front lifted neatly away from the thin nylon carpet, but she could not keep the cabinet far enough up to force her bandaged hands between it and the carpet to push up the bar. She needed a knife—a longish paper-knife.

There were no promising implements on the top of Scoffer's desk, or in its drawers, but there would probably be a carving knife downstairs. Willow was just stepping down from the hall passage into the kitchen when she heard a key in the front-door lock. Hardly thinking, she wrenched open the door under the stairs, and shut herself in.

She found herself not at the top of some cellar stairs, but in a musty cupboard filled with old paint pots and decorating tools. There was only just room for her to stand between the door and the piled tins. Hearing heavy footsteps coming towards her, she held her breath.

A police siren wailed in the distance, came nearer and then passed on, growing fainter in the distance. There was a tremendous crash as a thick shoe crunched into the fragile wooden door that was Willow's only protection. Expelling her breath through her nose as quietly as possible, and trying not to think of the people who might have been following her that morning, she pressed both bandaged hands to the inside of the door. It seemed a pathetic form of defence.

'Bloody fucking hell!'

It was a male voice, very angry, and slightly American. Its owner kicked the door once more, so hard that Willow's wrists were badly jarred.

'Fucking shit. Bloody, bloody, hell. What a shit. What a fucking shit.'

Through the stream of obscenities, Willow heard the coy sound of the front-door chime. The man outside her cupboard stopped yelling and kicking the door and for a moment there was silence until the chime sounded again. Then the footsteps retreated towards the front of the house. Willow let herself breathe more deeply. A click followed and then the angry voice, a little moderated, said, 'Yes? The funeral's at St Michael's, just down the road there. But you'll be late. They're half-way through already.'

'Mr Scoffer? Mr Martin Scoffer?' The second voice sounded vaguely familiar to Willow, but she could not place it.

'Yeah. That's me. Don't you want the funeral?'

'Not exactly.'

'Then what can I do for you?'

'My name's Harness.'

Willow stiffened in her dark cubbyhole.

'Chief Inspector Harness, actually. I was at the church, hoping to have a word with you after the service. When I saw you rushing off, I thought perhaps I ought… Could we do this inside, do you think?'

'Sure. Come on in.' There was a sound of heavy breathing gradually brought under control. 'You the guy investigating the arson?'

'That's right.'

'Then come on down to the kitchen and I'll make a cup of tea. I could do with one. There's not a lot I can tell you. I wasn't even in the country when the place burned. But I'll do what I can.'

Willow, whose left leg was beginning to ache and jump as cramp seized her calf muscles, realised that she was stuck. She could not emerge from the cupboard without humiliating herself in front of Chief Inspector Harness, and if the two men were going to settle down to tea-and-questions they might still be there when the mourners came back for their carouse. She leaned down to rub her calf and suddenly smelled gas. The meter was just behind her and the main gas tap on a level with her eyes.

Wonderful! she thought. Stuck in a cupboard with a leaking gas meter. Well, at least North Sea gas isn't poisonous, even if it does explode.

Despite all her desperate attempts at humour, her predicament seemed quite unfunny.

'Mr Scoffer, have you seen that the back door's open?'

Oh, shit! thought Willow with almost as much violence as the man himself had used.

'That's one of the few ways my poor mother could get back at my father,' said Martin, sounding as though he had been loosening his tie and rubbing his Adam's apple as he spoke. 'He was very security conscious, but she knew that there was nothing worth stealing in this hellish house, and so she used to leave the windows or the back door open as a kind of pathetic defiance.'

'You sound as though you disliked your father.' Harness spoke as though only mildly interested in the answer.

'Sure,' said the younger Scoffer easily. 'It's taken me nearly ten years in expensive analysis to be able to say it, but I hated him.' There was a pause and then he added cheerfully, 'And I can't say that I never fantasised about killing the bastard as I grew up, but in the end I ran away instead.'

'Perhaps that was wise.'

'Maybe, but it meant she was alone with him here. I'm not particularly proud of that. On the other hand my anger didn't help her any. In some ways it probably made it harder for her. Yup: I hated him all right, but I didn't set fire to his office.'

Willow thought she recognised someone who felt horribly guilty, trying to persuade himself that he was not nearly as bad as he feared. She wished that she could talk to him herself.

'I know that,' said Harness. There was a sound of chair legs being pulled along a hard floor. 'You were still in Maryland on the day he died, well alibi'd by all your colleagues at the lab.'

'You've been checking up on me, Inspector. Tea? Or would you rather have a beer?' There was the sound of the fridge door opening. 'That's another bit of rebellion. This was a wholly dry household until he died, but I took my mother to the nearest Majestic yesterday and loaded up with a couple of cases of lager, which she loves.'

'It's rather early for me, thank you, but I wouldn't say no to a glass of cold water.'

'How austere! You don't mind if I have a beer, do you?' A ring pull was ripped off the top of a can, but there was no sound of liquid being poured into a glass. 'Ah, that's better. You can't think how good it feels to give that bastard two fingers in any way available. How she put up with it I'll never know.' A tap was turned on and then off again. The cramp in Willow's leg was so painful that she started to bite the insides of her cheeks to make certain that she did not groan aloud.

'Sorry, I forgot; here's your water. Now, what do you want to ask me?'

'Anything you can tell me about your father—or his enemies.'

There was a short, barking laugh.

'There were plenty of those, I can tell you. Maybe one day
I'll let myself think what it must have been like for him to
hate everyone and be hated back—I don't suppose that there
can be anyone in the world who minds that he's dead—but I
can't yet. He didn't know how to be with someone else and
not bully them. He ought to have got help, but it would never
have occurred to him that there was anything the matter with
what he did. He thought he was right and the whole of the
rest of the world was wrong.'

'Poor man.'

'Easy for you to say, Inspector. You were never a target.'

'So who was, particularly?'

'I don't suppose I could even list them. Everyone he came
into contact with. Though to be fair I can't think of any I've
ever met who'd go to the lengths of burning down a whole
building to get back at him. Plenty might have liked to strangle
him or beat him over the head, but why torch the office? I'd
have thought that was someone who wanted to get even with
the Revenue, wouldn't you? A disgruntled employee, probably.'

Willow stopped trying to massage her agonising calf muscles for a moment. The smell of gas was still only faint, but
something had given her a frightful headache.

'Why d'you say that?' came Harness's voice, quite clearly
despite its quietness.

There was a short silence, followed by the sound of deep
swallowing and the complicated clinking rustle as a crumpled
can hit the inside of the garbage bin.

'I've been reading about the minds of serial killers and other
criminals recently,' said Martin Scoffer. 'One thing one of the
books said, which struck me as pretty sensible, was that someone who can't fit into an organisation or deal with the people
in it tends to want to destroy it for everyone else: maybe to
prove that no one else can succeed where he failed. See what
I mean?'

'Yes, I think so.'

'You look for a disgruntled employee or one who just
couldn't make it and you'll probably find the man—or

woman—who did us all such a good turn. Oh, fuck! I can't even say that without guilt. He was such a bastard, but he was my father. Look here, could we go outside? This place still stinks of him.'

'Certainly.'

As soon as she heard the sound of two pairs of feet leaving the kitchen, Willow slipped out of her cupboard and, hobbling, hurried to the front door. She let herself out and was back by Kate's car, hot, and full of questions eight minutes later.

The sun was beating down on the row of parked cars and shimmering around their edges, and there were no trees to provide any kind of shade. Waiting there, Willow narrowed her eyes against the glare and hoped that her head would stop aching soon. The only prospect of getting out of the sun would be to cross the roads to the church and she could not bear to risk meeting Mrs Scoffer.

It was no wonder, Willow thought, that Len's widow had not managed to sound convincing in her angry grief. The poor woman had obviously lived a miserable, sterile life, subject to constant tyranny, losing her only child to America, and forced to account for every penny of the miserly housekeeping allowance here husband allowed her. The most surprising thing was that she had not left him years earlier.

But could she have engineered the fire in the Vauxhall Bridge Road? She was one of the few people who would have known if he had really intended to stay late. But it seemed an unlikely way for a downtrodden, sixtyish woman to kill an unpleasant husband, however clever it might seem to make sure he died miles away from her. It was a pity that her son had such a strong alibi.

By the time people started coming out of the church, Willow felt ill. She was leaning against the car with her jacket laid on the roof, conscious of very little but her pounding head and a nausea that made her think she might actually be going to be sick.

'Are you okay?'

Willow opened her eyes and saw Kate peering at her.

'Just hot,' said Willow. 'I couldn't face the flog down to the railway station after all and so I came back here. Sorry.'

'Not at all. I ought to have left you with the keys so that you could at least sit down. Come on, get in, and I'll drive you back.'

'Thanks.' Willow sat back in the boiling car and closed her eyes.

Kate drove in silence until they were back in the middle of London. 'Will you be all right?'

Willow opened her eyes. 'I'll be fine. So sorry about that. It's partly my suit. You were much more sensible coming in that dress. How was the service?'

'Pretty grim, in fact. The address was a masterpiece of tolerant understatement, but the hymns were the most turgidly gloomy I've ever heard and the whole atmosphere was somehow unpleasant.' Kate paused for a moment and then added: 'From the few indiscreet comments I overheard, I got the impression that poor Len was as difficult at home as he was in the office.'

'I know he was,' said Willow and then closed her eyes again, silently cursing herself.

'Really? How?'

'Perhaps to say "know" was pushing it a bit. I mean, I assumed he was. No one could be quite as ferocious... Oh, you know what I mean.'

'I'm not sure that I do.'

Willow did not comment. Instead she asked what Mrs Scoffer was like.

'A poor sad little thing,' said Kate. 'As short as me and with terrible arthritis in her hands.'

Well that settles that, thought Willow. If Mrs Scoffer's small and arthritic she's most unlikely to have broken in to mess about with the electrics in the office.

Each absorbed in her own thoughts, they sat in silence for most of the rest of the way, until Kate said, 'Isn't your house somewhere along here?'

'If you take the second turning on the right, it's the first on the left, and there we are. Thanks, Kate. It was really good of you to drive me.'

'Not at all. Look, are you going to need to talk to any of us any more? I really should like to get all this wound up so that the department can get properly back to work. Morale hasn't been good in any case and you're hardly helping, poking about and upsetting everyone with the thought that they're being judged.'

'I want to get the job finished just as much as you,' said Willow with feeling. 'It oughtn't to be much longer. I've got one or two more people to talk to, but I've already roughed out the report.'

'May I ask what your conclusions are likely to be?'

Kate's co-operation and offer of a lift began to seem less disinterestedly kind than Willow had assumed. The ulterior motive was hardly surprising, but she felt disappointed; she had liked what she had discovered of Kate during the afternoon.

'I'd rather complete the report before I tell you that. But I can say that I appreciate the difficulties you had containing Scoffer.'

'Well, that's something, I suppose. I'd appreciate a copy of what you send the minister.'

'That's up to him, I'm afraid.' Willow smiled. 'I'm sure you'll get one in due course. Thanks for the lift.'

She opened the car door, longing for the day when her hands would heal properly and she could use them as unthinkingly as she had once done. Slamming the door with her hip, she waved at Kate and went to ring her own front door bell.

'Sorry to get you out of the kitchen,' she said to Mrs Rusham when the door opened, 'but I couldn't bear to squash my fingers down into my bag again.'

'That's perfectly all right. You look worn out. Shall I run you a cool bath?'

'Thank you. That would be heaven. But I must ring the hospital first.'

She went quickly into the drawing room, relieved that both

Serena and Rob appeared to be out, and dialled the number of Dowting's switchboard.

'Mrs Worth, I'm glad you rang,' said the ward clerk in the Intensive Care Unit. 'Mr Richardson would like a word with you. Can you hang on while I bleep him?'

'Yes, of course.' Willow suddenly remembered that she had been supposed to see the consultant the day after the fire. As soon as he came on the line she apologised.

'Please don't bother, Mrs Worth,' he said, sounding much more friendly than when they had first spoken. 'I could see from the newspapers what had happened to you. I wanted to talk to you because your husband's prognosis is looking better.'

Willow sat down heavily on the chair behind her.

'Are you there, Mrs Worth?'

'Yes, I'm here. D'you mean he's come round?'

'Not yet, but the signs are encouraging us to believe that he will.'

Released from her visions of Tom being kept mindlessly alive for years, perhaps retaining just enough brain power to make him long to be allowed to die and yet be unable to tell anyone, Willow could hardly speak. With a huge effort, she said, 'When?'

'We can't put any kind of time limit on it, but I thought you ought to know. Also, the latest scan is thoroughly encouraging. It looks as though there will be no permanent brain damage after all. Although, having said that, I must—'

'I know,' said Willow quickly. 'You can't promise anything. I understand. Thank you for telling me. I'll be round as soon as I can.'

'There's no hurry. I don't want to raise your hopes too steeply.'

'No. I see. Thank you, Mr Richardson.'

Willow sat in the chair with the receiver in her bandaged hand, her eyes closed, letting herself feel the beginnings of freedom from fear. She reminded herself that there were still no guarantees that Tom would make it, but even that could

not stop her spirits rising. Eventually she opened her eyes to
see Mrs Rusham standing in the doorway.

'They say that the signs are better. There's a chance that
he'll come round soon, and they don't think there's been any
serious brain damage.'

Mrs Rusham's dark face relaxed and she even smiled. 'I'm
glad. Your bath's ready. Would you like something cold to
drink?'

'Thank you,' said Willow. She knew that the gladness was
real and she was grateful all over again that Mrs Rusham did
not expose her own emotions. She seemed to have recovered
from the vulnerability into which Rob Fydgett's unhappiness
had plunged her.

'Oh, by the way, could you possibly ring the gas leak emergency number for me?'

'Certainly, but there are no leaks here, you know.' Mrs
Rusham peered forward, as though looking for signs of lunacy
in her employer's face.

'No, no, I know that. But I'd like you to report a possible
leak at number twenty-seven, Churchgate Row, Croydon.
Don't give your own name or mine, will you?'

'Very well.'

It was not until Willow went into her ivy-green bathroom
and started painfully to undress that she realised why both Mrs
Rusham and Kate Moughette had been so surprised by her
appearance. Not only was her face very white and rather dirty,
but her pearl-grey silk shirt was stained with sweat under the
arms and across the back, there were cobwebs in her hair and
a large hole in her black tights. But the bandages on her hands
were dry. It really did look as though the blisters must be
healing. She unwrapped the gauze and then wished that she
had not. The skin of her palms was still raw looking, and
exposing it to the air seemed to make it hurt more.

Taking two new sterile dressings from the pile the hospital
had given her when she last went to the clinic, she attempted
to rebandage the hands herself and got into such a mess that
she had to go in search of Mrs Rusham.

Five minutes later, her hands neatly dressed, Willow was

lying back in perfectly judged tepid water, sipping cold fruit juice through a straw.

It was only then that one of the worst ironies of the whole tragedy struck her. As Kate had pointed out, if Fiona Fydgett had responded to Len Scoffer's peremptory and possibly punitive demand for all her accounts, bank statements and related papers, he would have had all the proof he needed that her bank had given him wrong information about the interest she had earned. Equally, if he had answered her request for precise details of whichever figure in her accounts or tax return it was that he doubted, she would have been able to satisfy him at once. If Scoffer had been less aggressively mistrustful or Fiona less obstinate, there would never have been war between them.

Whether or not the depression that had made Fiona kill herself had been triggered by her battle with Scoffer, the battle's end might well have saved her.

Willow began to hope, with a fervour that made her breathless, that she would be able to prove Rob had had nothing to do with the fire. If it turned out that he had tried to burn down the tax office out of revenge for what Scoffer had done to his mother, that would turn irony into something much worse.

SIXTEEN

BY THE FOLLOWING Sunday there was still no sign of Tom's regaining consciousness. Willow had been so convinced by Mr Richardson's announcement of the improved prognosis that she had spent most of her time at the hospital, watching and waiting.

On Sunday morning she got up soon after eight, having slept badly again. She knew that she should never have allowed herself to hope for any improvement in Tom's condition until it actually happened, and decided that only work—lots of it—would save her sanity. There was not much she could do on a Sunday, but what there was would have to be done.

Rob Fydgett slopped into the kitchen just as she was making herself a cup of coffee to take back to bed. He was wearing baggy black tracksuit trousers and a vast white T-shirt with a slogan on it announcing the imminent death of the planet. Regretting her invitation to both Fydgetts and instantly ashamed of herself, Willow tightened the belt of her yellow silk kimono and offered him a cup of coffee.

'I don't like it,' he said gracelessly as he pulled open the fridge door. He did not look at her. 'Evelyn said I could always have a shake.'

Without another word, he took a large carton of semi-skimmed milk out of the fridge and a carton of orange juice from the freezer beside it and tucked them into the crook of his left elbow. Helping himself to two bananas from a large blue pottery bowl on the kitchen table with his right hand, he took his booty to the worktop where Mrs Rusham kept the blender.

Willow, wondering whether she had ever known that her housekeeper's first name was Evelyn, watched her young guest rip open the little drum of frozen juice and scoop half of it into the blender. He followed that with the two bananas, roughly chopped, and then topped up the blender with milk. Switching it on at the maximum speed, he kept one large floppy-looking hand on the lid to stop it flying off. Still without speaking or meeting Willow's eyes, he turned off the machine, reached across her for a tall glass and poured out a stream of thick, pale-yellow gloop.

There was, thought Willow in revulsion, no other word that would describe the viscous mixture.

'Ah,' said the boy, and wiped his mouth on the back of his hand.

'Good?'

'Yeah, great. Er, thanks. You know.'

Willow smiled. 'Let's sit down.'

The boy looked longingly towards the door, but when he had refilled his glass he pulled out a chair with one bare foot and sat down, tipping the chair on to its back legs and shaking his head once to clear the long fringe out of his eyes. Willow reminded herself how tricky his life had been, what a difficult age he had reached, how uncertain and miserable he must be, and that it behoved her to be both charitable and understanding as she interrogated him.

'You know, Rob, I'm really grateful that you've managed to get on such good terms with Evelyn,' she said eventually. 'I often think that she must be a bit lonely working here all day on her own.'

'She likes it,' said Rob with all the authority of one who knows. He looked directly at Willow for the first time. 'She doesn't like people much.'

'You don't either, do you?'

The boy shrugged and looked away again. The chair tilted dangerously backwards. Willow only just stopped herself reaching out a hand to steady him.

'Rob, will you tell me something?'

He shrugged again and lifted his milk shake to hide his face from her. His hair flopped forwards.

'We were talking once before about the last time you climbed out of school, and then the water tank exploded and so you never had time to answer. I know that the police were wrong when they tried to prove you'd been out of school on the night of the fire, but it would really help us all if you could tell me when it was.'

The boy muttered something into his drink.

'I'm sorry? What did you say?'

'Don't see why. It's got nothing to do with the fire.'

'No, I know it hasn't, Rob. But I'm as anxious as they are to find out everything about everyone involved. I'm sure you can understand that.'

''Course. But I'm not involved. I wasn't there. It wasn't anything to do with me, whatever the filth think.' He stared down at the remains of his milk shake.

His statement was longer than anything else Willow had yet heard from him, and it made enough sense to give her confidence.

'No, you're absolutely right. But I've got a problem with it.' She looked at him and as he glanced up at her for an instant she thought she saw understanding in his dark eyes.

'When we were talking before, you looked guilty. I don't think that you had anything to do with the fire, but I have to be sure. If you could tell me what made you feel ashamed when we were talking, I'd be in a better position to get everything cleared up. D'you see what I mean?'

His spots almost disappeared as his face reddened painfully. He scratched the patchy stubble on his chin.

'Yeah, I see all right.'

'Lots of us often feel guilty about things that are not our fault at all. For instance, your aunt told me that she feels guilty about what happened to your mother, and I suspect that you do, too. I think everyone does when someone they're close to dies, especially like that. If that's what it is, I wish you'd tell me.' Willow smiled at him. 'It might help you, too, to talk about it.'

A slight look of shock in his eyes was followed by a sulky glare. Whatever Rob was feeling was well under control and the sullen mask did not shift again. Willow thought that she could understand the frustration that the police must have felt when they interviewed him, and the difficulties the boy's teachers had with him; and probably his mother, too.

The chair shuddered as Rob let it clunk back on to all four legs. Something in his dully angry face gave Willow a clue.

'Was it the day she died that you climbed out of school?'

Tears appeared under Rob's eyelids and he pushed them away with the back of his sticky hand and then licked it.

'Did you go to see her?'

He shook his head. Willow could not see much of his face as he sat staring down at the half-empty glass he was gripping in his lap. His black fringe hung right down in front of his face.

'Can't you tell me about it, Rob?' she said with all the gentleness at her command.

He swung round in his chair to put the glass down on the table, leaned his elbows on it and, twisted though he was, buried his face in his hands. Willow waited.

'I thought she was just asleep.' His voice was muffled by his hands, but enough of it reached Willow to let her make out his words.

She got up from her chair and went to stand beside the hulking, weeping child. She did not try to stop him, perhaps remembering her own howls by the fridge on the day Tom was shot; she laid one hand on his shuddering back. When he had finished for the moment, she fetched a roll of kitchen paper and silently offered it to him.

He ripped off two sheets and blew his nose, then took two more sheets and mopped his eyes.

'Sorry,' he said, his voice even deeper than usual.

'Don't be sorry, Rob. What happened? Did you go home?'

'Yes,' he said, staring at the table. 'I needed my old squash racket for a match. It was in the attic at home. I had to get it.'

'But how did you get in? Your aunt said that the front door was bolted on the inside.'

He looked up for a second and Willow flinched at the misery in his dark eyes.

'It was. So I went round the back and got into the garden

over the wall. I always had a key to the back door as well as the front—Aunt Serena has, too—and I just let myself in.'

Willow thought that she was beginning to understand a little more, but there was still a lot of uncertainty. 'Did you see her?' she asked gently.

Rob shook his head, but he would not look at her, and something about his face made her think that he might be lying.

'Her curtains were shut. I thought she was asleep. I found the letter, but I didn't read it then and I didn't go in because I thought she was asleep. I didn't want to disturb her, see. I didn't read it then. I took it back to school and I didn't look at it till the next day.'

'What was the letter you found, Rob?' asked Willow very gently.

He sat still.

'I know it's probably the most private thing you have, but...'

He looked at her with a kind of miserable resignation that made her feel almost unbearably guilty for making him face his awful memories. At last he put his hand into the pocket of his tracksuit bottoms to take out a crumpled, grubby sheet of paper, and handed it to her.

Willow thanked him, unfolded the paper and silently read:

My darling, darling Rob,
   I am so sorry. I've been such a bad mother and made you so miserable. I can't help you at all. I wish I could. At least this way you'll be free to find a life for yourself that won't mean having to see me through any more of these awful times. I can't bear to go on hurting you like this. I'm sorry. I'm sorry. I'm sorry. I love you very much.

                                                        Mum.

Willow imagined some of the thoughts that would have gone through her mind if she had been in Rob's place. Intelligent as he undoubtedly was, he must have thought about the possibility that he could have saved Fiona. What could it be like to live with the thought that she might still be alive if he had only read the letter at the time or bothered to go into her room to see how she was? No wonder he had looked so guilty whenever questions made him think about that day.

'Thank you for showing it to me,' Willow said, handing it back to him. At least, she thought, since no one but she had ever doubted that Fiona had killed herself, no one else need see or even know about the letter. She could leave the boy that bit of privacy at least with a clear conscience.

'Can I go now?' he said, still staring at the table.

'Of course you can. You're not any kind of prisoner here, Rob. I'm sorry to have put you through so much,' said Willow. She had not time to say anything else before he was out of the door.

Having given him plenty of time to get into the sanctuary of Tom's study, she followed him upstairs to bathe and dress in cool, baggy Chinos and a thin grey-blue shirt. She looked at the John Buchan novel that had kept her company during some of her vigils at the hospital and shook her head.

With almost all her doubts about Rob banished at last, she hoped that she would be able to think constructively about the fire and her report on Fiona Fydgett's death—and whether the two were connected—while she waited for Tom to come round. Her hands felt better, too, and so she slid her notebook computer into its carrying case, slung that over her shoulder and set off for the hospital.

Out in the street the air was even stuffier than it had been during the previous few days, and she was glad that she had managed to leave the car under one of the few trees at the edge of the pavement. The steering wheel was hot even so, but at least her bandages protected her from the worst of that.

There was not much traffic and she reached the hospital ten minutes later. Since it was Sunday she parked in the main road. Locking the car behind her, she felt sticky in spite of her light clothes, and pulled her shirt away from her sweaty back.

The main foyer of the hospital was even more crowded than usual and very noisy. Willow made her way through hordes of patients, visitors with little children, and volunteer helpers selling flowers and cards and baskets of fruit from a fancily decorated stall opposite the entrance. She ignored them all and shook her head at a woman with a clipboard, who started forwards and looked as though she wanted to ask questions for some kind of market research. Through the crowds at last, Willow headed for the lifts and the tenth floor.

The Intensive Care Unit was still and wonderfully cool in comparison with the mayhem downstairs. As usual all the blinds were down across the windows and the light was dim. The nurses moved smoothly past the beds, checking monitors and drips, replacing dressings and talking with soothing efficiency to anyone who was awake and frightened. One of the women nurses saw Willow and smiled at once.

'It is difficult waiting, isn't it?' she said, talking quietly but without any suggestion of a whisper. 'But Mr Richardson is quite pleased with his condition. Come along. I'm just going to check his drip.'

Willow smiled back, not trusting herself to talk about Tom, and followed the nurse into his room. He looked just the same as he had done on the day of the shooting. His chest was pulled up and down by the ventilator, the drip still fed life-preserving fluids into his bloodstream, and the catheter collected the urine his kidneys produced. But nothing else moved. Willow tried to believe in the encouragement that the doctor had given her three days earlier.

'I brought this word processor to do some work,' she said when the nurse had finished attaching a new bag of fluid to the frame above the bed. 'Will it interfere with any of the monitors?'

The little nurse laughed so loudly that Willow looked at Tom to make sure he had not been disturbed.

'This isn't the flight deck of Concorde, you know,' said the nurse cheerfully.

'Good.'

The nurse put a chair ready beside the bed and rolled forward a table.

'It's a bit high for you to work at. Will you be all right? And will you have enough light?'

'You are kind. Yes, I'll be fine. I can use it on my knees.'

When the nurse had gone, Willow took the computer out of its case, switched it on, and found the relevant floppy disk from her handbag. She called up the first draft of her report for the minister and cut and edited what she had written as well as she could, but it was not gripping enough to keep her mind off Tom for long.

When she realised that she had retyped the same paragraph four times without actually changing anything material, she filed that document again and let her mind turn instead to the question of who could have killed Len Scoffer.

It was clear from Harness's appearance in Croydon that he, too, was still searching for convincing suspects. Either he had crossed the Fydgetts off his list or he had never wanted anything more from them than background information.

Tom's necessarily discreet accounts of some of his cases had gradually taught Willow that a great deal of police work in a murder investigation is like using a shotgun. If you fling enough pellets in the air you are almost bound to hit something. If you interview enough people, talk to enough possible witnesses, ask enough questions of enough people, you are likely to stumble on something useful in the end.

There was a slight movement somewhere in the room and she looked instantly at Tom. He seemed to be lying utterly still. Her raised hopes were making the waiting even harder than it had been before. She felt as though she would not be able to bear the suspense for much longer.

Gritting her teeth, aware that she had no choice, she wrenched her mind back to the investigation and ran through the things she still needed to know until she remembered Miss Andrea Salderton. Brian Gaskarth was obviously having trouble tracking her down, but Willow suddenly thought of a way to find out what her connection with the minister might be.

There was a telephone just outside the Intensive Care Unit.

It had no privacy, but on the other hand there was no one else in the shiny, clean-smelling lobby, and anyone using it would be able to see possible eavesdroppers long before they could get close enough to hear anything.

Willow dialled Jane Cleverholme's private number.

'Jane, is that you? It's Willow here.'

'How are you feeling?'

'So so. My hands are better and my brain's less fogged, although it's still pretty slow.'

Jane laughed. 'And?'

'And I've been thinking about your proposition. I really can't go poodlefaking in some pseudo-romance with the climber while Tom's still unconscious, but I am prepared to write a piece for you about what it felt like to be trapped in the fire and helped down by his expertise.'

'That's great. And I do understand. How is Tom?'

'The consultant says that the… This is off the record, Jane,' said Willow, suddenly afraid that her friend's interest might be professional.

'Oh, my wretched job! I know it's off the record. Don't be silly.'

'Good. Apparently the signs are encouraging, but I've been sitting with him all morning and I can't see any change. It's hell waiting.'

'I can imagine. Look, d'you want to come in and have lunch one day next week?'

'That would be nice,' said Willow, recognising Jane's affectionate intent. 'It depends on how Tom is. Could I ring you next week when I know more? Would that be all right?'

'Fine. Ring any time so long as it's soon. Oh, I can't do Wednesday.'

'It will be soon. Thank you. By the way, Jane?'

'I might have known it.' Jane's voice was heavy with resignation, but Willow thought that there might be a hint of amusement in it, too. 'What little titbit do you want now?'

It was Willow's turn to laugh. 'Okay, fair's fair. But you do it to me, too. I just wanted to know what the buzz is about

George Profett, you know, the Minister for Rights and Charters.'

'What d'you mean by "buzz"?'

'Come on, Jane. You know perfectly well. I know you're not on gossip any more, but journalists always know about cabinet ministers' private lives. What have you heard about him? Does he have a mistress? Is he gay? Does he gamble? What?'

'Sorry. I can't help you.'

Willow was about to use her possible co-operation with the paper's romantic feature as a persuader when Jane added casually, 'In fact we've graded him SCDD for the moment at least.'

'That's an acronym I've never come across.' Willow was interested. 'What does it mean?'

'Squeaky clean; deadly dull,' Jane said, laughing again. 'It was the most dreary outcome imaginable. Some of us were so unable to believe that of any politician that we wanted to do some really deep digging, but the editor wouldn't authorise it. We couldn't decide whether he was being hardheaded or sentimental, or,' Jane laughed, 'best of all, whether he himself has something to hide in connection with Profett.'

'You journalists are a bunch of paranoid conspiracy theorists, aren't you?'

'We have to be. Reluctantly, though, in this case we had no option but to drop the whole thing for the time being. I've decided since that the killer, as far the editor was concerned, was probably the fact that even Profett's most disaffected colleagues couldn't think of anything bitchy to say about him, and so he really may be unassailable.'

'Oh, is that where you usually get dirt from? I'd never—'

'No, no, of course not,' said Jane in a tone that sounded as if she really meant: where on earth did you think we got it?

'Anyone else I can help you with before I get going on cooking my Sunday lunch?'

'Actually, since you offer, I'm also trying to find out a bit of background on Andrea Salderton.'

'Who's she?'

'Haven't you heard of her?' Willow let herself sound surprised.

There was silence. Jane must have been running all the people she had ever written about through her computer-like memory.

'Can't say I have. Give me a clue.'

Willow knew that she had painted herself into a corner. She could hardly tell the truth, that she knew nothing whatever about the woman except for the money she received every month from the reputedly SCDD minister, and yet if Willow gave Jane nothing, she would probably make the connection herself and might cause trouble.

'Just a hot new writer from the States,' Willow said eventually. 'Someone was talking about her the other day in such glowing terms that I thought I ought to have heard of her and didn't want to expose my ignorance. I'm glad it wasn't just me who didn't recognise her name.'

'She can't be that hot or we'd have had something here, and it would have come to me. The Lit. Ed. knows I like to keep abreast of publishing tittle-tattle. Well, I'd better get the beef in the oven or the delectable new man in my life will discover what an undomesticated slut I am and bugger off home to perfect mummy.'

'If he's like that, he's not your type.'

'He's shown no signs of it yet,' said the journalist, sounding much less tough than usual, 'but they nearly always turn out to be that sort in the end, however. promising the packaging.'

'Not a good picker, eh?'

'Rotten so far. I'm just keeping my fingers crossed this time.' Jane laughed again, and Willow wished her luck.

She rang off and went back to Tom's bedside and leaned over him, trying to see any signs of awakening. Failing again, she sat back in her chair, switched her computer back on and tried dismally to do some more work. Remembering the way John Blackled had talked of Rob Fydgett as fitting the likely profile of a criminal, Willow got as far as typing a few ideas about the characteristics she thought might be likely of an arsonist and possibly deliberate murderer.

Ten minutes later the words she had typed disappeared in front of her eyes and bright orange fish glided peacefully across the black screen. She tapped a key and her text reappeared. Then, like the fish swimming across the screen, a sluggish thought appeared in her mind and she cursed herself for having wasted so much time on ever less likely suspects.

If the arsonist had not been a member of Kate's staff, and Willow had reluctantly come to the conclusion that not even the mischief-making Jason was a reasonable suspect, he or she must have broken into the tax office to damage the wiring and set the timer—or the photosensitive tripswitch—that had triggered the fire. No taxpayer was allowed further into the building than the public parts on the ground floor.

The fire could have been started simply by pouring petrol through a broken window, but it had not been. It had been started on an upper floor of the building, in a specific office, and it had been started electrically. Whatever that vague description implied, it must have involved personal contact with the wires. Therefore, the person who did it must have got into the building without setting off any burglar alarms or leaving a trace of his entry that would have made the security people call the police.

Willow could not imagine why she had fiddled about trying to uncover evidence of corruption in the office, and searched Len Scoffer's home and worried about Kate and Cara and Mrs Scoffer and the minister, when there was such an obvious line of enquiry. She looked at Tom's unconscious face and blew him a kiss as she remembered, all too late, one of his precepts: 'Never ignore the obvious. In most criminal investigations, the "obvious" means motive and suspect are the right ones. Check those out first and then let your imagination fly free. Otherwise you'll only waste time.'

'As I have been doing,' she said to her unconscious husband. 'Time and terror. In this case the most obvious suspect is someone with experience of breaking and entering. All I need to know is which of the people who had a reason to hate—or fear—Len has a criminal record for burglary, and Bob's your uncle.'

Since it was Sunday, there seemed little hope of getting hold of Brian Gaskarth at his office, but even so she went back to the telephone outside the ward so that she could at least leave a message on his answering machine.

To her delighted surprise, he answered the telephone himself and made no difficulty about checking her list of names against the police computer. He told her that he would try his contacts there and then, but that if none of them was on duty he might not be able to get back to her until Monday.

SEVENTEEN

THAT NIGHT Willow was so tired when she went to bed that she fell asleep within a few minutes of turning off her bedside lamp. One moment she was thinking about Tom, and the next she was unconscious, only to wake, sweating and terrified, from a nightmare in which she was trying to reach him through a burning, noisy, stinking barrier of flame.

Although she could not get through it, she could see everything that was happening to him on the other side of the fire, and it was terrible to watch. Eventually, sobbing in her sleep, she came near enough to waking for her brain to tell her that she could pull herself right out of the dream if she would only make the effort. She opened her eyes.

It took several minutes before she could free herself of the effects of the dream and even then the smell of the imaginary fire seemed to stay in her nostrils. She pushed herself up the bed, propping her back against the headboard and switched on the light so that she could pull a paper handkerchief from the box on her table. When she had wiped the sweat off her face and poured herself a glass of cold lemonade, she began to feel slightly better. Having drunk it, she turned off the light and let herself slide down the bed again until she was lying flat.

She wondered what was happening in Tom's brain and whether he might have been suffering foul and terrifying nightmares since the shooting. That was something she had never thought of until then, and she longed to be able to save him from being trapped in terror. Her hand reached towards the telephone before she even realised that she wanted to ask the nurses caring for him whether he was dreaming. Feeling foolish, she put her hand back under the sheet and tried to go back to sleep.

It was then, as she was trying to make herself relax, that she heard the quiet footsteps in the passage outside her bed-

room door. At first she laughed at her fear, assuming that the
footsteps were Serena's as she went to the bathroom, creeping
as quietly as possible in order to let the others sleep. But there
was no sound of the bathroom door opening or any running
water.

Straining to hear what was happening, Willow thought that
she could hear someone breathing fast and nervously just outside her bedroom door. All her own and Stephen Harness's
doubts about Rob rushed back into her mind. She remembered
his unexpected dexterity, his anger and unhappiness, the questions she had asked him, and the fire.

The smell of it seemed all around her again and she silently
slammed her hand across her mouth to stop herself making a
noise. She thought that she heard the handle of her door begin
to creak. Peering through the thick darkness, she saw a faint
greyness around the door and knew that someone had opened
it. She bit into her bandaged fingers and felt saliva soaking
through the gauze. Her mind seemed suddenly clear and her
imagination was working furiously.

She felt as though a whole troop of facts was being re-
viewed in front of her. Rob had been to his mother's house
on the day she died. He climbed like a cat. He hated his mother's lovers. No one had seen the suicide letter except for him.
He had shown Willow a letter, but it could easily have been
a forgery for all she knew. The handwriting was like that on
the letters she had seen in the tax file, but Rob might well
have been able to copy it.

Staring at the darkness ahead of her, with her hand still
jammed against her mouth, Willow thought of the tall, gangly,
furiously unhappy boy discovering that his mother was in the
house when he had got in through the back door. Had he gone
into her room, perhaps, and overcome with jealousy or resentment or some other emotion held a pillow over her face
until she suffocated? Had he subsequently tried to exorcise his
guilt by burning down the building from which most of her
torment had come? And had Willow been asking too many
questions and getting too close to the truth of what had actually happened?

The grey line around her door widened and she saw Rob silhouetted in the gap, apparently listening. She flexed her free hand, trying to decide whether it would be strong enough to fend him off. He took a step forward into the darkness and she could no longer see him.

There had been a post-mortem on his mother's body, but it had been a formality, Serena had told her, once they found a high concentration of tricyclic anti-depressants and whisky in her blood. Perhaps they had not bothered to look for fluff or feathers in her larynx.

'Willow?' The question was so quiet that she doubted that she had really heard it. She lay silent and still, and realised that she had been holding her breath. Letting it out as quietly as possible against her hand, she knew that she was sweating all over and was terrified that he knew she was awake. A surreptitious pillow over her face was something she could deal with; a more violent attack—perhaps from further off— would be harder. Vile though it was to wait, she knew that she had to make him come close before she would be able to fight back.

He took another step towards her. She could hear his breathing, ragged now and very quick. It sounded frightened, or excited.

Why did I let them come into my house? she asked herself in silence. I must have been mad. Tom's getting better now. I want to survive. Why did I take such a stupid, hideous risk? Oh, God! I want to survive. What should I do? If I make the first move that might spark off something I can't control. I must wait. I must.

Rob came steadily closer to the bed. He was moving far more neatly than he ever did during the daylight. She could not see him in the darkness, just the faint grey patch where the less well-curtained passage window let in a little light. But she could hear his breathing and she could smell him. He was sweating, but it was not only the acrid smell of young male sweat that hung about him. There seemed to be smoke as well.

Perhaps that's a hangover from the dream, she told herself, trying to keep up her collapsing courage.

The bed creaked and the mattress was pressed down as he lowered himself on to the foot of the bed. She nearly screamed.

'Willow?' The almost silent whisper came again.

She did not move, determined not to give him any excuse to attack her.

Tom, she thought, I'm sorry. I don't want to die. I won't. I must be strong enough to fight. He may weigh nearly the same as I do, but I've got the advantage of surprise. What if he's got a knife or a hammer? What the hell is he going to do?

There was another movement at the end of the bed as he stood up. Willow longed to be able to see. She heard his foot-steps again and braced herself. Astonishingly he seemed to be moving away from the bed.

His silhouette appeared against the grey patch by the door and then disappeared. The door closed. She took her hand away from her teeth, noticing that it hurt, and waited, listening.

Eventually there was another click, further down the pas-sage, and she thought that he must be back in his own bed-room. Reaching for the light, she knocked over her Thermos flask. And then she heard footsteps again. They came back along the passage towards her room, and then sounded on the stairs. She listened to him reaching the ground floor. Then there was a pause when she could not hear anything at all.

It felt like at least five minutes before she heard footsteps in the hall and then on the pavement outside her bedroom window. When they had dwindled to silence, she turned on her bedside light at once and saw that the table and all her books were covered with lemonade from the Thermos. Fling-ing a batch of tissues into the spreading pool of yellow liquid, she looked down her bed and all round it in case Rob had left anything there.

There was nothing to see, and yet there was still the elusive smell of burning that had clung about her ever since her dream. Then she thought she understood. Rob must have set the house on fire and come to check that she was deeply enough asleep to die of suffocation before she woke and called for help.

Devoutly thankful that she had not betrayed her wakefulness, she thought suddenly of Serena and ran into her bathroom to wet a towel. Holding it around her face, she went quietly out into the passage, turning on the light outside her bedroom. There was no sign of any smoke, let alone any flames. Pulling the towel away from her nose, she sniffed again, and then saw that Tom's study door was open.

Running silently in her bare feet along the passage, she looked in. It was empty and there was no fire. Determined to find out what Rob had done so that she could stop it, she turned on the light. There was nothing in the room that seemed at all out of order, and she could not smell anything either.

Beginning to think that she must have imagined everything except Rob's flight, Willow went downstairs. There, the smell of burning was slightly stronger, and she went first to the kitchen. It looked in its usual pristine state. There was nothing poking out from under the lids of the Aga's hotplates and the oven doors were firmly closed. She checked them even so, and found them all empty. The microwave oven was switched off and, as usual, Mrs Rusham had removed its plug from the socket, as she had done with the coffee grinder, the blender, the toaster and all the other bits and pieces of machinery that were ranged at the back of one of the long worktops.

Following the faint smell that held such horror for her, Willow went on into the drawing room. There, too, everything looked as it should. But the burning smell was stronger.

She ran her hands over all the electric switch plates, all the lamps and even the telephone, but none of them were hot—or even warm. Then she turned on the lights and saw, at last, where the smell had been coming from. There was paper smouldering in the fireplace. She leaned against the wall, panting. She felt a fool, and she let the damp towel drop on the parquet floor.

It must have been Rob, she thought, and went to kneel before the fireplace, poking at the mass of blackened paper with the tongs. Most of it disintegrated into ash, but there were some sheets that were only blackened around the edges. Manoeuvring the tongs with difficulty, she pulled the papers on to the tiled hearth and spread them out. Each one was covered with the same big, sloppy writing, which she had never seen before.

Testing the paper with her unbandaged wrist to check that it was cold enough, she picked up one piece and read.

'I'm sorry. I'm sorry. Mum, I'm sorry. I'm sorry. I'm sorry. I'm sorry.'

Willow castigated herself bitterly for the fear that had kept her pinned to the mattress when Rob had come. Probably all he had wanted was comfort from the only person whom she had told about his mother's letter.

'Oh, God! What ought I to do now?' she said aloud, thinking of all the things that Rob might be doing to himself. 'When am I going to learn that people's emotions aren't dangerous? It's Tom all over again: all that need, which frightens the life out of me and makes me shut myself off.'

Checking the front door a few minutes later, she found it was closed. Rob had taken her keys from the pewter plate. She was relieved to realise that at least he intended to come back and she could not decide whether it would be hysterical of her to wake his aunt or irresponsible not to.

Eventually she did go to Serena's room and explained simply that she had woken to hear the front door closing and found that Rob had gone, taking the keys.

'But why?' said Serena, pushing the tousled hair out of her eyes. She turned to look at the small clock by the bed. 'It's two-thirty in the morning.'

'Perhaps he just couldn't sleep and went for a run or something. It's possible.'

'But you don't think that, do you? You think he's gone off to set fire to some building.' Serena sounded almost hysterical.

Knowing how irrational anyone could be when suddenly woken out of a nightmare, Willow only shrugged and shook her head.

'Well, I don't know what we can do now,' said Serena, rubbing her eyes with both hands. 'I'm hardly going to ring the bloody police and send them after him, and there's no point our trying to find out where he's gone.'

'I don't know what we can do either,' said Willow, sounding as tired and defeated as she felt, 'but I thought you ought to know he's up and about. Perhaps he's gone back to your sister's house for something. Look, I'll let you go back to sleep, but if there's anything you want me to do, tell me.'

Serena frowned. 'I don't understand what's been going on. If he wanted to go to Fiona's for something he could have told me. Do you know something I don't?'

'No,' said Willow, lying out of a determination not to break her promise to Rob. Then she thought of another possible meaning of the half-burned note, and added, 'Except that he was burning this in the fireplace downstairs.'

Serena read it and then looked up at Willow, her face quite white between the straggling dark hair. Before either of them could say anything, she flung back the duvet.

'I'm going round there.'

'Shall I ring Harness?'

'Certainly not. I can cope with Rob. If he…I don't believe it for a minute, but if there is anything… Well, he needs help.'

'Shall I come with you?'

'No, I'll manage. Thank you for waking me.'

Serena started to pull up her nightdress and Willow backed away. Later, lying in bed with the light on, she felt horribly torn between wanting to believe that Serena could deal with her nephew and the thought that she was being ludicrously irresponsible in not warning Stephen Harness of what might happen.

Eventually exhaustion took the decision out of her hands, sending her to sleep with the light still blazing.

She did not wake until nine the following morning, when she opened her eyes to see Mrs Rusham standing at the foot of the bed with a tray in her hands.

'You were very tired,' she said with a faint smile. 'I thought you might like to have breakfast in bed.'

Willow ran her tongue around the inside of her mouth, which felt stale and dry. 'Thank you,' she said, and then remembered the events of the night. 'Oh, have you seen Rob this morning?'

'Yes.' Mrs Rusham looked puzzled. 'I gave him his breakfast at seven-thirty as usual and he left in time for school, just before Ms Fydgett went off to chambers.'

'How did he seem?'

'Tired and not very happy.'

'Poor boy,' said Willow, deeply thankful that Serena had managed to bring him back.

'Yes, indeed,' said Mrs Rusham, laying the tray across Willow's knees. 'Call me if there's anything else you need, won't you?'

'Yes, thank you. Oh, did Ms Fydgett leave any message for me?'

'No. She just said that she would see you at dinner.'

When the housekeeper had gone, Willow quickly drank the orange juice she had provided and then picked up the cup of frothing cappuccino. Lying back against the pillows, she tried to decide what she ought to do next. Before anything occurred to her, the telephone rang.

'Hello?'

'Willow, is that you?'

'Yes. Jack,' she said as she recognised the superintendent's voice. 'What's happened?'

'I'm not sure quite how to put this,' he began and then waited.

'Directly. Whatever it is.' The only thing that would really have mattered was bad news of Tom, and Willow knew that the hospital would have told her anything like that long before they bothered with his colleagues.

'The CPS are going to drop the case against the young men we arrested for the shooting.'

'What? They can't. I thought you said it was cut and dried.'

There was a silence before Willow let the cold anger take over her remaining doubts.

'You've cocked it up, haven't you? What didn't you tell me? You had the weapon. You had the fingerprints. What?'

'The CPS felt that there wasn't a realistic prospect of conviction because a jury might believe the defence.'

'Which was?'

'That they had found the gun abandoned on a skip outside the estate where they all live,' he said reluctantly.

'Why didn't you believe it?' asked Willow.

'Because it's a ludicrous story on the face of it.' There was a pause, which she did not even try to help him fill. 'We weren't to know at the time that there's a witness who saw them do it—or says she did.'

'Oh, shit!'

'My words exactly.'

'Who found the witness? Surely it's not the CPS's job to truffle about for that sort of thing.'

'No. She happened to have reported what she'd seen to another station. It took a while to filter through to us, but when it did…we had to pass it on to the CPS. You must see that, Will. We are doing the scrotes for possession of an unlicensed weapon and for class A drugs. Don't worry about it, they will go down; but it'll be for a lot less than they would have got.'

'You don't have to sound so pleading,' she said impatiently. 'I told you once that revenge isn't one of my things… Still less is the desire to have anyone punished for a crime they didn't commit.'

'We won't stop looking for proof, you know. I'm pretty sure they are the ones, although I don't know how they squared the witness. But we'll get them in the end.'

'I'm sure you will. Thanks for letting me know.'

She replaced the receiver and the telephone rang again almost at once.

'Yes?' she said, sounding breathless.

'I hope I haven't rung at an inconvenient moment. It's Brian Gaskarth here. Those names you wanted checked against the police computer…'

'Yes,' said Willow. 'That's remarkably quick. I'm most impressed.'

'The only one with a record is Daniel Hallten. Breaking and

entering in the late seventies. He did a couple of years in Wandsworth.'

'Did he though? I don't suppose you've any information on the offences of the men who shared his cell?'

'Sorry. No can do.'

'Never mind,' said Willow, who had been optimistically hoping to hear that the electrician had been banged up with an arsonist. 'You've been very helpful. Send me a bill.'

'Sure. And don't hesitate to call on me again.'

'I won't. Goodbye, Mr Gaskarth.'

Willow slowly ate her croissant and decided what to do next. With vivid memories of Tom's past distress when she had risked confronting violent suspects, she felt that she had to involve Harness before she did anything else. When she had wiped the buttery crumbs off her fingers she telephoned his office, only to be told that he was very busy.

'Can I take a message?' said the young officer who had answered her call.

'No, I don't think so,' Willow said, reluctant to make a fool of herself—and therefore Tom—in front of someone who might not feel constrained from publicising it by loyalty to him. 'Except just that I rang and I'll try him again later.'

'Very well. Has he got your number?'

'Yes.'

Putting aside the breakfast tray, she got out of bed and bathed, trying out first one plan and then another. Eventually, she decided that she would have to find out at least whether Hallten had an alibi for the night of the fire. She rationalised away Tom's possible objections by telling herself that, as a self-employed electrician with large tax debts, Hallten was bound to be away from home on a job during working hours. Calling on his wife, who the tax files had told her had no paid work, to ask where he was on the evening before the fire would hardly constitute wild recklessness.

EIGHTEEN

BUILT OF THE SAME RED brick as Len Scoffer's house, the Halltens' also had a bay window on the ground floor and two flat ones above it. A small garden, about four foot deep at the most, separated the house from the pavement. It was a lot less tidy than the Scoffers'.

In fact the whole house was less well maintained, but to Willow's eyes at least it was more attractive. The windows were the original softwood sashes and, although the white paint was old and peeling, there were no signs of rot. The door was the original, too, or one very like it, made of cream-painted wood with two narrow, engraved glass panels set into it.

Willow pressed the bell. No one came to the door. Stepping back so that she could peer in through the net-curtained windows, she could not make out any signs of life. She tried the bell again.

'All right, all right. I'm coming,' called a plaintive female voice.

There was a pause during which Willow noticed a fish-eye lens in the wooden part of the door, then she heard the sound of keys being turned and bolts being undone. The door opened to reveal a pretty young woman with untidy brown hair and a harassed expression. She was wearing a loose flowered cotton dress, and she carried a naked baby on her hip.

'I am sorry,' said Willow at once. 'I thought that the bell hadn't worked the first time. Am I disturbing you horribly?'

'I was just changing her. Can I help? Are you looking for Dan? He's out on a job.'

'Don't let me hold you up,' said Willow, looking anxiously at the baby's powdered bottom. She remembered the script she had invented on her journey south of the river.

'I had hoped to see your husband, but perhaps I could have

a word with you?' She took her driving licence out of her handbag and held it up. 'My name's Willow King. I am a civil servant.'

'I'm not sure,' said the woman, not moving. 'Oh, no! Tammy! Couldn't you wait?'

Willow looked at her and saw a damp stain spreading between the baby's plump legs over the pink and blue flowered skirt. The legs waggled suddenly as though in pleasure and the baby smiled at Willow, revealing a bright friendliness. She could not help responding to it with a smile of her own.

'Look, you'd better come in,' said Mrs Hallten, perhaps reassured by Willow's obvious approval of the baby. 'I must put a nappy on her.'

'Yes, of course. I'll shut the door.'

'Go on into the lounge, will you?' said Mrs Hallten over her daughter's head. 'I won't be long.'

Silently blessing the child for her excellent intervention, Willow went into the room and sat down on a tightly upholstered bucket chair in the bay window, from where she could watch the street. No one approached the front door and the only figures she could see were a languorous postman, slowly stuffing letters through a few front doors and an angry young woman in jeans and high heels dragging two crying children along the pavement, shouting at them.

Mrs Hallten came back ten minutes later. The baby in her arms had not only had a nappy put on but also a pretty red and white gingham dress with bright blue smocking across the front. Mrs Hallten had also changed her own dress.

'I hope you didn't put clothes on her just because I'm here,' said Willow, smiling at them both. 'It's so hot.'

'I know. Isn't it awful? I can't wait for it to rain again.' Mrs Hallten pushed her hair away from her damp face. 'What did you say you wanted to know? I'm so tired at the moment that I keep forgetting everything.'

'It's all right. You haven't forgotten anything today. Tammy intervened before we got that far.'

'That's all right then. You said your name was King, I think.'

'Yes. Willow King. I'm a civil servant, working at the moment for the Minister for Rights and Charters.'

'Oh yes?' Mrs Hallten was clearly puzzled but too tired to ask questions. Willow felt such sympathy for her that she decided to be a little franker than she had planned.

'He's been worried about the way that a man called Leonard Scoffer…'

Before Willow could get any further, Mrs Hallten's face changed. She dumped her baby in the netted playpen in the centre of the room and went to stand in front of Willow. 'Who are you and what do you want?' she said, sounding quite different from the gentle, worried mother of a few moments earlier. The baby heard the difference too and started to howl. Mrs Hallten went over to pat her head, but it did not stop the cries. 'I don't like that man's name mentioned in my house. He is…oh, I don't want to go into it all again now.'

'As I was saying,' said Willow, noticing that the other woman had used the present tense, 'the minister is worried about the way Scoffer has been conducting some of his investigations. Your husband's file is one of the ones I have been reviewing and I wanted to talk to you to find out whether my instincts are correct.'

'Oh, yes? And what are your instincts, then?'

'That Scoffer crossed the line between reasonable and unreasonable behaviour in the way he dealt with taxpayers. But I need some facts to support my instinct. I hoped that you could give me examples of unreasonable behaviour.'

'Ah.' Mrs Hallten's tight shoulders relaxed and she started to breathe again. 'Look, what about a cup of tea? We could go into the kitchen and talk. Tammy'll be all right in her pen for a bit, and it'll be easier not to worry about sounding angry. She'll calm down in a minute.'

'Fine,' said Willow, not wanting to drink anything hot but more than willing to go anywhere to hear the information she needed. 'Look, I can't call you Mrs Hallten. My name's Willow. What's yours?'

'Sally. It's this way.'

She led her guest down a passage exactly like the Scoffers' towards the kitchen. As they passed the cupboard under the stairs, Willow grimaced.

'Is tea all right for you, or would you like something cold?'

'Oh, I would. Thank you.'

'There's lime or Tammy's Ribena, oh, and some Diet Coke, I think.'

'Lime would be great.'

When they were sitting either side of the pine table, Willow drank some of the iced cordial she had been given. 'Well?' she said.

'I don't know where to begin. Scoffer's done his best to ruin our lives.'

'Just tell me anything that comes into your head then. Start with how your husband is at the moment.' Willow took her black notebook out of the bag and unscrewed her pen.

Tears welled up in Sally Hallten's warm brown eyes and she shook her curly head. 'It's awful. He's upset and broke and bad tempered all the time now. It's even worse than when he started giving up smoking to save money. And Tammy cries all night so he can't sleep, and he doesn't know how we're going to pay the rent and we'll never get another mortgage. So it'll be bed and breakfasts as soon as we get evicted. And now he's so worried that even when she's not crying he can't sleep. He was tossing and turning all night and when I tried to help, he just yelled at me. Our own house went, you see, months ago.'

'This one doesn't seem too bad,' said Willow, looking round the kitchen, which was infinitely more up to date than the Scoffers' had been.

'I know. It's okay and we're really lucky to have it. But we won't have it for long if we can't keep up with the rent. I just don't know what we're going to do.' She started to cry, pulling a ragged handkerchief from the pocket of her dress.

'You had an Individual Voluntary Agreement with your creditors, didn't you?' said Willow when Sally Hallten had begun to get herself under control.

'That's right.' She sniffed and smiled bravely. 'And we thought it would be all right then. If everything had gone on as it was, we'd have been able to pay the four hundred a month, just. It would've been a squeeze, but we'd have done it.' She sobbed loudly and then got up to turn her back on Willow while she blew her nose.

'But now we've had another huge tax bill, and we've discovered that the old tax doesn't seem to be part of the agreement. Scoffer's told us that they've got a charge against our future profits, which I didn't know and I don't think Dan could have understood at the time.'

There was another pause, during which she took out the handkerchief again, rejected it and found a roll of lavatory paper, from which she tore off sheets to blot her tears. There was a surprising dignity about her, in spite of her misery.

'It all seems obvious now. But you see everything was agreed at thirty-five pence in the pound, so we thought the tax would be too. When we got the next big tax bill—assessment they call it—we thought that would be part of the agreement, too. It wasn't till later that we realised none of it was. And then the van broke down. That cost a fortune to mend, though less of course. Much less.' She mopped her eyes again. 'And then we got the real horror.'

'What was that?' asked Willow as the other woman relapsed into silence.

Sally coughed to clear her throat and blew her nose, before stuffing the paper handkerchief into the pocket of her dress. 'Danny got this huge job, which was going to salvage everything. We worked out the estimate really carefully together. Everything seemed to be all right. He was talking to me again about work and money, and I typed up the estimate for him after I'd checked his sums and he'd checked mine and we were happy again. And the profit was going to clear a lot of the new tax bill and give us a bit of breathing space.'

'It sounds perfect.'

Sally's eyes filled again and she shook her head. 'He got some of the money up front. He always does, you know, for materials and things. But it wasn't very much this time; not nearly enough to pay for all the materials he needed. He bought the stuff as he needed it and did the work. It half killed him there was such a lot, but it was going really well. He fitted in with the other subcontractors, even when it meant working far longer than usual, even at night. Tammy and I hardly saw him. And then the developer went bust, owing us a fortune. We're not going to get anything, not even thirty-five pence in the pound like our creditors get. But we've still got to pay all the tax we owe. It's so unfair, it's just broken his spirit.'

'Oh dear.'

'I sometimes think if it had happened before he could have coped, but once he'd relaxed and got hopeful again after the IVA, it was just too much.'

'What happened?' asked Willow, not feeling as triumphant as she might have done. It was pretty clear to her that Hallten must be the man she had been looking for, but all she could feel was pity for them both—and for the child howling in its playpen in the front room.

'We wrote to the insolvency people, suggesting a lower repayment over a longer time so that we could try to pay the extra tax bill, but they wouldn't accept it. And we're already four months behind. And now there's yet another lot of tax to pay.' She looked at Willow in horror. 'Scoffer's said that they'll bankrupt us, and we'll lose everything.'

Willow drank some more of the lime cordial, bumping her nose on a piece of ice. 'But that's not so bad, is it? All the debts will be wiped out and you can start again. Your husband will be able to go on working. He just can't be a director, but I don't suppose you're a limited company, are you, so that's hardly an issue?'

'You don't understand.' Sally blew her nose loudly and took the lump of paper tissue to the kitchen bin. With her back to Willow, she added: 'It's not just the shame, although he feels that dreadfully. It's…he was a bit of a fool when he was young, you see, but he went straight ever after, and we got married and got the house and had Tammy, and now… And then there's the lack of credit. If he's bankrupted he'll never get it again, so he'll always have to have far more money up front, and that means he just won't get the work. There's not enough around at the moment anyway for everyone who's qualified. And no one will choose him in favour of people who…who can get credit. And no one will ever employ him because of his record.'

'I can see it's the most awful worry for you.'

Sally looked round, her flooded eyes swollen and her lips trembling. 'What's frightening us both so much, only he won't even talk about it, is that he won't be able to stop himself going back to thieving again. Oh, I shouldn't ever have said that. You'll forget it, won't you?' She started to cry again and then burst out: 'My nan always said, "once a tealeaf, always a tealeaf". It's being able to talk to someone that's making me like this.' She tried to wipe her eyes but they kept filling with tears. 'I haven't said a word to anyone except Tammy and I've been going mad with it all.'

Willow watched her struggle to stop crying. Then they both heard the sound of heavy feet in the street walking towards the front door.

'That's Dan,' said his wife, looking shocked. 'Look, I don't want him upset all over again, before he understands that you're on our side against Scoffer. Will you wait in here while I explain to him? Please?'

Willow had no chance to say anything before Sally left the kitchen, closing the door behind her. Sitting at the kitchen table, Willow could hear whispering, placatory on Sally's part, aggressively questioning on her husband's, and then the kitchen door opened with a crash. Willow turned to face the newcomer just as his hands reached for her.

She dodged but merely hit the wall as his tattooed hands closed about her neck. Opening her mouth, she tried to talk and felt her throat squeezing against his hands. Over his shoulder, she could see Sally looking desperate as she pulled at his arms and yelled out protests.

'Leave me alone,' he shouted as his fingers squeezed tighter and tighter around Willow's neck. 'Why can't you bastards leave me alone? I've done my best. I can't take it any more. Damn you, damn you to hell.'

'Stop!' Willow gasped, reaching for his eyes. The bandages around her hands made it impossible for her to do him any damage that might make him stop throttling her. She felt her head swim. Panic overwhelmed her. Dimly she heard Sally's voice.

'Dan, don't. Please, Dan. For God's sake. She's here to help. Dan. Dan.'

The unseen baby's cries rose to a single, sustained shriek. Willow felt her head banging against the wall as Hallten pulled her towards him and flung her back again, all the time squeezing her throat, choking her.

'Stop him,' Willow tried to say, but no sound came out of her mouth. In desperation she forced her burned hands up between his arms and tried to push them apart, but he was far too strong for her.

Sally loomed out of the mist that was all Willow could see, holding something large and brown between her hands. She brought it down heavily on her husband's right arm. All of them could hear the bone snap. Dan screamed as his wife gasped and dropped the heavy pottery bread crock. It smashed on the floor.

Letting Willow's throat go, Dan Hallten cradled his broken arm with his other hand, muttering, 'You stupid, stupid bitch.'

Willow, backing away from him with both her hands over her throat, said hoarsely, 'Not stupid. Listen to her. Tell him.'

Hardly any sound came out of her mouth. Sally pushed a chair towards her, saying, 'Sit down. I'm sorry. I'm so sorry. Are you all right?'

'It's not her you ought to bloody worry about. It's me,' said Dan Hallten as Willow nodded, painfully swallowing saliva. Standing between them, Sally turned to face her husband and put her hands on his good arm.

'You've broken my fucking arm.'

'Dan, sit down and don't make it worse than it already is.'

'Stop talking and get me a bloody doctor.'

'I will, but you must listen first.'

'Later. It's agony. Get me a doctor, damn you.'

Sally turned to look at Willow, who was still standing on the other side of the table.

'There's not a lot he can do to me with a broken right arm,' Willow said, relieved to find that she could speak almost normally again. The damage to her throat must have been much more superficial than it seemed. 'You go on and telephone.'

When Sally had left them for the telephone in the hall, leaving the kitchen door wide open, Willow stared at Daniel Hallten. He was sitting hunched over his damaged arm, his face contorted with pain. Willow's sympathy for him had died at the moment when he seized her throat. She looked down at her bandaged hands and then back at him, thinking of the horror of the fire.

Fury raced through her, removing the last traces of fear. She hated him, and despised him too. She picked up the abandoned glass of lime and drank it down. When she tried to speak again, she found that she could use her voice almost normally.

'What would you do to the wires in an office where you wanted to start a fire?' she asked quietly.

'I don't know what you mean.' He spoke sullenly and did not look at her, but the sagging of his shoulders and the defeat in his voice confirmed all her suspicions.

'Really? We can play it like that, but it seems a bit silly now, doesn't it? I can have you charged with assault and when I explain why I'm here, the police are going to start asking all kinds of questions about the fire in the Vauxhall Bridge Road. D'you really think they're not going to make the connection?'

There was a long pause. Then he raised his head. He looked terrible, but Willow had no pity left in her.

'Did you tell her? Sally.'

'What, that you killed Scoffer? No. She didn't even know he was dead. You are a fool. How did you think it would help your case to kill me? Scoffer's death could conceivably be manslaughter. Killing me would have been murder.'

'I didn't mean to kill him. Christ! This hurts. I hadn't a clue anyone would be there. I just wanted to get rid of the files to give myself a bit of time. I thought if I had a breathing space even, I could have got straight and paid it all. But now...'

'The doctor can't come,' said Sally, returning. 'But he says they'll set it for you in casualty at the hospital, only I can't drive the van, and...' She looked from one to the other and then said breathlessly, 'What's happened?'

Dan Hallten looked at Willow with a pleading expression that seemed surprising in a man who had recently been trying to throttle her.

Willow looked from him to his wife. 'Will you both wait here?' she said. 'I'll ring and make some arrangements.'

'I must get Tammy.' Sally ran out.

'Don't tell her,' Dan Hallten said to Willow as soon as they heard Sally crooning to the child. 'Please don't tell her.'

'It's up to you, but she'll have to know soon enough. It would be better coming from you. You can explain how it happened. The police won't make her feel sorry for you. You might. She seems to love you.'

Willow waited until Sally returned with the panic-stricken,

screaming baby pressed against her shoulder. 'I won't be long,' she said and went to the telephone, shutting the door between her and the sad little family. She did not think that Dan Hallten would try to escape out of the back door, and even if he did he could not get far with a broken arm.

'Chief Inspector Harness,' she said when her call was answered. 'It's Mrs Worth speaking, and it's extremely urgent.'

'Just a minute please.'

'How urgent?' said Harness's voice a moment later.

'Exceedingly,' said Willow drily. She told him why and explained who Daniel Hallten was.

'Yes, I know who he is.' Harness sounded furious. 'But what the hell are you doing there?'

'I'll explain all that later. But he's here and he has a broken arm and you ought to come and get him.'

'I'm on my way. Get out of there and wait outside—somewhere where there are other people.'

'I told you, he's got a broken arm. There's not a lot he can do to me now,' said Willow, but Harness had dropped his telephone. Another voice told Willow that he had left and she replaced the receiver.

She looked into the kitchen and saw that Sally Hallten was cradling her husband's head against her breast while Tammy knelt at her feet, clinging to her leg. Willow went out of the house to sit on the edge of the low wall that edged the Halltens' front garden. There was a large hawthorn in the next door garden, and it threw enough shade to make the midday heat bearable.

Willow heard the sirens from streets away. Two crested white cars stopped, double parked just beyond her perch and Harness came rushing out of the second one.

'Where is he?'

She gestured towards the open door of the house and stayed sitting in the shade, waiting.

It was not long before Harness reappeared, followed by Dan Hallten, still holding his broken arm with the other hand, and two uniformed officers. Sally Hallten, looking grey-white and sick, followed with their baby in her arms. She caught sight of Willow.

'Is this why you came here?' she demanded, coming to stand a foot or so away.

Harness moved to stand at Willow's side as his constables helped Hallten into the back seat of one of the cars. Willow did not answer.

'Why couldn't you have left us alone?'

'Look, Mrs Hallten,' said Harness, ushering her away, 'why don't you find a neighbour to take care of the baby and then come with me to the station. Mrs Worth can hardly—'

'She said her name was King.' Sally Hallten no longer looked at all harassed or pathetic. She was angry and deeply suspicious.

'My maiden name is King, my married one Worth,' said Willow, knowing perfectly well that Mrs Hallten did not really want to know. 'All I can say is that I'm sorry, and I'm very grateful that you saved my life.'

Sally Hallten shuddered as violently as though someone had poured a deluge of icy water over her.

'I must go,' Willow said.

'Will you be all right?' asked Harness urgently. 'Do you want a lift?'

Willow looked at him in surprise and shook her head. 'He didn't do me any real damage. I'll be fine. I've got the car here and I'm going to the hospital.'

'Good idea. Get them to check you over. I'll be in touch, but I have to go now and get this sorted.'

Willow nodded at him again. She could not bear to say anything more to Sally Hallten and so she left without looking back. Knowing that they must both be watching her, she found it almost impossible to get her car out of the tight space and bumped both the car in front and the one behind. When she had at last driven out into the road again, she had to wait for Harness's constable to move his car forward to the end of the street to let her past.

She did not want to think about what had just happened, or what might have happened to her if Sally Hallten had not intervened. It was not until she got to the hospital that she started to shake and found that she could not even make herself get out of her car.

NINETEEN

THANK HEAVENS they got hold of you!' cried Willow's favourite nurse as she appeared at the doors of the Intensive Care Unit nearly half an hour later.

Willow had stopped shaking and had regained enough self-control to remember her bruised neck and want to disguise it. Fortunately she kept a thin, printed silk scarf in the glove box. She had wound it loosely about her neck and tucked the ends into the collar of her shirt. 'Why? What's happened?' she asked, grasping the other woman's arm. 'Tell me.'

'He came round. Didn't you know?'

Dizziness swept through Willow's head, making her whole body sway. Waves of heat passed through her, followed by chilling cold. The nurse's voice seemed to come from a great distance.

'Sit down. Put your head between your knees. Come on.'

Willow could feel the pressure of a firm hand on the nape of her neck, pushing her head towards the floor.

'Fainted, did she?' said a deep male voice. 'Well, not surprising I suppose. Ah, here she comes.'

Willow raised her head, feeling that it must be twice as heavy as usual.

'Mr Richardson?'

'That's right. He's asleep again now, but he was conscious and talking not half an hour ago. It's looking good.'

'Thank God! Can I see him?'

'Certainly, but you'd do better to have some tea first.'

'Can't I do both?'

He smiled and looked at the nurse, who nodded.

'I'll get her some.'

'Good. Come along then, Mrs Worth.' He offered her his arm and, clinging to it, she got up and went with him to Tom's bedside.

At the sight of him, lying exactly as he had been the previous day, Willow felt her knees sagging again. She could understand exactly what Sally Hallten had meant about the devastating effect of reawakened anxiety after hope had been given back. Richardson pushed forward a chair and helped Willow into it.

'He really is going to be all right,' he said. 'I must go, but I'll see you later.'

Willow, who had hardly heard him, said nothing. All she could think of was the possibility that she might have missed her last opportunity of talking to Tom. She stared at his clay-coloured face, much thinner than the first day she had sat beside the bed, and waited.

A different nurse, whose name she did not know, brought her a cup of tea and sat with her while she drank it.

'Thank you,' said Willow at last. 'It's hard to know that he was back and not... Sorry.'

'It's all right. I know what waiting does to people. Here are some tissues.'

As Willow was mopping her face dry, she heard a movement from the bed.

'I'll leave you to it,' said the nurse, backing away on slightly squeaking shoes.

Willow, not quite sure what was happening, leaned forward and saw Tom's eyelids flutter and then open fully. His lips parted.

'Will?' His voice was no more than a whisper.

'Yes, it's me.' She put her right hand over his left one. 'Oh, Tom.'

He smiled, with an obvious effort, and his eyes closed again.

'Perhaps things do come right,' said Willow aloud.

Tom slept on through the afternoon. She left his side once to go to the lavatory and then a second time to telephone Mrs Rusham.

'I know,' she said when Willow had given her the news. 'They told me when they rang this morning, trying to find you. I couldn't tell them where you were. They'd tried the tax office and the minister's staff.'

'Yes, I had to go and see someone else. I never thought to leave the address. Stupid of me.'

'Well, it hardly matters now. You're with him. I'm so glad that he's all right.'

'Thank you, Mrs Rusham. You've been a real stalwart through all this. And I—'

'I know,' she said, choking off whatever expressions of gratitude or affection Willow was about to make. 'Now, there have been several calls this morning; the most important seem to be Mr Gaskarth and the minister. He sounded very anxious to talk to you.'

'Oh, thank you. Well, I suppose I'd better ring him. I'll be here for a while yet. Will you explain to Serena and ask her to eat whenever she's ready, without waiting for me?'

'Yes. Certainly. Goodbye.'

Willow smiled, hoping that she might one day be able to tell Mrs Rusham how much she had done during the crisis and thank her for it properly. Pushing a new Phonecard in the slot, she called the minister's office. She had the usual difficulty getting through to the man himself but eventually she heard his voice, colder than usual and sounding angry.

'Thank you for calling back. I want to see you.'

'Well, of course, but need it be immediately?' she said, surprised by the peremptory tone. 'My husband has just come round. I'm at a payphone in the hospital. I can't leave him.'

'I see. Well, I suppose I can say what I have to say over the telephone.'

Whatever's coming now? Willow asked herself.

'It took me a while to find out that it was you behind the questions about Miss Salderton. I should like first to know exactly what you thought you were doing and second to get from you an undertaking that you will never mention her name again or ask any more questions.'

'I'm sorry you're so upset,' said Willow. 'That was never my intention. All I was trying to do was...' She broke off, hardly able to say that she had wanted to find out whether he had any scandalous secrets that might have led him to want Leonard Scoffer dead—or at least discredited.

'Yes? Explain to me just exactly what it was that you've been trying to do.'

'Find out as much as I could about everyone concerned with the enquiry,' said Willow, her own voice growing cold as she thought of the past few days. 'Quite frankly, neither of your explanations as to why you wanted me in that office convinced me. I was merely trying to find out whether there could be anything else behind your interest in Scoffer's activities.'

'I see. Well I am not going to satisfy your curiosity about Miss Salderton and I will reiterate what I told you: I wanted to find out what was going on in Scoffer's office because I am exceedingly concerned by the possible misuse of power by any employee of the state. Now, that having been said yet again, when may I expect your report?'

'Within forty-eight hours,' said Willow crisply. 'Goodbye, Minister.'

She pressed the follow-on button, and dialled Brian Gaskarth's number to find out what had been happening. He was both frustrated and illuminating.

'The minister,' he explained, sounding coldly angry, 'has taken it upon himself to threaten to have me prosecuted under some provision of the data protection legislation.'

'Has he, though? What is it he's hiding?'

'Ah, well, Miss Salderton is an alias.'

'As we suspected.'

'Yes, but for quite a good reason. I'm reluctant to say anything more on the telephone.'

'Why?' demanded Willow, suddenly scared. 'You can't think this one is tapped?'

'No, but I suspect mine is.'

'Because of the enquiries you've made for me?'

'Good God, no! It started long before that. There have been a few signs over the past year or so. I may be paranoid.'

'But it's extremely difficult to get a Home Office warrant for phone-tapping.'

There was a superior-sounding laugh down the telephone. 'If you genuinely believe that only legal tapping goes on, I'm afraid that your ideals have got the better of your common sense.'

'Have they indeed? When shall we meet?'

'I could drop in on my way to a meeting this afternoon.'

'I'm not at home, in fact. I'm with my husband at Dowting's. I don't terribly want to leave, since he's...'

'Well, it's hardly urgent. Why not call me when you're free?'

'Fine. Thank you. Just tell me how old she is, if you know that.'

'I do indeed. She's forty.'

Well, she's clearly not his daughter, thought Willow as she was left holding the receiver and trying to contain her curiosity. Slowly she walked back into the Intensive Care Unit and down the long vinyl-floored passage to Tom's room. She was not even looking at him when she opened the door and his voice took her by surprise.

'Will, I thought you'd gone.'

She looked at him then, her face softer than he had ever seen it. 'You must have known I wouldn't do that. Not now.'

He held out his hand, still tied to the bags and bottles. 'How are you?'

'Me? I'm fine.' She stood at his side, gazing at him and then suddenly remembering the last time she had looked at herself in a mirror. 'Although I know I must look like the wrath of God.'

His lips widened into the smile that she had almost forgotten. 'Not wrath,' he said in his faint voice. 'Just irritation.'

For a minute or so she could not think what he was talking about and then remembered their last breakfast before the shooting. It felt as though it had happened years before. She sank down on to her knees beside the bed and laid her forehead against the back of his hand. With some difficulty he reached his other hand across his body so that he could stroke her head.

MUCH LATER, when she was back in her chair and had drunk yet another cup of hospital tea, he said, 'What have you been doing while I've been dead to the world?'

'Didn't you hear anything? I used to chat to you sometimes when I visited.'

He shook his head. 'I didn't hear anything. As far as I knew last night was the night I was shot. But from the look of you, Will, I'd have said you'd been up to something.'

'You could put it like that.' She wondered how strong he

was feeling and whether he was up to hearing an account of her activities.

'How are the tax gatherers?' he asked when he realised that she was not going to tell him.

Inexpressibly touched that he should remember what she had been doing when he was shot, she smiled a little. 'A pretty peculiar bunch, but you were quite right that I'd find them interesting.'

Before she could get any further the door of Tom's room opened and they both looked round. Superintendent Blackled strode forward and put his hand on Tom's left shoulder.

'They told me you'd come round. How're you feeling?'

'Not too bad at all, sir. Good of you to come. Do you know my wife, Willow King?'

Black Jack turned and winked at her. 'Of course I know her. Hasn't she told you how she's our latest heroine?'

'What?' Tom squinted down at his bandaged chest. 'Because of all this?'

'Not exactly, but if she hasn't told you, I won't. It's her story.'

'Will?'

'It's all a bit melodramatic, Tom. I'm not sure you want to hear it quite yet.'

He closed his eyes and said: 'Have you been going after the people who shot me?'

'No. I haven't done anything about that at all. There wasn't anything I could do.'

'We'll get them, Tom. Now you can give us a statement and identify the little toerags, I don't suppose we'll have any more trouble with the CPS,' said the superintendent. 'Don't you worry about a thing, my boy.'

Tom opened his eyes and looked up. 'I wasn't worrying about that, sir, just about what my wife has been up to. If not my attempted assassins, then who? What's under those bandages and behind that scarf, Will?'

It was obvious that he was not amused any more and seemed to be trying to struggle up.

A nurse came running into the room. 'Now, now, calm down,' she said. 'What's the matter?'

'What do you mean?' demanded Willow.

'I suspect my heart monitor's going bananas,' said Tom grimly. 'I'm fine, but I want to know what's been happening. Someone's been strangling you, haven't they?'

The nurse looked horrified. Black Jack told her that there was nothing to worry about and, after checking Tom's various drips, she stood back away from the bed.

'Will? Has someone been strangling you?'

'Not very effectively,' she said, upset that they could not have kept the news from him until he was stronger. 'It's too early for you to bother about it. When you're stronger, I'll tell you the full story.'

'No. Tell me now. I'll have a relapse worrying if I don't know.'

'Don't you fret yourself, Tom. Your little woman here is the toughest thing since Pocahontas.'

'Pocahontas died of cold, sir. Will, what the hell's been going on?'

'I think you should tell him whatever it is he wants to know,' said the nurse. 'He'll rest more easily.'

'Thank God someone's got some sense.'

'All right,' said Willow. 'As your superintendent has so tactfully raised the subject, I'll tell you. Someone set fire to the tax building. I escaped without too much difficulty, guided down the wall by a passing mountaineer.' Seeing her husband's glinting smile, she smiled too. 'Perfectly true, in fact. You'll probably meet him.'

'But you didn't get bruises round your throat from that. I can see them now that scarf thing's slipped.'

'No. They were from the arsonist. I'll tell you all...' Willow broke off as she saw tears seeping out from beneath Tom's closed eyelids. She turned to Blackled and jerked her head to send him out of the room. He grasped the nurse by her wrist and took her with him out of the room.

When they were alone again, Willow took a tissue from the box on Tom's bedside table and clumsily wiped his eyes. 'It's all right, Tom. It just happened. But I'm fine. Don't worry about it. It's all over. A nice chap called Stephen Harness, who seems to know you, has the bloke in custody. He's confessed. The bloke, I mean, not Harness. It's all over.'

Tom lifted his eyelids. 'I wish you wouldn't do these

things,' he said, sounding unutterably weary. 'I'm sorry if it makes me seem like a caveman, but I wish you could remember... You take such dreadful risks, and you go on doing it and on and on and on.'

Willow, hurting for him and longing to apologise, to swear never to step outside the house without permission, kept a firm grip on reality. By then she had learned the better way, and knew enough of herself to understand how much she would come to resent any of the things she wanted to promise. She stood beside him, smiling down.

'For a man who's been lying in a coma for a week or more, that's pretty rich, I must say.'

To her immense relief he grinned weakly, sniffed, and then said: 'Give me one of those tissues, damn you, and tell me the whole story.'

She did, censoring some bits, telling him every minute detail of others. She scored her greatest success with a description of the walk through the royal parks when she had been caught talking to herself. At that Tom laughed until his breath gave out, and told her she was wonderful.

EPILOGUE

MUCH LATER, when Tom had been out of hospital for about ten days and felt up to receiving visitors again, Stephen Harness was allowed to visit him. Tom was lying along one of the silver-grey sofas in the drawing room, dozing over a new book recommended by Eve Greville. Willow was stretched out on the other sofa, writing letters to the last of the many people who had sent them both flowers, and keeping an eye on Tom to make sure he was not in too much pain.

He was still pale and looked much thinner than he had ever been before. Small frustrations tired him out and he could not gauge when his energy was about to fail him. Food, even Mrs Rusham's food, gave him no pleasure, and he had to force himself to eat more than a mouthful at any meal. He slept badly at night, tormented by headaches. During the day he tended to become fretful if Willow was away for too long or if one of the neighbours started making a noise or a car backfired.

Visitors were carefully screened and well briefed either by Mrs Rusham or Willow herself to stay no longer than half an hour. She longed for the time when Tom's old easy, teasing tolerance would return and he would be himself again.

That evening the air felt fresher than it had during the heatwave, and they had been sitting out in the little courtyard garden until Tom began to feel uncomfortable in his deck chair and they moved indoors. The French windows were still open and the late evening sun was flooding into the room, casting a warm light over the silver greys and calm pinks of the room. Tom seemed relatively relaxed.

When Mrs Rusham brought in Chief Inspector Harness, Willow got up to greet him. He handed her a large bunch of red and white roses, wrapped in cellophane and tied with ribbon.

'You won't mind if Tom doesn't move, will you?' said Willow, ushering the visitor towards Tom's sofa. She gave his flowers to Mrs Rusham to put in water. 'It's bad for him to keep popping up and down.'

'She's turning into a terrible tyrant, Steve. How are you?' said Tom, holding out his right hand.

'Pretty good,' said Harness. 'What about you? You look a lot better than reports that have filtered through to me suggested you would.'

'I'll leave you to it,' said Willow, heading towards the door.

'Why?' demanded Tom. He sounded petulant, which was so unlike him that Willow stopped at once and smiled at him. 'We're not going to bore you with shop talk, you know.'

'I'd be riveted with shop talk. You know that. I just don't want to get in the way.'

'Don't be a clot. Drink, Steve? And do sit down.'

'A drink would be very nice if you're having something. But don't trouble just for me.'

'We will be. What have you got in the fridge, Evelyn?'

Mrs Rusham smiled cosily at him. 'There's some champagne, of course, and a couple of bottles of that rather nice Alsace wine that Mrs Worth ordered last month. Or there are all the ordinary things.'

'The wine'll do fine.' Tom stopped as though he had thought of something and deliberately smiled at Willow. 'Unless you'd rather have champagne, Will? I'm sorry. I was being selfish and remembering the awful wind that last bottle we had gave me.'

Mrs Rusham blushed and backed out of the room.

'Now you've shocked her,' said Willow, glad to see his smile.

'Nothing I could do or say would shock her while I'm an invalid,' he announced with all the satisfaction of a child who has got away with a piece of deliberate naughtiness. He added in more adult tones: 'I'll know I'm better when she starts to freeze me out again and demands that I call her Mrs Rusham.'

'How did you know that she's called Evelyn?'

'Rob told me.'

Willow smiled. She had packed off both Fydgetts to live in Fiona's house as soon as the hospital told her that Tom was fit enough to go home, but Rob had been back several times and it had begun to look as though he might become a fixture in their lives.

Tom was nodding as Stephen Harness decided it was time he joined in the conversation.

'How is young Fydgett?'

'Getting on all right, I think, though no thanks to your lot. He and Tom are quite matey these days. They play chess together after school, but I don't think they talk to each other at all.'

'Talk?' repeated Tom, laughing and looking much more familiar. 'Certainly not. You don't think me and Rob have gone all girly, do you, Will? He does me good, you know, Steve. All these affectionate women keep wanting to know how I feel. Rob wouldn't ask me anything so personal in a hundred years.'

Willow made an undignified face at her husband and stuck out her tongue for a moment, glorying in his mockery. Harness looked surprised and turned to Mrs Rusham in relief. She had come back without the roses and was offering him a glass of Hugel's Gewurtztraminer and a plate of miniature pancakes rolled around a mixture of smoked salmon mousse and chips of cucumber.

'Thank you very much. They look delicious.'

Mrs Rusham let him have a pancake and then took her tray of goodies to Tom's sofa.

'Can't I tempt you to a little food? It's all fish—good for your brain cells.'

Tom laughed and accepted one tiny stuffed pancake. When she had gone, leaving the plate of pancakes and the bottle on a table near Willow's sofa, Harness turned to Willow.

'You'll be glad to hear that Hallten is standing by his confession and the CPS is going to run with it. The trial will go ahead as soon as possible. Probably next winter some time.'

'Did he get bail?' asked Tom.

'Yes. The view was taken that he's been so chastened by what happened that he's hardly likely to be a danger to the public. And that sensible wife of his has got him in the hands of an excellent shrink, who seems to be sorting him out.'

'What about the money?' asked Willow.

Harness turned to smile at her. 'It's all on the National Health.'

'I didn't mean the shrink. I meant the tax he owes and the other debts. From what his wife told me, he hasn't a hope of paying them.'

'I understand that he's filed for bankruptcy, which will clear all the debts, including the tax, and she's working as a secretary again to bring in enough to feed them and pay the rent. He takes care of the child while she's out. It all looks as though it'll work out reasonably well.'

'Until he's sent down,' said Willow.

'As he must be, even if it is manslaughter and not murder,' said Tom from the further sofa. 'Willow tells me he has a record.'

'That's right. He did some time in Wandsworth. Oh, by the way, Mrs Worth,' Stephen said, feeling in his jacket pocket.

'Do call me Willow,' she said, 'and take off that jacket. You look awfully hot.'

Harness smiled and did as he was told, neatly folding his jacket and laying it across his knees. She was amused to see that over his pristine blue shirt he was wearing bright green braces decorated with pink hummingbirds, and she wondered if he indulged in such eccentricities of dress at work.

'I forgot to let you know about those four lifers you warned us about.'

Willow looked warily at Tom, who had heard the story of most of her activities during his time in hospital, but he had come to terms with it all by then and grinned at her. Much relieved, she turned back to Harness just as Tom was saying, 'Don't worry about it, Steve. Black Jack reported to her a while ago, thank God. The pair of you really put the wind up her, you know.'

Thinking he heard anger behind the amusement in Tom's tired voice, Harness looked from him to Willow and back again and then seemed to make a decision. 'We were just shaking the tree really.'

'You what?' said Willow.

'You had a better opportunity than anyone else for lighting that fire. Given that you escaped and the only other inhabitant of the office died, I had to find out if you were on the level.

The superintendent insisted on chaperoning you and pretending we were worried that you had been targeted by Tom's would-be assassins, so that you didn't get upset by the thought that you were among my suspects. Given Blackled's rank I couldn't stop him coming with me without making more of a fuss than I wanted.'

Thinking of the waking terrors and the nightmares she went through after the fire, Willow was furious. 'I don't know that I want you drinking my wine,' she said, trying to make a joke of her dislike.

Tom heaved his battered body off the sofa and padded across the floor in his bare feet to stand beside her with his hand on her head.

'He had to do his job, Will, you know that.'

Harness's delicate skin had flushed a vivid blood red. 'All I can say is that I'm glad that you turned out to be as you are. Until I'd interviewed you, I knew nothing about you. You must understand that, Willow.'

Tom raised his glass. 'Now, we've had enough of all that. The case is over and done with and ought to be forgotten. Budge up,' he said, sitting down beside Willow and taking hold of her right hand in both of his. 'Tell me when you first knew that it was Hallten, Steve.'

As Stephen Harness began to explain the course of his investigation, Willow lost some of her anger and listened in growing interest as he laid bare the ideas that had been running in parallel with her own. In the end she laughed. Tom leaned his shoulder against her in a gesture of pleasure and perhaps of gratitude, too.

'We ought to have shared our information right at the beginning,' she said. 'We'd both have got on to Hallten a lot faster if we'd done that, eh, Steve? And I wouldn't have had a bruised throat.'

He looked at her for a moment and then bowed his good-looking head. 'That's pretty generous, if I may say so. I'd better be off. Tom, I'm sure I'll see you when you're back at work. Willow, I hope that our paths will cross again, although perhaps not in the way of business.'

Tom got up to shake hands with him and was all for escorting him to the front door, but Willow sternly sent him to lie on his sofa while she herself saw Harness out. At the front door, he apologised for upsetting her.

'That's all right,' she said. 'But if you feel you owe me anything, you could pay with a scrap of information.'

'Oh, yes?' he said, looking at her warily.

'Who was Serena Fydgett's alibi?'

The guarded look in his eyes was transformed into a smile. 'I can't tell you that, you know perfectly well.'

'Yes, but I am terribly curious. I'm also completely discreet. I'd ask her myself except that we've become friends and I don't want to risk that—or Rob's trust in Tom, which is good for both of them.'

Harness waited for a moment and then nodded. 'I shouldn't tell you, but for some reason I'm going to. I only hope *my* trust isn't misplaced. It was Malcolm Penholt, the MP.'

'Aha,' said Willow as several other pieces of the jigsaw fell into place. Penholt's relationship with Serena would easily explain why he had been prepared to give George Profett time to make his enquiries before raising a fuss in the House of Commons. Any publicity he gave Fiona Fydgett's case could have backfired if his relationship with her sister had been exposed, which it probably would have been.

Their intimacy was obviously the reason why Serena had been less surprised to hear from Willow than might have been expected, and it could also explain what had made Serena so angry with her sister a short while before she had killed herself. From what Willow had learned of them both, it did not seem to be beyond the bounds of possibility that Fiona might have had a go at seducing her elder sister's lover.

When she got back to the drawing room, Tom smiled up at her.

'Steve's not such a bad egg, you know, Will.'

'No, I know. But I feel a bit… Oh, I don't know, used, I suppose. He charmed me into thinking how civilised he was beside Black Jack. I despise myself for having succumbed to his charm and believed his stories. It was plain old "good cop, bad cop" stuff and I fell for it.'

'We all have our ways of getting people to talk. He couldn't have known that you are as unlikely to set fire to a building as Rob Fydgett is to swap intimacies with me. Although…'

'What is it?'

'Rob did tell me one thing, which I think I ought to pass on to you. I know you'll never let the boy know I told you.'

'What is it?' Willow said again in a different voice.

'He did go into his mother's room that day she killed herself.'

'I thought he must have. Didn't he guess what she'd done?'

'No. He said she was lying in bed looking incredibly beautiful and he suddenly needed to talk to her, to tell her things he felt and find out what she felt about him. You see, sometimes she was full of affection and a kind of dependence, and at others he says she seemed to loathe and despise him. She'd tell him he was tiresome and clumsy and stupid and that if he'd never been born she'd have been fine and never had any of her depressions or tried to kill herself. He said it just washed over him then that he needed to know which was right and so he tried to wake her up. He called her name a couple of times, but she didn't stir.'

Willow remembered the way Rob had whispered her name on the night he had been burning paper in the drawing room fireplace and she wished passionately that she had given him what he needed. She nodded to make Tom go on.

'He said that he needed her so much that he bent down and kissed her forehead. When she still didn't move he kissed her on the lips. At that she sort of grunted, he said, and pushed his face away. He said he felt sick and desperate and he shook her, but she still didn't wake. Miserable, rejected as he saw it, and frightened by everything he felt, he just ran out of the room. He didn't notice the pill bottle or the whisky glass. He said that at that moment he hated her. But he had no idea she was dying.'

Willow said nothing but her face was quite expressive enough.

'I know,' said Tom. 'He told me that he felt utterly disgusted with himself for kissing her and bolted back to school. It wasn't until much later, when he'd read her letter, that he understood and realised that he could have saved her life. I've tried to explain to him that he didn't kill her and that it wasn't his fault, but it's going to take him a long time to come to terms with it all.'

'Poor boy. No wonder he always seemed so guilty. I can't have helped, asking my questions, and the police interview must have made him feel even worse than he already did.'

'Yes, I think that's probably right. But it had to be done. I know Harness hurt the boy, but you can't blame him. Rob just got caught in the crossfire.' Tom looked profoundly sad. 'That's what crime does: its ripples affect huge numbers of innocent people who are simply in the wrong place at the wrong time.'

Willow said nothing, feeling obstructive. Tom tried again.

'Look, you can't blame the police if, faced with a dead body, they trample over the sensibilities of the innocent in their search for the guilty.'

'I suspect that that's pretty much what Len Scoffer thought about his job of hunting down tax dodgers, but I don't know that I can accept it. I don't think he ever actually broke a rule, let alone a law in his life, but he harmed people…innocent people.'

Tom sat up in defiance of her orders and patted the cushion beside him. 'Come and sit down, and stop looking like an avenging angel, Will. Rob's going to recover. He'll find a way to tell himself the story that makes it all less awful. We can't help him by agonising over his feelings, just as we can't help Scoffer's victims by blaming him for the things they did in response to his bullying.'

'No,' agreed Willow. 'I've done my bit on that score by laying out for the minister exactly how Scoffer operated. If there's anything that can be done to prevent it happening again in the future with another cast, he'll do it. It's his pigeon now.'

Willow made herself smile. Tom took her hand.

'One thing you haven't told me is who Miss Andrea Salderton turned out to be,' he said in a lighter tone.

'Ah, now she is interesting,' said Willow following his lead away from the thought of Rob Fydgett and what he had had to face.

'Oh?'

'She's a protégé of the minister's from his days with Amnesty. Some years ago she was a political prisoner of one of those awful South American regimes. I'm not sure which one. But she was tortured, repeatedly over several months. Some-

one got her out in the end and George Profett has been paying
her an allowance ever since. She's getting better and doing
bits and pieces of translation work, but she'll probably need
his help for years yet.'

'Good for him,' said Tom seriously. 'Really good.'

'I know. You can see why he got so angry when Gaskarth
and I started truffling about trying to find out about her. As
you can imagine, her hurts aren't only physical and the last
thing she needs is any kind of publicity. But I think he was a
bit naive not to realise that someone might notice he was sub-
sidising her and start asking questions. Quite frankly, he's
lucky that no one's tried to expose her as his mistress.'

'You mean the tabloids haven't got on to her at all?'

'Apparently not,' said Willow, thinking of the SCDD clas-
sification Jane's paper had given him. 'Perhaps they don't
bother with bank accounts unless there're some other clues to
a good story, or perhaps the editors have a pact with him to
keep off it.' Willow took off her glasses and rubbed her eyes.
They had almost recovered from the effects of the fire, but she
was still reluctant to wear her lenses again.

'Is he in love with her?'

'I think he probably is, from what Gaskarth gathered from
someone who knows them both; but she can't bring herself to
trust anyone and needs to live alone. You can understand it.'

'Yes, I think you can. And perhaps his fear of officials misusing their power comes from the same thing. From what
you've said it does sound a trifle exaggerated, if not actually
neurotic.'

'Perhaps a bit. And not knowing any of the background, I
just assumed he'd invented it to cover something else up. It
kept me from seeing what was really going on for days.' Willow paused to rub her head against his shoulder. 'That and my
terror for you.'

'Ah, Will,' he said, putting a hand under her chin to turn
her face up. 'Do you know, I think I rather like you in glasses.'

'You can't,' she said, peering at him over the top of them
to see whether he was teasing her. 'I look ghastly.'

'Don't be so hard on yourself.'

Willow looked round the beautiful room and, thinking about
the ease and self-indulgence of her life, laughed.

'You are, you know,' said Tom. 'You give yourself a very hard time.'

Before Willow could answer, the door opened and Mrs Rusham reappeared, holding a brown envelope. 'I quite forgot the post in all the excitement this morning,' she said, flushing. 'I am sorry.'

'I don't suppose it'll matter at all. It looks fearfully boring.' Willow took the proffered envelope and ripped it open.

'What is it?' asked Tom as she started to laugh.

'That bloody little Jason Tillter! I bet it's him.' Willow handed Tom the short, printed letter, which he read aloud:

Dear Sir/Madam,

   I am writing to enquire whether you are certain that all your income for the years 1989/90, 1990/91 and 1992/93 has been declared in your tax returns.

                                        Yours faithfully

The letter was signed with an illegible ballpoint squiggle over the printed title of Her Majesty's Inspector of Taxes.

'Well, I expect that'll give you quite a lot of fun now that you know the way they operate,' said Tom, putting his arm around her. 'And with luck it'll stop you doing anything else dangerous for a bit.'

'In the circumstances, I suspect it will. It should keep me nice and busy while you're recovering your strength.' Willow eyed her husband for a moment and then added, laughing: 'And perhaps it'll distract me enough to stop me asking how you're feeling every two minutes.'

'That's m'girl!'

MURDER IN
RETIREMENT

First Time in Paperback

A Laura Michaels Mystery

CURTAINS...

Timberdale is having its very first murder-mystery weekend. After the show, the residents of the Oklahoma retirement community will play detective and solve the crime. Or so the script goes.

But the script takes an unexpected twist when the role of the corpse, being played by the acting troupe's acrimonious director, becomes the real thing.

Resident troubleshooter Laura Michaels is quickly on the trail of a desperate killer, who must be found before stealing the scene again—with murder.

JOHN
MILES

"A refreshing brash sleuth."   —*Murder ad lib*

Available in July 1997 at your favorite retail outlet.

To order your copy, please send your name, address, zip or postal code along with a check or money order (please do not send cash) for $4.99 for each book ordered ($5.99 in Canada), plus 75¢ postage and handling ($1.00 in Canada), payable to Worldwide Mystery, to:

In the U.S.	In Canada
Worldwide Mystery	Worldwide Mystery
3010 Walden Avenue	P.O. Box 609
P.O. Box 1325	Fort Erie, Ontario
Buffalo, NY 14269-1325	L2A 5X3

Please specify book title with your order.
Canadian residents add applicable federal and provincial taxes.

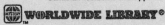

WRETIRE

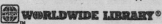

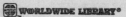